Prai

"A gem of a book that focuses on a small-town teen struggling to find her place within a fractured family and a world that's larger than she could have imagined. Mart artfully balances authentic relationships and light romance against a backdrop of dangerous intrigue and American folklore come-to-life."

—C. J. Stilling, author of *Rust, The Goblin King's Skull,* and *Death Warden.*

"Mart integrates Native American lore as a backstory to develop a twisty and intriguing story of a teen's search for Bigfoot. In addition to encounters with the beasts, Mart meaningfully explores the complexity of family dynamics and examines how uncovered truths can help mend relationships."

—BookLife Prize Critic Review

"Packed with deceit and deeply layered secrets that turn deadly, this book is perfect for a YA reader looking for an adventure romance. Mart's writing style is addicting, and her craft of storytelling will leave you wanting the next book in the series."

—Laura L. Zimmerman, *The Banshee Song Series.*

"Mart skillfully weaves a narrative that not only delves into the possible existence of Bigfoot but also explores the complexities of human relationships. As Ellie Mae and Jake venture deeper into the forest in pursuit of the truth, their bond deepens, and hidden secrets begin to emerge. This intertwining of adventure and personal growth adds depth to the plot, making it a satisfying read for fans of both mystery and romance."

—Sanesha Sammerson, Online Book Club

Hidden Truths

A Living Lore Novel

Tammera Mart

May you soar on wings of truth

– Tammera Mart

ISBN: 979-8-9885739-0-6

Published by HT Press
https://tammeramart.com

For any inquiries regarding this book, please email:
tammeramart@tammeramart.com

Cover Design by Lynn Andreozzi.
Cover Image Credit:
Oscar M Vargas—hawk
Andrew Soundarajan—Sunset in the Smokies

For my daughter, Melissa.
You have inspired so much of this story. My life would not be the same without you in it.

Long, long ago, hidden within the caves and forests of the Appalachian Mountains, lived majestic creatures known to locals as the Nun'Yunu'Wi. These large animals shared hunting grounds with the Native Americans, and both populations thrived cohesively until men from across the great water brought danger.

The natives moved inward, deeper into the mountains, taking the Nun'Yunu'Wi with them. But as disease and exposure ravaged the creatures, the Nun'Yunu'Wi dwindled. By the time the natives were forced out of the land completely, few—if any—of the great creatures remained.

Today, some say if you know what to look for and how to track them, deep in the hills, in the darkest corners of a river gorge, you might get a glimpse of the Nun'Yunu'Wi, also known . . . as Bigfoot.

Chapter One

Grandma said a person's defining moment could be found in life's darkest corner. In my case, I found it at the bottom of a river gorge. It was when I'd come face to face with my greatest fear and decided risking my life was better than not finishing what my mom had started.

The journey began weeks ago on an early June morning after several days of rain left everything a muddy mess.

"Ellie Mae." Grandma stopped me halfway out the back door, holding my jacket. "Make sure you bring me those eggs before you head over to the clinic. Yesterday, you left them on a bale of hay, and the cats broke half the lot."

I winced. "Got caught up trimming the goats' hooves. Sorry about that."

The air was cool as I slipped out of our two-story farmhouse and walked down the hill toward the barn. I pushed my arms through the blue zip-up and pulled my hair into a short ponytail, using the band I had placed on my wrist earlier. After chores, Dad and I planned to go into town for breakfast, deliver shoes to a family in need, then visit Mom's grave. Depending on the time, and his mood, I'd ask if he wanted to trek through the mountains to the old weeping willow she'd often gone to when she wrote in her journal.

Talking about Mom was the only thing I had asked for on my eighteenth birthday, a month earlier. And Dad agreed . . . *finally*. I don't know if he thought being an official adult entitled me to know the truth surrounding Mom's death or if he feared I'd never return home from the university if he didn't open up. I'd never made that threat, but I thought it more than once.

Dogs barked. I glanced across the barnyard to Dad's vet clinic. The front door stood ajar—Dad's way of saying he wouldn't be staying out there. Just long enough to feed the boarders and maybe leave a note for Sarah, his office manager.

From out the back, two beagles raced across the kennel to the fence that lined a hillside full of birch and pine. Joining them, a beautiful Irish Setter trotted out—Dad's late afternoon spay.

Chickens fluttered inside the coop, and the goats bleated like they'd been starved for a week. I shoved open the large, sliding barn door. Daisy stepped on the bottom rung of the gate, lifting herself up so her head cleared the top. She let out another wavering cry. Lulu hopped up beside her and joined in.

"Enough. You're just hearing those noisy hounds. Nothing to worry about." I brushed a hand over her nose and planted a kiss on the short, wiry hair. "One molasses-and-grain breakfast coming up."

Carrying two flakes of hay back with the feed, I didn't dally like normal. I'd give Daisy and Lulu extra attention this evening. Right now, I was anxious to get a move on. But Dad was still in the clinic when I walked to the house, the bottom of my sweatshirt bulging with a dozen eggs. Grandma held open the back door, letting out a sweet apple-and-cinnamon aroma. I inhaled deeply.

"You made turnovers?"

"Just warmed up some I had stashed in the freezer." She smiled, aged dimples forming tracks along each cheek, but her ice-blue eyes didn't flash with the usual spark. Not even with Frank Sinatra crooning in the background. He always pulled a hum and a smile from her, so something was off. Or maybe it was just the day.

"You remember Dad and I are going into town for breakfast, right?"

Her lips folded into a straight line. An apologetic expression that warned me not to get all worked up. I'd seen the look plenty enough to know what it meant.

"Dad changed his mind, didn't he?" I lifted the eggs from my jacket into the kitchen sink, resisting the urge to smash a couple.

"Another animal attack. This time over at the Hansen's." Grandma washed her hands beside me then moved the spigot so water splashed over the eggs.

"What happened?" Concern edged in as I rinsed off the eggs and placed them on a towel, a little hurt that Jeanine hadn't texted me. I could think of a couple reasons she might be avoiding me. The main one centered around her brother, but I thought we'd all moved beyond that.

The oven timer buzzed. Grandma draped the towel over my shoulder. "I have no idea. You'll have to ask your dad." She pulled the sheet of pastries out of the oven. At the same time gravel crunched, the sound of a car rolling down the drive.

Drying my hands, I walked through the house and glanced out the living room window. "Uh-oh. It's Simsy. I better get out there. Who knows what stray she's brought him this time."

Grandma handed me a double-layered napkin with a warm turnover on top. "Good idea. I'm not sure he'll have the patience this morning."

"Or any morning when it comes to her." I lifted the treat. "Thank you for this. You're the best." I gave her a quick squeeze and hurried out the door, hoping Dad would hold onto his temper. Dorothy Simms, or Simsy, as most people called her, tended to be a little eccentric, but her heart was in the right place. At least that's how I felt.

Two months ago, she'd brought in a baby raccoon and wanted to make sure it was healthy before turning it into a pet. Dad had scolded her and let it loose right then and there. Simsy left madder than a mule chewing on bumblebees and had sworn she was never coming back.

Yet here she was. Like always.

Three bites into the turnover, I entered my dad's office, placing the uneaten portion on his desk next to a week-old invoice. I picked it up and glanced at the customer's name. "Jaxon. Figures."

"You can't keep an owl as a pet!" Dad's voice boomed through the wall.

I tossed the paper on the desk and raced into the room next door. "You have an owl?" I grinned at Simsy, who was sitting in a chair across from the exam table, but frowned when I saw Dad's face. Eyebrows drawn over fiery green eyes and a tight mouth, he looked like a weather-worn lumberjack who'd just broken his last axe handle.

"Not for long, if your daddy has his way." Simsy blew a strand of salt-and-pepper hair out of her face. The rest was wrapped tightly in a bun at the nape of her neck. The baby was only about the size of Dad's hand and still sported some gray fuzz between brownish feathers. It barely squawked as Dad set it back in the cage.

"It's against the law, Dorothy." Dad fixed his gaze on me. "Ellie, I want you to take it over to the bird sanctuary. Rebecca will know what to do with him." He placed his gloves on the table next to the cage.

"We're kind of busy today. Maybe Simsy would like to take it over."

His nostrils flared. "I'd rather you do it."

"I can't. The brakes on the Jeep need fixed, remember?" I intended every ounce of venom lacing my tone. He wasn't ditching me without a fight. He made a promise.

"God in Heaven above, Neil, what's happened to your manners?" Simsy stood and grabbed the cage. "Besides the owl, I'll be sure Rebecca gets an earful. Ellie Mae, good luck at college. I'm sorry to say you won't be seeing me out here anymore."

I scowled at Dad for being rude and followed Simsy out the door. "Here, let me help you with that." I took the cage. "Don't mind him. You remember today's the anniversary of Mom's death?"

"'Course I remember, and I'm sorry for that." She opened the backseat door on her oversized Buick. "Don't know why I thought we could share a civil conversation."

I tightened my hold on the cage. "Maybe just come by without an animal sometime. Visit."

"I'd be as welcome as a tick on a dog's ear."

"Don't know if you don't try."

"Hmpf!"

Unsure what to say, I nodded at the owl. "Dad'll call the game warden if you don't take him straight over to the Rescue. Why don't you let us do it? Then you won't risk getting a fine. And you can go over to visit the owl whenever you want."

The lines in her face softened. "I hadn't thought about a fine."

"Dad means business when it comes to wild birds. A couple weeks ago, I brought home a hawk with an injured wing. Scratched the heck out of me. I thought I earned the right to nurse it back to health." I jerked a thumb toward the office. "But he said no and threatened to call the warden if I kept it." This was only a half truth. I knew as well as Dad that the bird needed to be at the Rescue, but it didn't keep me from wishing I could have held onto it for a few days. And it didn't keep Dad from sharing the consequences if I followed through on my desire.

"Tsk." Ms. Simms shook her head and closed the back door. "What you have to put up with."

"He's right, though. Rebecca has the equipment and facilities. She knows what she's doing."

Simsy plopped behind the wheel, reached across the front seat, and produced a cherry pie. "Here, you and your grandmother share this. Although you might give your daddy a piece to try and sweeten him up. Just be sure and tell him I didn't make it for him. Oh, and I wanted to tell you the boys are coming home this weekend. They'll be at church on Sunday. If you wanted to sit with us at the potluck, you'd be welcome."

I held the cage with one hand and took the pie in my other as my mind raced then stopped at the faint memory from last week's church announcements. "The church's anniversary potluck. Right. Sure. I'll be there, and I'll tell Dad and Grandma. Can't wait to see them."

With that, Simsy pulled the door shut and let gravel fly as she tore down the driveway.

I set the cage beside Dad's truck and carried the pie into the clinic, not sure whether to laugh at Simsy or be mad at Dad's rudeness.

"So, what's going on?" I dropped the pie in the middle of his desk.

"Nothing." He grabbed his blue University of Kentucky windbreaker off a hook by the door and slipped it on.

"That's a lie. We're spending the day together, aren't we?"

Dad let out a sigh. "I can't. I have an emergency over at Hansen's, and then I guess I need to drop off the bird at Rebecca's. You did get it from her, didn't you?"

I nodded once. "I'll go with you. We'll still have time to do everything else. Including this." I held up the overdue bill. "Jaxon Reid. We can tag team. It might even be fun."

"I'm writing that off. Stay away from Jaxon."

"Since when are you writing it off? He'll think he's won if you do. Reason he bullies people is because everyone tiptoes around him. I've heard you say it yourself, so why are you enabling him this time?"

Dad grabbed the tranquilizer gun off the top of a cabinet. "That's a discussion for another day." He walked out the clinic door. "Lock up and make sure the closed sign is visible."

I stuffed the invoice in my back pocket and pulled the door shut behind me. "I'm coming with you. Why the gun?"

"Animal attack at Hansen's. And you're not coming." He placed the owl in the backseat of his truck and paused, looking apologetic for the first time. "I'll be home in time for the surgery."

I couldn't let him bail on me again, so I pushed. "You might need help at Hansen's. What kind of attack? Were the livestock hurt?"

"I don't know yet. I'll call if I need you." He nodded toward the dog run. "Take care of the animals." Then in the space of a heartbeat, he closed the door, backed up, and turned around. I watched as he left our property and disappeared down the road.

He wouldn't call. Just like past years, he'd spend the day somewhere else. The attack was probably an excuse to make a quick getaway. I used to try and find him. I went to Mom's grave, the willow tree, the hills behind the pasture where Mom and Dad often went on walks. I never figured out where he went, and when I asked, he always said, "Nowhere in particular."

The past couple years, between school, work, and helping others, I hadn't dwelt on Mom much. But ever since my birthday, when Dad gave me one of her journals, I'd been thinking more about my treks through the hills with her, the stories and singing, her lessons on tracking and botany. The memories, combined with not knowing the truth of what happened to her, left a hole in my heart the size of Mammoth Cave. Dad needed to answer my questions, help fill in the gaps before I left home, but more and more I sensed him pulling away.

I retrieved the pie and marched into the house, allowing the screen door to slam behind me. "Dad bailed."

Grandma took the pie out of my hands, set it aside, and gave me a long and firm squeeze. "I'm sorry it didn't work out, but don't let it spoil your memory of her." She pulled back and brushed fallen hair out of my eyes. "You look more like her every day, you know that?"

My chest tightened, and I struggled to swallow. Mom and I shared the same dark hair and eyes that stemmed from her Cherokee heritage—Cherokee as far as anyone knew.

"Do you think I remind him of her? Is that why he leaves every year?"

"Sweetie, he's trying his best. Emotions creep up, and he doesn't know how to cope."

"He knows how to shut me out." A hot tear burned the corner of my eye. I blinked fast to keep it from falling and stormed out of the house.

Chapter Two

We'd lived on Dillard Hollow my whole life. The rutted gravel road ran past our place, turned, and went dead on straight into Hush Briar. The little town, nestled between two mountains, was pretty far off the beaten path and didn't offer much in the way of entertainment, but it was enough for me.

Atop the four-wheeler, I swerved around a mud puddle at the end of an abandoned coal mine road and came upon Johnny and Bessie Stroh's property. Bessie picked cherries from atop a wooden stepladder that sat half cockeyed in the wet ground.

She waved and hollered, "Hi, Ellie Mae. Fine morning, ain't it?"

I slowed to a crawl. "Best one yet," I called back but felt the nice day was wasted on me.

"Tell your daddy Missy's getting along real good with those stitches."

"I will. You take care." I sped up. It'd been Bessie's small collie that crossed paths with Jaxon Reid's rottweiler and nearly lost her life. And there was Jaxon, blaming the little dog for leaving the yard when his own had jumped out of a moving truck. Just thinking about his arrogant excuse made my insides boil. And I couldn't believe Dad wanted to write it off.

Dad would be mad that I confronted Jaxon, but right now, I didn't much care. Good people were being taken advantage of, and I wasn't about to stand by and do nothing. I just needed to be careful not to ruffle too many of Jaxon's feathers.

Jaxon used to work in the coal mines before they closed a few years back. Now, he operated a tow truck for his cousin and hung out at Willie's Tavern between runs. Only one of the two restaurants in town, Willie's opened early enough to capitalize on the brunch crowd. And sure enough, Jaxon's truck sat at the edge of the lot. I parked the four-wheeler facing the wrecker and climbed off, never pausing, unwilling to lose my nerve.

I unzipped my blue hoodie and yanked the two halves of my short ponytail in opposite directions to tighten it. A few stray hairs still fell across my face, so I tucked them behind one ear as I hauled open the bar's front door.

The place was dark and dank, and the smell of scrambled eggs blended with the aroma of stale smoke still embedded in the ceiling beams and wooden floor even though no one could smoke inside anymore. Fox News blared from a flat screen near the ceiling on one wall. Two men sat at the bar eating plates of eggs while they talked to Big Travis—bartender and the owner's son. A few others dotted the place.

I tossed Travis a wave and beelined toward a table in the back corner where Jaxon sat, playing cards with the McGraff brothers.

At ten in the morning? Not the scenario I had hoped for.

Jaxon alone didn't bother me too much because I could hold my temper around him, but Rodney and Todd McGraff brought out my worst. The twins were two years older than me and lived with their uncle out on Southbend Road. Old man Josiah took them in after their momma ran off with a truck driver passing through town. While those boys turned over stones looking for trouble, their uncle believed his wayward nephews were better than no family at all. Guess it shouldn't have surprised me to find them hanging out with Jaxon.

Rodney mumbled to his brother and cast a resentful glare my way. I swallowed an equally resentful scowl and allowed my dislike for Rodney to fuel my courage. Jaxon glanced over his shoulder, and a slow smile split his face. All three looked a wreck, like they'd been up all night. On the other hand, this might be just another Wednesday for them.

I walked over and slapped the vet bill down on the scarred wooden table in front of Jaxon.

He fell back into his chair. "What's this?"

I straightened my shoulders and spoke businesslike, careful to keep my sarcasm hidden. "Cost for damages from when your dog attacked the Stroh's collie."

Jaxon scratched his head and exchanged a look with Rodney, who turned and spit into a tin can on the table.

"Hard to believe, but me and the boys here was just talking about you."

Hard to believe was right. It'd been months since I'd so much as nodded a head their way. I narrowed my eyes, unwilling to appear intimidated or show that I cared a wit what they'd been talking about. "I didn't come for small talk, Jaxon. Just to bring you the bill."

"I have a question for you first."

On the surface, when he washed his ash blond hair and combed it halfway decent, Jaxon looked all right. Same with the scruffy mustache and beard. All he needed to do was give it an even trim. But when he smiled, decent-looking morphed into creepy. Brown stains from the chaw outlined his teeth and accentuated those missing on his left upper side.

I folded my arms, my only invitation. Glasses clanked. I looked behind me and caught Travis watching as he dried the dishes from the other side of the bar. He and his dad co-owned the place and were decent guys who listened to as much gossip as any beautician and kept a close eye out for potential trouble. Wish I could say I knew this from hearsay, but I'd spent my fair share of time in this place trying to rescue my former boyfriend from the dufus sitting on the other side of the table spitting tobacco like some beady-eyed grasshopper. At least my bartender-friend wouldn't run off and tell my dad he saw me talking to Jaxon.

"You hear about them animal tracks out on Hansen's land? Behind the pasture leading up into the forest?" Jaxon jabbed at the chaw in his lower lip with his tongue and stared at my face.

"No." While a million questions scorched a trail through my mind, I didn't trust a word out of Jaxon's mouth. I pointed to the bill. "Pay up. I want to get out of here."

Jaxon pulled out his wallet and tossed three twenties on the bill. On top of the money, he placed a padlock, the shackle twisted until it had snapped.

"What's this?"

"Came from Hansen's, and I believe it has to do with the animal attack your daddy's investigating right now. Only it weren't no attack. Cows went missing completely."

"How do you know what my dad's doing?" I glanced around the table, hating that these guys possibly knew more about my dad's whereabouts than I did. Rodney's thumbs moved across the screen of his phone while his brother watched the news.

"When I have an interest in something, I make it my business to know what's going on."

I resisted the urge to roll my eyes. "What kind of animal could even do this?" I picked up the lock and shoved the money in my jean's pocket before he had an opportunity to change his mind.

"Exactly. Instead, ask yourself what kind of *creature* could do this? Could leave footprints the length of my forearm in Hansen's back pasture and carry off a couple of his cows?"

I frowned. A blanket of cold fell over me. The past zoomed to the forefront of my mind, bringing with it a head rush of embarrassing memories filled with pain and ridicule. Jaxon's words faded in and out as if he were speaking through a tunnel.

"You know what I'm saying. Your momma used to study and track all kinds of wild animals 'round these parts."

He was lying. Just like everyone else had been lying when they gossiped about my mom and spread false rumors. I swallowed, sucked in a deep breath, and focused on the lock, forcing my nerves to settle and my vision to clear. I wouldn't let him shake me or let on that he knew something I didn't. "So?"

"So, you go on and have a look at those tracks. Ask your daddy about 'em. By the way, tell him I'd like to have a word. It's been a while."

Outside the overdue bill, what business did Jaxon have

with Dad? The two never shared the same space, and besides the nosey undercurrents of the town, I didn't believe Jaxon knew much about my mom. But his eyes carried an arrogant sheen, a confidence that meant I stood in the wake of secrets.

I fixed my gaze on Rodney because my good sense had abandoned me when I left home that morning and because a piece of me desperately needed to reject Jaxon's implications. "Maybe you should be asking these two what they know about the missing livestock, animal attacks, and whatever tracks you're talking about."

Rodney looked up from his phone. "You got a point in making that kind of statement?"

"You seem fixated on tearing up other people's property. I wouldn't put it past you to pull a hoax or steal someone's cows."

Rodney stood, the chair clattering against the wall behind him. "You accusing me, after you vandalized my property?"

"Maybe. How could an animal do this?" I held up the lock. "Who else would stoop to such a low kind of entertainment?"

I'm not sure who burned with more hatred. So much anger ran through me that I welcomed another confrontation with Rodney. Except I didn't have my shotgun this time, or a car, and antagonizing a bully, even in the middle of the day, was about as stupid as trying to catch a badger with my bare hands.

"Settle down, Ellie Mae." Jaxon took a sip of coffee. "I can vouch for Rodney's whereabouts last night. He's not Hansen's thief. Rodney, sit down."

"How do you know all of this?"

Jaxon picked up his cards and nodded for the boys to do

the same. "The hills have eyes," he said hauntingly and laughed.

To accuse Jaxon of lying was not the same as yanking Rodney's tail. Older, smarter, and related to a crooked sheriff over in Breathitt County, Jaxon operated on motive. And that scared me a little. I turned to leave, but Jaxon caught my arm. "Don't forget to talk to your daddy. Your momma wasn't as crazy as people said. Go take a look at them tracks." I glanced around. Travis watched openly as he wiped down the bar, but everyone else ignored us.

I pulled my arm away and left. Outside, I squinted against the sunshine. No way was I telling Dad I'd talked to Jaxon. I intended to put the money in the safe, swear Sarah into silence, and spend the rest of the day mowing the barnyard in solitude.

"Hey, Ellie Mae."

I glanced across the parking lot as I hefted one leg over the four-wheeler. JT strode toward me in full police uniform. His real name was Justin T. Long, and his daddy was the reverend at the Methodist church we attended. He was a few years older than me. Early as I could remember, folks called him Pokey. Not because he was slow or anything, but he was ramrod thin and his bones were sorta pokey at the joints. I don't think he minded being called Pokey, but it felt a little offensive, so I stuck with JT. We got along real well, but others had been mean to him in school. Even though he took it all in stride, I knew he'd wanted nothing more than to become a cop so he could hold those bullies, or others like them, accountable.

"Hey, JT, what's up?"

He stopped next to the four-wheeler, hooked his thumbs over his belt, and hem-hawed. I tipped my head in question.

"What were you doing in Willie's?" he blurted out, nodding his head toward the coal-stained building.

"Why?"

"You got nothing in your hands like you might've ordered food. You didn't go with anyone, and you weren't in there long enough to eat in. I heard tell you might be looking for trouble." He tipped back on his heels and smiled like he'd caught me in the act of something disorderly. Not out of arrogance or spite, but more like a friends-don't-let-friends-start-fights sort of smile.

I dropped my shoulders and growled. "Grandma sent you to check up on me, didn't she?"

"We all know what today is, and we know what happens when your temper gets riled. She called Doc, worried you might do something stupid again. He called me. You know I can't fudge over another one of your tantrums." The smile broke through. Such a cute smile I never could get angry at him.

"No one said you had to."

"You want to go to jail? A judge will only allow so many warnings."

"How'd you know I would be at Willie's?"

"Where else do you go when you're looking for a fight?"

That's the trouble with a small town. Everyone knew everyone else's business. I pulled at a tear in my jeans. "For your information, I went in there to talk to Jaxon Reid about a vet bill. According to what he said, seems like you should be looking for an animal thief instead of following me around town."

"And for your information, I knew McGraff was in there, and you still have a bone to pick."

"Do not."

He snorted. "Whatever you say."

"Hey, did Mr. Hansen or my dad call you?"

He furrowed a brow and turned dead serious. "We talked not too long ago. Why?"

"Because I know someone caused trouble for Mr. Hansen. My guess is it's those nim-wits sitting inside."

"You mean McGraff's. Why them?"

"Who knows why they do what they do. Attention. Boredom. Sociopathic tendencies."

He snorted. "Suppose'n you leave the speculation to us."

"Fine, but do you know anything about those tracks out on Hansen's land?" I put Jaxon's words to the test. See if they held any weight.

He pursed his lips. "Never mind those tracks. There ain't no truth to 'em. Leave 'em be, you hear?"

"I hear, but Dad said there was an animal attack, and Jaxon said cows were stolen. Which is it?"

JT grimaced, like speaking to me was going to cost him more than he wanted to spend. I snorted back at him. "Your look says it all. How is it Jaxon knows so much about what's going on and finds it important to include me?"

JT shook his head. "I'm not sure what's going on. Just steer clear of Hansen's place . . . and Reid . . . and McGraffs. In fact, why don't you just go on home so we know you aren't part of the trouble."

I glared at him. Trouble? How was holding people accountable or expecting the truth trouble? Frustrated and feeling like an outsider, I left him staring after me, a cloud of gravel-smoke in my wake.

A half-mile from home, I paused at the abandoned coal mine road that meandered up the mountainside on the south side of Hansen land. I pulled the lock out of my pocket and examined the twisted steel. No animal or man could do this without a tool. I wouldn't put it past the McGraff's to try and pull off a prank. Maybe they convinced Jaxon to yank my tail. See if I'd squawk. But it didn't figure in with Dad blowing me off and rushing over to Hansen's first thing this morning. That, along with JT's warning to stay away, fired up my curiosity. Just who was prowling around up there on our neighbor's land, and what did they hope to accomplish?

As much as I believed those tracks had nothing to do with my mom and was simply Jaxon running his mouth, I needed to see them for myself. Just so I could comfortably tuck the childhood rumors back where they belonged. But I couldn't go now, not when Mr. Hansen might see me. Later, after dinner. I'd slip away without Dad knowing.

Chapter Three

Words from Sinatra's "The Way You Look Tonight" drifted into the kitchen from the living room. Grandma turned from the stove, where fried chicken sizzled in the large cast-iron skillet and reached for a platter on the adjacent counter. Her quick frown and blue eyes flashed a reprimand.

"Ellie Mae, don't ya think a nice skirt and blouse would be more appropriate?"

I knew she wanted the evening to be special. Every year, she made an amazing meal, attempted a nice atmosphere, and convinced me to be respectful of Dad's need to avoid the topic of Mom. Most years, she pulled off a pleasant evening, but tonight, she'd fallen flat by inviting Doc and his grandson out.

I faced her, five plates in hand. "This is my best flannel." I spun in a circle, showing off the yellow-and-gray plaid. "I even tucked it in."

"And why the ponytail? Your hair isn't long enough for it."

"It's out of my face. I like it that way. Besides, I'm just

being myself." I opened a drawer and piled silverware on top of the plates. "I'm not about to change my appearance for some city boy passing through, and Doc wouldn't recognize me if he saw me in anything else."

She turned back to the stove. "One of these days, a boy will come along, and you'll want to look nice for him."

Even though she had pulled up her silver hair into the usual bun, I noted the floral skirt and navy-blue blouse under the apron. Had she dressed up for Doc? I sensed something brewing between those two, but she'd swatted me down like a pesky fly the one time I asked.

"This isn't that boy, Grandma. Trust me. He ain't my type. I don't understand why you had to go and invite them to supper."

"Because it's neighborly. And what is your type?" She forked a piece of chicken onto the plate.

Good question. Only boy who'd caught my eye had turned to drugs and since left the state. I crossed the hardwood floors into the adjoining dining room but could still see Grandma through the doorway. "Someone normal who enjoys simple living, but not too simple, if you know what I mean. Book smart but outdoorsy."

"Careful expecting too much. You might end up a lonely old woman."

"Are you lonely?"

Grandma gripped the skillet with both hands and drained most of the oil into a small silver bowl then set the pan back on the burner. "No, but I'm not old either." She winked. "My life became extra important after your momma passed away. Being here with you and your daddy is the only place I want to be."

I went back into the kitchen, opened the cupboard on the right side of the sink, and pulled out five glasses. "I'm glad you're here because it sure isn't where Dad wants to be. At least not today." I held a glass under the spigot and filled it with water.

Grandma dropped a spoonful of butter in the chicken drippings. It sizzled as she used the back of the spoon and smashed pieces of crispy chicken. My stomach growled, the aroma drifting around us.

"Sweetie, he's trying his best. Emotions creep up, and he doesn't know how to cope."

"He knows how to shut me out."

"He's not the only one who has trouble expressing their feelings. Now promise me you'll be civil tonight. Especially toward Ethan's grandson."

"Oh, please. I'll bet he isn't interested in anything more than throwing a ball down a football field."

"Careful assuming too much when you haven't even met him." Her gaze drilled mine before she turned back to the skillet and sprinkled two large spoonfuls of flour over the melted butter.

I carried three glasses of water into the dining room and returned for the other two. "Doesn't take much to form an opinion. If this grandson cares about Doc then where's he been this past year? More than likely he wants a vacation from the rest of his spoiled family and is using his grandpa to get it."

Last night, when Grandma mentioned Doc was picking Jake up at the airport, my first thought had been what kind of person waits until after they're needed to show up? I saw Doc cry when none of his family came to Gertie's funeral. I sat with Doc and kept him company the days after. Maybe I had missed some important tidbit of information, but I didn't think so, because I only remembered thinking how selfish they all must be.

Grandma added milk to the skillet and quickly whisked it. "Well, mind your manners tonight. The day's been rough enough as is. I'm hoping to lighten the mood, have some good food, enjoyable conversation, and end the day well. Sound okay to you?"

I skewed up a corner of my mouth. Having fun and entertaining someone I had no intention of even talking to would only slow my efforts to get over to Hansen's. I looked into Grandma's pleading eyes. "I'll try to behave."

The front screen door opened and fell shut, bringing laughter and talk into the house.

"Perfect timing." Grandma poured the gravy into a small pitcher and motioned for me to help carry the chicken, potatoes, and biscuits, while she brought the gravy and turnip greens. Not the healthiest meal but all of our favorite comfort foods. I loved her so much for it.

I sucked in a deep breath and entered the dining room, ordering myself to not make a scene and ruin the evening for Grandma. Besides, there was a tiny speck in the corner of my mind that was curious about this boy who'd decided to show up out of nowhere.

As soon as I placed the food on the table, my gaze went straight to Doc's grandson. Hard to miss him when his body consumed almost as much of the dining room as my dad's. He was taller than Doc by an inch or two and made my five-seven feel short. Brown hair combed neatly to one side, he'd tucked a gray T-shirt with a big, faded, orange T logo into worn jeans. Typical jock.

Doc introduced us. Jake held out his hand, blue eyes scanning my face and clothes as he quietly sniffed and produced a half-smile. Was he smirking at me? What, did he think I was one of those girls who prattled on and on acting silly for attention or just a simple piece of mountain trash? I sidestepped his hand and wrapped Doc in a hug.

Ethan Dillard, also known as Doc, was my surrogate grandpa. The Dillards were a long line of outstanding doctors who served more out of a love for people, and the Hush Briar community, than for money. Dillard Hollow had been named for Doc's great-granddaddy, and folks out this way respected the whole lot of 'em. Long as I could remember, his belly'd hung over his pants, and he'd had a full head of silvery-white hair. Recently, he'd lost weight and his hair had thinned, but Grandma said he looked a lot like he did when he was younger.

Always around for important events, Doc kept up on my schooling and even helped me out with a project on occasion. When I was younger, I'd spill every sad detail about the arguments I'd had with kids at school or with Dad when we didn't see eye to eye. After he listened, Doc never failed to reassure me the rain would pass and the sun would shine again. He'd been there to clean up scrapes or dry tears as often as Grandma and my parents. I used to think he did it for all the kids in Hush Briar until around age eight when Jeanine set me straight. She said Doc liked me best because my dad was a doctor, too. Maybe. He and Dad had become pretty good friends over the years.

After he turned off the music, Dad settled at the end of the table and pulled out my chair. We locked eyes for several seconds, and I saw the apology, as if he wanted to explain. In past years, I would offer a grim smile to let him know we were good, but today, my resolve lay smothered under a mountain of half-truths. I wasn't waiting another year to dig for details.

I jerked the chair from his grasp and pulled it out for myself. He hadn't come home until the afternoon spay, and then afterward, locked himself in his office, not even giving me a chance to ask about the animal attack.

I sat down and pulled the padlock out of my front pocket so it wouldn't jab me. And so it'd be handy if an opportunity presented itself. I slipped it under my leg. Jake sat next to me and Doc across from him, next to Grandma.

Dad said grace, but the tone of his voice sounded sad. His movements were tense, and he squinted like he had a terrible headache. His blond hair was a mess, and he'd failed to shave. Regret chiseled at my anger. This happened every year. I didn't want to be mad. I wanted Dad to understand me, spend time with me, talk to me about Mom. Not about school, or work, or our crazy wildlife projects. I fought the burn behind my eyes. I loved him, but this year, I wouldn't relent. I couldn't, or nothing would change.

I kept quiet, glancing off and on at Jake. His manners were impeccable as he conversed with Dad about the vet business and asked Grandma about her garden and volunteer work down at the mission. Come to find out, he volunteered for the Red Cross Disaster Relief and was planning to follow in Doc's footsteps to study pre-med at the University of Kentucky.

To avoid gagging over so much perfectionism, I passed a glare between Jake and Doc. "So, how long had you two been planning Jake's pre-college visit to Hush Briar? And how long is he staying?" I directed my last words at Jake as if they were a punch to his side. He ignored my insult by stuffing another jam-laced biscuit into his mouth.

Doc stared at me, weighing his words like always. "He's spending the summer here. Let's just say it's been a work in progress."

I picked up my glass and mumbled, "A top secret work in pro—"

"Ellie's attending the University of Kentucky to study medicine as well," Dad said, and I choked.

"Veterinary medicine." I coughed. "Not quite the same thing."

"Only a couple years difference in the amount of schooling."

"While studying entirely different species," I swiped a napkin across my mouth and placed it in my lap next to the lock.

"Hey, don't sell yourself short. Every human has two hundred and six bones—"

"Here we go." Doc rolled his eyes and grinned at Jake.

Dad took a quick sip and set his glass down. "Animals are all different. Cows, two hundred seven. Cats, over two hundred and thirty. And dogs, three hundred and nineteen."

Doc picked up his water. "But you don't have all the variables of the human psyche."

"Then you haven't met Dorothy Simms. Isn't that right, Ellie?"

I stuck my fork into a chicken thigh, tore off a chunk of meat, and shoved it in my mouth.

Dad went on. "She brought in an owlet this morning. Wanted to raise it. Keep it as a mouser for the barn."

I jerked my gaze up. "Owls make good mousers."

"But not good pets. How'd you get the owl from her anyway?"

I lifted a shoulder. "Told her you'd call the warden, and she'd be fined. Just like you did me."

His forkful of greens paused midair. "Thought we were on the same page about that hawk."

We were. I knew as well as Dad that the injured hawk I found a couple weeks ago needed to recover at the Raptor

Rescue, but reality hadn't kept me from wishing I could've held onto her for a few days.

Poor Simsy. She loved animals. Dad needed to realize other people had feelings even if he didn't. "The owl was just an excuse to come over. Today's probably hard on her, too."

He swallowed the greens. "She has her boys."

I lifted my chin in acknowledgement, but not wanting to lose sight of my goal, I slipped the padlock onto the table. "This came from Hansen's. What happened over there?"

The room fell silent except for the tick of the mantle clock in the living room. Dad looked at the lock then my face. "Where did you get that?"

"Doesn't matter. What did this?"

"We'll talk about it later."

"No."

"Let me see that." Doc stretched an arm across the table. I placed it in his hand, noting Jake's curious stare.

Dad scowled. I scowled back. *Why did you bail on me today?* I willed him to read my mind.

"Same thieves, you think?"

Dad cleared his throat and looked at Doc. "Maybe. Hansen lost a couple cows."

I sat up a little straighter, capitalizing on the opportunity. "You see any tracks from an animal that might have dragged them off?"

"No possible way for that to happen." He said it with as much indifference as if I'd suggested a porcupine took them.

"I heard there might be some tracks out there. Bear or something."

"Where'd you hear that?" Dad cast a glance at Grandma, who tightened her mouth and looked apologetic.

What sort of exchange was that? Had he told Grandma

to keep an eye on me today? Was that why she'd called Doc, and then had Doc call JT?

I sat in the midst of a conspiratorial group, and still, I hated that I'd put Grandma in a tough spot. If she knew about my confrontation with Jaxon and Rodney, she'd take it personally, as if she'd somehow failed in the mothering department. Just like she did when I shot out Rodney's tires. She'd cried for two days, fearing I would go to jail because she hadn't talked better sense into me when it came to boys.

For Grandma's sake, I backed off. "Down at the mission yesterday when I was sorting through the shoes . . . someone mentioned bears were in the area. I assumed—"

"Not a bear. These footprints were a hoax. Checked them out myself." Dad's eyes drilled mine, a warning that if I didn't change the topic, I'd be asked to leave. But if the prints were hoaxed, what did it matter?

"Right," I relented. "A hoax. Makes sense." Except his reaction didn't make sense. And what about Jaxon's comment? *Your momma wasn't crazy. Go look at those tracks.*

Grandma stood, capturing everyone's attention. "I have apple turnovers. Who wants one?"

Doc pushed his chair back. "Always have room for your turnovers. I'll help with the coffee."

Jake grinned. "I think those turnovers might be why we came. He's been talking them up ever since she invited us out."

Dad chuckled as if all was right with the world and began peppering Jake with questions about hurricane relief efforts still happening around New Orleans.

Once dessert and coffee had been served, I took mine out on the front porch, allowing the screen door to slap shut behind me. Air was chillier than usual, but I'd take it over the heat and humidity soon to roll in. I sat on the porch swing, folded one leg up under me, and pushed with the other. A few frogs sang as the sun began to set on the opposite side of the house.

How would I get over to Hansen's without a confrontation? Could take the truck or four-wheeler, but Mr. Hansen wasn't likely to let me snoop around. Too far to walk. But I had to go, see what Jaxon was talking about and why Dad was acting so antagonistic. I didn't believe Mom was one of those Bigfoot researchers like some people had said. She never talked about mythological creatures or strayed away from practical science. But I also didn't know everything about her. She had secrets. Ones that Dad wouldn't share. Possibly ones that got her killed.

I took a sip of Dad's favorite instant decaf. Almost too gross to drink, but hot and totally smothered by apple-cinnamon heaven as I bit into Grandma's crispy pastry. The screen door opened. Jake slowly stuck out his head like I might snap it off if he weren't careful.

"Mind if I join you?"

Chapter Four

"Free country." I stretched out my leg and touched the porch railing with the toe of my worn-out tennis shoe, stopping the swing.

"Quite a bit chillier than what I'm used to this time of year." With the mildest hint of an accent, Jake showed off a nice straight smile, which only complimented everything else.

The swing jostled as he sat beside me. I gave it another push. "Give it a month, and you'll feel right at home."

"Not sure about that." He took a bite of turnover and groaned. "Wow."

Poor rich boy. Probably missed his poolside lounge chair and being waited on by his housemaid. "S'pose life 'round here's not quite what you're used to either." I tossed my last bite in my mouth and licked the frosting off my thumb.

"S'pose not." Jake deepened his accent, obviously poking fun at my hillbilly speech. Yeah, I needed to clean it up a bit before I went off to school, but at home, relaxed, I enjoyed the comfort and cared little what he thought.

"So, what was that about the missing cows, animal

tracks, and that broken lock? Noticed you were cut off."

"You noticed that, huh? Let's just say things around here aren't always as they seem."

"Like you?" He took another huge bite of turnover.

"Excuse me?" I searched for hints of teasing, but his expression remained neutral.

He spoke around the food. "Acting cold when there's actually a friendly girl underneath. Or at least that's what Pappy says. My verdict is still out."

"Well, don't waste too much time thinking on it. Your opinion matters more to girls impressed by southern football jocks than it does to me."

"Wow. Why don't you say what you really think?"

"Okay." I unfolded the foot tucked under me and let it fall to the porch. "These past few months—since Gertie's death—I've watched your grandpa nearly grieve himself to death. It broke my heart there was no one here for him. Why was that?"

"He didn't want us here."

"He doesn't want me around half the time either, but I go anyways. He's stubborn like that. You show up when family needs you whether they want you to or not. Or is it different down in New Orleans?"

Jake narrowed his eyes. "Sure you aren't jealous because now you have to share him?"

"Me, jealous? Listen to you. At least I have some right. As far as I knew, you didn't even exist outside his *occasional* visits to Louisiana. Doc didn't even talk about you."

"Obviously."

There was no sound beyond the frogs, crickets, and the creak of the porch swing. I took a sip of coffee, sensing I'd sucker punched him with words. Staring into my cup, I gnawed on the corner of my lip and thought how I would feel if Grandma talked about someone else's grandkid and didn't acknowledge me.

"Sorry. If it's any consolation, you've accomplished in one day what I've been trying to do all year."

He lifted a brow and swallowed the last bits of his turnover.

"His smile touched his eyes tonight."

I wasn't sure if he was contemplating a thank you or buying himself time as he dredged up another insult.

"That does help. Thank you."

"Since we're clearing the air, why don't you tell me why you looked down your nose at me when you first came in?"

"Me? Looked down on you?" He said it accusingly, like it'd been the other way around.

"Yes, you smirked like I was an insignificant piece of mountain trash."

His eyes widened. "You got all that from a look?"

"Yes."

"Wow. Your perception needs help." He took a drink from his mug and grimaced. "Ugh! What is this stuff?"

"The one thing I know is that you're an absentee grandson."

"One thing. Maybe you should find out more. You might be surprised." He tossed his coffee over the porch rail. "And when I looked at you, I was thinking *so this is the great Ellie Mae.* I thought when I met you, you'd be wearing a tiara and glass slippers."

"What! Why?"

"Because I have a photo of you wearing them."

I stopped the porch swing from moving. "That's weird. Why in the world would you have a picture of me?"

"Pappy sent it." His voice took on a smug tone. "We've emailed each other since I was about seven. Trust me. To him, you're a superstar. I probably know more about you than you realize."

Confused, I looked down at my tennis shoe and skimmed my toe along the porch floor, setting us back in motion. Why would Doc send pictures of me to his grandkids? How did he even get them? I'd not even seen Doc or Gertie hold a camera. Except maybe one of those Polaroids. When I was eight or nine, Doc had taken me over to Hatley's Pumpkin Farm and snapped a picture while I held one of their pups. I remember shaking the photo to speed along the development.

"I had no idea." I met his gaze, wondering what else Doc told him about me.

"I know."

"What does that mean?" It was my turn to study Jake. Serious, confident. Not a measure of doubt. Unless my perception was as bad as he said.

The screen door opened and Grandma stepped out, holding the phone. "Ellie Mae, Jeanine would like to speak to you. Said she's been trying to call ya."

"Left my phone upstairs to charge." I hesitated before lifting myself off the swing. As neighbors, Jeanine and I had been friends by default our entire lives, best friends at times. But after graduation she'd started ignoring me.

"Thank you." I took the phone and held it next to my ear. "Hello?"

"Ellie, why haven't come over and seen my baby yet? You need to. He's so cute!"

"Josey's calf? The one that came a couple days ago?"

"Yeah. He's just the sweetest thing."

I blinked. She didn't usually get this excited two days after the birth of a calf.

"Come on. You know you want to come over," she

coaxed.

True. I loved babies, but I didn't need to go over to her place to see one. "I have company, so—"

"Bring him! I mean, that's okay, bring your company. I don't care."

Holding back a snort, mixed feelings stirred through me as I caught on to why she really invited me. Figured. Well, who cared? Showing off Jeanine's calf to Jake offered a legitimate excuse for me to get over on Hansen land. How I'd get back beyond their pasture without being noticed would require some thought, but I had time.

I glanced at Jake. He pushed the swing lightly, staring out across the lawn.

"We'll be over soon." I pushed the off button and smiled wide as Jake met my gaze. "That was my friend, Jeanine Hansen. I'm gonna check out her new calf. Wanna ride along?"

"Hansen?" He narrowed his eyes then lifted his chin along with the corner of his mouth. "Because I'm the ticket for your dad's approval to go over there?"

"*Pfft!* No..." I reared back. "I'm just being friendly. Stay here if you want."

He stood and grinned. "Sure, I'll go along"—he opened the screen door and held it for me to pass in front of him—"but it's gonna cost ya."

"We don't have a coffee shop in town, and the only Starbucks is in the Food City in Hazard. That's about ten miles north, and they close at nine. But I can make a decent pot of coffee if you want."

Jake stood aside as I unlocked the pole barn. "You won't

poison it, will you?"

I drilled him with a glare. He grinned and held up his hand. "Joking. Okay, your coffee tonight, but tomorrow—"

"I'll buy you something frou-frou."

"Hey, there's no shame in liking cappuccino."

"There is when it costs five dollars a cup." I flipped the light switch, revealing Dad's truck, surrounded by a menagerie of dog kennels, farm equipment, and tools. An old, broken freezer we used for storage sat along one wall. I pulled out a backpack.

"Here." I handed it to Jake. "Hold it open." I dropped in two heavy-duty flashlights, a couple rain jackets, and a half dozen shotgun shells.

"Wait! We're taking a gun?"

"Yes."

"Why do we need a gun?"

"Because . . . crazy things can happen." And their names ended in McGraff, but Jake didn't need to know about them. "There was an animal attack or something. Best to be prepared." I crossed to the other side of the barn and rummaged through the toolbox until I found a tape measure.

"What's the last thing you shot?" Jake held open the pack. I dropped in the measuring tape.

"A deer tangled in some barbed-wire fence."

"Ouch. Sorry."

I heard the wince in his voice. The kind words caught me off guard. "Thanks." I closed the bag and my gun inside the cargo bin on the four-wheeler. "Would you get the door?"

I straddled the seat and backed out. Jake closed the door and climbed on behind me. If he noticed, Dad would wonder why we didn't take the truck, but by the time I returned, we'd hopefully have more important things to talk about. Like *why* I disobeyed him.

Jake and I drove down the road, gravel crunching under the tires. Slowing near the mouth of the Hansen's drive, I spoke over my shoulder. "Better hold on and lean in close. It's a pretty steep climb." Not that I'd mind dumping him if I didn't think it'd slow me down.

I'd made the trip a hundred times in the dark and hadn't been one bit concerned about making it up the hill until Jake scooched closer and put his hands on my waist. Warmth under the pressure seeped through my flannel shirt, and every nerve inside me jumped to life. Annoyed at my reaction, I wriggled closer to the handlebars, leaned forward, and pushed the throttle.

Water-filled ruts disguised as shadows splashed as I unsuccessfully swerved. Under our weight the tires slipped and threw up mud, threatening to send us backward at times. Eventually, we made it up the drive and pulled to a stop. A light atop the barn illuminated the area.

Jake hopped off, grinning. "Nice driving! That was awesome." Mud speckled his face and coated his pants and arms.

I bit back a laugh, knowing I had a bit of mud in my hair and on my shoes, but nothing compared to him. "I kinda forgot about how muddy it'd be. At least you look less like a city boy."

"So that's how it is?" He scooped four fingers of mud off the side of his jeans and held them up with a playful, threatening look.

My eyes widened. "You do not want to do that."

"Why? What happens if I smear mud on the great Ellie Mae? Does the Earth crack open? Does the sky rain down fire? Are you going to shoot me and hide the body?"

"You'll wish." I fisted my hands and faced him, ready to throw a punch if he came near me. He tipped his head, a glint in his eye.

In two steps, he intercepted my moving fist and wiped mud across my face. How did he move so fast? My mouth fell open. "You did not . . ."

"I did, and I gotta say, that felt good." He stepped back and crossed his arms, assessing his work as I used my flannel sleeve to clean off my cheek. He laughed, and my stomach lurched, betraying everything I wanted to feel. Everything I should feel. Jake was the enemy. I couldn't like him.

"Good to know you're not risk averse 'cause the evening's not over." I grudgingly flung a clump of mud at him as we walked into the barn.

We found Jeanine inside, standing on the bottom rung of a gate. Beyond her, the new baby nursed from his momma. At the other end of the barn, a couple dozen Angus had been shut in for the night. A few expressed their unhappiness with repetitive mooing. Jeanine jumped down when she saw us.

"Hey there, Lills. Who's this?" She held out her hand. "I'm Jeanine."

"Jake." He held up his muddy hands. "Sorry."

"He's Doc's grandson. They were at our place when you called." As if she didn't know. Whatever Jake thought of her too-tight cropped T-shirt and cutoffs would mean the opposite for me in my muddy jeans and flannel.

I didn't care. Princess, indeed. I tossed Jake a cheeky smirk as I rubbed the mud off my fingers. "You owe me. I rescued you from a checkers tournament."

His cocky sniff said he knew better.

"How long you in town for?" Jeanine propped an elbow on the top rung of the gate.

"The summer. I'm helping Pappy around his place. See if we can fix it up a little."

"The whole summer. That'll be fun." Jeanine tilted her head and ogled him as if she'd found a new toy. With her blonde ponytail and big blue eyes, she was pretty and would have been more so if it weren't for the dark cavity in one of her eye teeth.

"Where you from?"

"Small town north of New Orleans. I was under the impression news traveled fast and y'all would know everything about me."

It was true. Even though Jake'd just arrived last night, gossip flew faster than a hawk on a mouse. Grandma knew. That's why she'd invited them to dinner. Dad knew and had prepared a passel of questions for Jake about his course of study at the university. And by all appearances, Jeanine knew—the real reason she'd invited me over. Had I been the only one who didn't care two wits about his presence? He'd get what he wanted and then move on. Surely everyone else could sense an underlying self-serving motive.

After fawning over the calf and talking about plans for the summer, I walked us back into the barnyard.

"Don't need to hurry off. You can stay and hang out for a while. Caleb's back from Knoxville today. Said he planned on calling you. It's a little cool, but the four of us could take a dip in the pond, clean your clothes up a bit." Jeanine looked Jake up and down.

Alarm shot through me. I hadn't seen Caleb in almost a year, and last time we were in the pond together, horsing around turned serious, one kiss led to another, and the night ended with me telling him I wasn't ready. That had been the beginning of the end, and I had no desire to revisit those memories.

Was Caleb the real reason Jeanine called? If he'd put her up to it, wouldn't he be out here? Didn't matter. I didn't want to see him. Fear of a confrontation and how I might react sent a streak of panic through me. "Can't. Need to get Jake back."

"Maybe the four of us could go out another time? Shoot some pool or something."

I gave her a questioning look. Caleb and I weren't on speaking terms.

She ignored me.

Jake climbed on the four-wheeler as Jeanine laid a hand on his arm. "If you find yourself bored, give me a call. I'll be happy to help you find some entertainment."

I gawked at her.

"I'll keep that in mind. Thanks."

I heard a definite hesitation in his words and felt relieved, which startled me. After breaking up with Caleb Hansen, I wasn't looking for another boy to occupy my thoughts or time. Especially this one. Still, when Jake touched his hands to my waist, that undeniable current set me off-balance.

"See you in church, Jeanine." I said pointedly and hoped she'd back off and stop acting like a cow in heat.

Smiling and unfazed, Jeanine waved. "See ya."

Jake chuckled.

More aware of Jake's nearness than what I was doing, I popped the clutch and slammed him back against the cargo bin.

"Sorry."

He resettled and we started down the hill, entering a dark cavern of trees that snuffed the moonlight as all light from the barnyard faded.

Chapter Five

The four-wheeler moved along easily, headlamps cutting through the darkness just enough. About halfway down the hill, I slowed to a crawl and veered right on a path leading into the woods. Weeds brushed at our ankles, and a sapling slapped my arm. Caleb and I had ridden four-wheelers up and down this area enough that I knew my way, but it'd been over a year, and the terrain and overgrowth had shifted in places.

I half-turned toward Jake. "Watch your face." If I hadn't been so focused on the tracks, I would've remembered to bring the helmets I took out of the cargo bin earlier today. Rocks and holes caused us and the lights to bounce. I slowed.

"Where we headed?" Jake hollered in my ear.

"Wait and see."

The next landmark was a large boulder. Easy to find. We turned right onto the coal mine road. The tires spun and flipped mud as we climbed back up the hill. Our bodies jerked side to side as I hit one hole after another. The rain had done a number on this trail.

The four-wheeler pulled hard to the left near a drop-off that bordered North Fork River. I could tell because the space was completely black, not even the silhouette of a tree. Jake must've seen it too because his hands tightened on my waist as he mumbled a few words I couldn't quite make out.

I slowed even more, switched gears, and leaned to the right. Another five yards and the front tire popped out of a rut. We started to tip. Jake let go and catapulted himself off the back. I stood and leaned forward. The ATV slammed down on all four wheels and lurched ahead. Within seconds, I hit level ground, killed the engine, and jumped off.

"Jake! Are you okay?" I fumbled in the bin for the flashlight, slammed it shut, and hurried down the hill, half-sliding as I went, praying Jake hadn't slipped over the edge of the drop-off. He stood near where I lost him, shaking mud off his arms, his body covered. Beyond the darkness at the base of the gorge, the river rushed by.

I expelled a heavy breath. Thank God he was alive. Then, releasing all the nervous energy generated from the climb, I laughed, probably more than I should have. "The whole mud look suits you. I'd say I'm sorry, but . . . you kind of asked for it."

"Glad you find it funny." He stormed past me and hiked up the path.

I caught up to him, slightly concerned he'd want to go home. Probably wasn't the best idea to take him trail riding at night. "You okay?"

"I'll live." He ran a hand back through his hair and flicked the mud on the ground. "Where are we?"

"South side of Hansen land. We have to walk the rest of the way."

"Rest of the way to where?"

"The tracks. I brought us this way because I didn't want Jeanine or her dad to know we were out here. He might not take kindly to us snooping around. Not to mention, he'd tell Dad."

"Then why are we doing it?"

An owl screeched, and a breeze circled around, sending maple seeds twirling to the ground.

I looked at his face under the waxing moon. Should I trust him with the secret I'd kept to myself for so long?

At the four-wheeler, I handed Jake a towel and spoke over the sound of the river. "Thanks for jumping off back there. We would have rolled otherwise." I pulled my gun out of the bin and slipped the strap over my shoulder.

Jake wiped off his arms and face then tossed the towel on the seat. He pulled out the backpack and one of the flashlights. Extending his arm, he indicated I should lead the way. He was mad. Well too bad. He knew I was going after the tracks, or he wouldn't have made that comment about being my ticket for Dad's approval. What did he expect—an easy night hike through a prairie? I bit one corner of my lip. I did almost dump him over a cliff.

"So what's New Orleans like?" I hoped to smooth over his annoyance.

"Hot, muggy, noisy."

"Bet there's always something to do." I shooed a buzzing mosquito aside.

No answer. We walked on in silence until the question nagging me spilled out.

"Was coming here something you wanted to do?"

"I'm here, aren't I?"

"But why now?" I made a conscious effort to keep accusation out of my voice.

He stopped, staring at the ground for two seconds, then made eye contact. "I've always wanted to come, but it's complicated. Or at least it was."

I let the flashlight fall against my leg and tipped my head to one side. "Can I be blunt?"

He blew out a chuckle. "You're asking now?"

"This is important. I don't want you to think I'm being rude."

He folded his arms across his chest. "Okay. Be blunt."

"I'm about to trust you with a major secret. I'd like you to trust me back. I promise not to tell anyone about whatever is complicated in your life, just help me understand why no one was here for Doc after Gertie's death."

"I told you. He didn't want us here."

"That's not true. Doc's crazy-happy you're here."

Sucking in a deep breath, Jake started walking at a slow pace. "Okay. I'll tell you why visiting Pappy is complicated, but first tell me what you've heard about my family."

"Doc has a daughter. She went off to college and never came back. Gertie used to leave for long stretches to visit you guys, but Doc only went a few times I'm aware of. He'd come over to our house after Gertie left, but he never talked about any of you. I always thought it was because his feelings were hurt for not being invited. That's all I know."

We walked in silence for a full minute before Jake spoke, a bit of an edge to his tone. "I hate that Pappy was alone during Gertie's visits, but he was invited. I invited him. Even if no one else wanted him to come, I did. But he always said he needed to work."

"Wouldn't your parents let you visit?"

"No. My mom is . . . Well, she's an attorney and can be very hard to argue with. My dad manages the farm. He's barely home."

"Wait." I stopped out of shock. "You're a farm kid?"

He chuckled. "Not exactly. We live next to my grandparent's organic farm. Dad runs it, but I work there. And by the way, Jeanine's calf wasn't the first newborn I'd seen. My grandpa raises grass-fed beef."

I adjusted the gun over my shoulder. Somewhere nearby bushes rustled, a coon or fox maybe. "Sorry for misjudging you."

He shined his light in my face, but I could see his smile in the shadow. "Guess I can forgive you. Wanna start over?"

"Only if you move that light out of my eyes." I playfully pushed it aside and stuck out my hand. "Nice to meet you, Jake Harris. What made you decide to visit your Pappy this summer?"

He squeezed my hand. "It's the first summer since I turned eighteen, and no one could stop me. But I had to move out." A hint of sadness surrounded his last few words.

"Why?"

"The million-dollar question. Rules and expectations. No one, besides Pappy, wants me to go to the University of Kentucky."

"Why'd you choose it?"

"Scholarship, good medical program. It's Pappy's alma mater."

I tipped my head. Why hadn't Doc told me about Jake following in his footsteps or about their relationship? "All good reasons. Your family should be proud of you, not making you feel like you need to do what they want."

He bumped me with his elbow. "Thanks."

For a brief second it felt like we existed on common ground. The place where people are pushed aside when they become too much of a burden to their families. Maybe Jake wasn't that spoiled after all.

We continued to trek upward on the narrow road, which was no more than a tractor's width of low-growing weeds. Sounds of the river dwindled away, replaced by the hum of crickets.

"Want to know the real reason we didn't come up here when Gertie died?"

"Yes." I swatted a mosquito on my cheek.

"Mom had Gertie's body shipped down to New Orleans for a memorial service."

I squinted at him through the darkness. "But she has a grave marker here. I saw her casket at the cemetery."

Jake slapped at a mosquito on his bicep. "But you didn't see her put into the ground. She went from the cemetery in Hush Briar to another funeral home in New Orleans. Gertie signed a document, giving my mom permission to move her body. Mom had her buried down there."

My mouth fell open.

"But that wasn't the worst. Mom told Pappy he wasn't invited to the memorial. I can't even begin to describe how wrong it felt. When I asked why, she tried to convince me that Pappy didn't deserve to mourn *his wife*. She brought up a bunch of stuff from the past I didn't need to hear. I finally worked up the courage to confront my parents and made plans to leave. I'm here to find out Pappy's side of the story."

My insides froze. "Don't even try to tell me Doc did something bad to Gertie or your mom. I won't believe it."

He glanced my way. "I won't, at least not until I know a little more. But he never laid a hand on Mom or Gertie. Nothing like that."

"Then what happened between Doc and your mom? Why doesn't—"

Thwump! Thwump! . . . Thwack! The loud noise vibrated in the space around us. Jake and I stopped, looked at one another, then panned our flashlights over the area, listening to the darkness.

"What was that?" Jake whispered. The crickets had quieted. Nothing moved.

Thwack! Thwack! Thwack! Three short fast noises answered from farther away.

The faintest whoop sounded in the distance, not too far off from the cry of an owl, but it wasn't any owl or coyote I'd ever heard. Maybe someone trying to imitate either one.

"Probably just hunters or pot growers signaling to one another." But the sound came from the ridge directly west of Hansen's pasture where the terrain was pretty steep and rocky. I'd hiked over there not too long ago. No one was growing out that way. What were people doing out here in these woods? A follow-up theft at Hanson's? Or some other kind of harassment?

"Maybe we should go back." Jake pointed his flashlight straight up so it illuminated both our faces. "Finish this in the morning."

"No! The tracks might be gone by morning. I have to do this now. Another hour and we'll be done. I promise."

Jake leaned in a little closer, drilling his eyes into mine. "Why would we stay out here with hunters and drug dealers?"

Good question, but how could I explain my need to prove the prints were fakes? And that deep down inside I feared they might not be. Jake would develop the wrong impression about Mom. I needed to see the tracks first then decide if telling him the full truth was worth it.

"That noise was far enough away that whoever made it can't even see our flashlights because of the hills. Noise always travels farther at night. I promise, if we come across anything remotely out of place, we'll leave right away."

He moved the light to my face. "I'm going to hold you to that because someone obviously caused trouble here last night."

We walked on until the trail opened into a clearing. At one time, the old road had continued along the edge of the forest. Today, this was where it ended. I pointed my flashlight beam across the expanse, snaking it over the ground as we crossed at an angle. The temperature was dropping, creating a low-lying mist that drifted up and mingled with the tall grass.

"You cold?" I scanned his bare arms.

"A little."

I stopped, pulled a jacket from the backpack, and handed it to him. At least the mosquitos stopped biting. We continued side by side, our beams of light intersecting now and again as we crossed the prairie-like green space. Another five minutes and my light bounced off a flash of color.

"Over there." I pointed. "What's that?"

Jake moved his light in the same direction.

"Looks like some kind of orange marker."

We had hit the back edge of Hansen land. Off to our right, a fence closed in the backend of the pasture. In the daylight, the farmhouse wouldn't even be visible. I felt comfortable no one could see or hear us. And whoever had made those sounds had quieted.

I moved my light. The beam passed over a series of roped-off areas that led, one after the other, in the direction of the ridge. Seven patches, each four-foot by four-foot, lay an equal distance of about six-feet from each other. Someone had tied orange nylon strips on the ropes. The first two sections were inside the pasture. The others, outside. We approached the first one on our side of the fence.

I dropped to my knees, expecting to see a prefabbed footprint like the ones I'd seen in the zoo a long time ago. To be funny, the zoo personnel had mounted a set of Bigfoot prints next to other human and primate footprints. The memory of Mom rolling her eyes flashed through my mind. I remembered her pointing out everything wrong with the Bigfoot print—the arch, the ball of the foot, the lack of weight shift, the perfect toe position, and the absence of material between the toes. *If the tracks are uniform without variation, if they don't tell you a story, then they're probably not real.*

At the time, I thought her words were meant for all footprints in general. Now I wondered. My heart pounded harder as I touched the impression in front of me. It was deep, about two inches, and at least twenty inches long.

Jake knelt to my right. "Think these were faked by whoever stole the cows?"

"Look at the details." A scant amount of water pooled at the deepest point where it looked like the upper portion of a padded foot struggled for balance after jumping over the fence. There was no clear outline, almost as if the potential bandit had hurtled and nearly fell. "Look, this one is smaller, and they slightly overlap. The toes are longer than a human and they vary in position, gripping for balance." I swallowed hard and glanced at Jake. "Could that be faked?"

"Has to be. Your dad said they were planted to throw suspicion off the cow theft."

"Yeah, well, all my dad's cylinder's aren't exactly firing the truth right now. He said that because he didn't want me to see these and ask questions."

"Questions about what?"

Mesmerized in a whirlwind of confusion, I pulled my phone out of my back pocket and tapped the camera icon. I had only wanted to prove to myself these prints were fake and shake the notion Jaxon had planted in my mind. I never believed my mom studied the Bigfoot. She was a respected naturalist. She didn't talk about cryptids and that kind of stuff. It was only after her death that I'd heard whispered rumors that she tracked them. Now, I wondered if the rumors held some truth.

Instead of answering Jake, I pointed to where the long toes of one foot smashed into the wide heel of another. "It looks like two creatures are running, one behind the other. How can this be?" I whispered, tracing the outline with my fingertips.

I walked to the next section, stepped over the rope, and knelt beside the impressions. *The tracks will tell a story.* No foot angle or pattern was an exact replica of the others. Some toes varied in width, none uniform. Where the feet overlapped in the previous section, now I could clearly see where two . . . animals? Humans? . . . caught their balance and separated slightly to run side by side.

They didn't run like humans. I moved to the third set. Humans landed on their heels and propelled off the balls of their feet, leaving behind an obvious arch. These tracks showed wide padded feet that landed flat, then pushed off on long toes.

I took several pictures and started for the next roped-off area.

Snap!

Jake crouched beside me. We turned off the flashlights and scanned the pasture. It was too dark to see anything but the silhouettes of trees and rolling ground.

Hunched, we hurried away from the footprints toward a

thicket down a slight incline. I slipped the gun off my shoulder as we backed our way into the brush. My mind whirled in confusion, trying to process what my eyes had seen and rationalize it with facts. There was no sound beyond our breathing. Not even a cricket.

I half-expected random hunters to invade, but they'd have to get past Mr. Hansen first. Unless they were familiar with the gorge and coal mine road, which I doubted. Not many people wandered around this territory at night.

But what if Mr. Hansen was allowing someone to investigate on his property? What if he was planning to sell a story? Did Mr. Hansen enlist Jaxon's help to fake the prints and bring in investigators, or worse . . . Bigfoot hunters? Was that why Jaxon had the lock? False proof? Why would he give it to me? And why would they create such detailed tracks? Could they even do that?

Was it remotely possible these footprints were real?

You go on up and have a look at those tracks. Did Jaxon think my affirmation would give him credibility? I could see the headline. "Hush Briar graduate follows in her mom's footsteps to track Bigfoot."

Realization hit. I grabbed Jake's arm and whispered, "I think we're being followed. He knew I'd come out here."

"Who?"

"Remember the lock from supper?"

"Yeah."

"This guy my mom used to know gave it to me."

"So?"

"He thinks I'll track this animal . . . or whatever it is. Lots of folks around here know I can track. Not as well as my mom, but I know enough. But why would he follow me tonight? I can't track anything in the dark."

"You're talking like those footprints are real." Jake shifted his weight, balancing on his haunches.

"I know. I didn't expect to find something that looked so real. I'm not sure what to think."

"What do you want to do?"

"Wait." We sat in the tall weeds another ten minutes. Moisture soaked through my knees and thighs. I clenched my jaw to keep my teeth from chattering. When nothing happened and it was obvious no one followed, I slipped into the second rain jacket and crept back to the fourth set of footprints.

"Look at this." I pointed to dark brown spots on a broadleaf weed. "Blood."

Only two drops of fading blood separated the fourth and fifth set of prints. I studied the last pair—more a half print than a full impression. "Whatever it was, it picked up speed." I glanced up the dark, forested hill.

"Ellie, it looks like a large human. Shaquille O'Neal has feet about this size. It's probably a well-staged prank to throw off the police."

"Did you see any footprints or tire tracks outside the barn?"

"Didn't really look."

"Even our four-wheeler left ruts in their driveway. A heavy truck would have done more damage. No way they'd have even gotten up the lane last night with all the rain we had. And if the thieves walked the cows out of the barn and down to the road, there would have been hoof and boot prints all over the place."

"What are you saying exactly?"

Now was the moment of truth. It might also be the moment of goodbye. I hoped not. I was beginning to think Jake's presence would be a breath of fresh air this summer.

Still, I couldn't deny the truth just because I wanted to. I stood tall and placed both hands on my hips.

"What I'm saying is that I think these footprints might belong to a real Bigfoot."

Jake stared at me for several seconds. I stared back, daring him to laugh. But he didn't. He glanced at the tracks, skewed up a corner of his mouth, then nodded as he hefted the backpack over his shoulder. "Okay. What's your next move?"

Chapter Six

After I dropped off Jake, I hurried out Dillard Hollow toward home, the dark road a longer stretch than usual. My nerves pinged as gravel crunched under the tires. At every turn where I slowed, swaying trees silhouetted against the sky created wavering shadows. All kinds of animals lurked in those shadows. If there was an oversized humanoid creature out there, would it follow me?

I sang a Sam Hunt song loudly, only I wasn't *taking my time*. Three times through the song and I'd be home. Wished I'd taken up Jake's offer to follow me back, but it seemed a waste of time, gas, and a little pride on my part.

Think I could've sacrificed some pride. If an overly large creature was out here roaming the woods, I didn't want to be its sole object of interest. For the first time tonight, I allowed my mind to imagine what a Bigfoot might look like, how they lived, if they were dangerous, and how I would find them. Wrong thoughts because my vision morphed from friendly gorilla-like creatures to monstrous beings that had murdered my mom.

I shivered and shifted my thoughts to Doc's face when I'd dropped off Jake all covered in mud. He'd belly laughed like I hadn't seen in a long time.

Jake had been a good sport the entire night. And when he didn't laugh over my speculation Bigfoot might be roaming the surrounding hills, admiration set in. I'd misjudged him in more ways than one.

Headlights appeared around the bend, followed by the rumble of a diesel engine. I sighed, thankful someone else was out and about, until the pickup passed. The front tire hit a puddle and splattered me. I stopped, shocked by the cold spray. Red brake lights appeared in my rear-view mirror, and the truck backed up to where I sat wiping muddy water out of my eyes.

"Ellie Mae, what're you doing out here?" Caleb Hansen stuck his head out the window, elbow draped over the door frame. My heart did a little flip before nosediving.

He shifted the blue TCAT ball cap on his head. I always liked his sandy blond hair, a natural mess, but it looked good on him. His eyes were a dark blue that lit up with simple pleasures like midnight ice cream cones or jumping out of hay mows.

"Hi, Caleb. I'm headed home, and thanks to you, I won't be needing a shower."

He looked me over. "Sorry. Don't think I helped as much as ya might think. You okay?"

"Yeah."

Silence. I picked at a piece of mud on my jeans.

"Jeanine said you were out at our place."

"She said you were home."

Silence.

"New calf is gorgeous." I flicked the mud onto the ground.

"You would think so. Excited to start school?"

"Yeah. How's TCAT? Still studying Diesel Mechanics?"

"One year left. Listen, Ellie, I'd love to sit here in the middle of the road talking to you, but someone's bound to come along and move us. Can we get together soon?" He smiled, and while I couldn't see it, I knew there was a single dimple in his right cheek.

"I don't think—"

"Not a date. Coffee. To talk."

A year ago, I was glad to see him leave. He broke my heart in so many ways, and the sting of betrayal hurt enough I didn't care if I ever saw him again. I'd heard snippets about him working and going to school full time, keeping so busy there wasn't time for fooling around, that being away from Rodney McGraff helped him refocus.

I missed him something awful the first few months, but it got easier. Now, I wasn't sure I wanted to share coffee with him and dredge up old feelings. Even the good memories still hurt. But a part of me longed to talk to my old friend. While it might end as a mistake, I wanted to find out for myself how he was doing instead of relying on the latest gossip.

"Tomorrow evening. Seven o'clock. Meet at the diner. Not Willie's."

"Sounds good." He shifted the cap again. "It's nice to see you, Ellie."

I didn't reciprocate, because I wasn't sure if I was glad to see him. Years of the best and worst memories haunted me with heart-slicing pain. Today—being reminded of lost time with Mom, experiencing Dad's rejection, and now seeing Caleb after a year of no contact—pushed me to a place I hadn't been in a while. A dark and lonely place in my mind where a familiar shadow of fear chased me home.

Exhausted, I stowed the four-wheeler and entered the house through the back. In the utility room, I grabbed a towel out of the aluminum cabinet hanging on the wall, went into the bathroom, and ran water as hot as I could tolerate. I stood under the spray and thought about Jake, probably still washing the mud out of his hair. I frowned as I lifted my face into the water. He'd been forbidden to see his grandpa and had to move out to do so. Why did his mom hate Doc? Made sense that Doc wouldn't go see them if he was treated badly. But why had Gertie allowed it? I refused to believe Doc had done anything wrong. It simply wasn't possible.

My thoughts flittered to Caleb as I soaped up my hair. I hadn't prepared myself for a summer return. Guess I thought he would stay in Knoxville and work. Honestly, I didn't know if I had forgiven him yet. We all did stupid stuff, but he'd been hurtful on a personal level.

A knock sounded on the door. "You okay in there?"

Dad waited up? Maybe with Grandma in bed, he finally wanted to talk.

"I am," I hollered over the spray of water. "Had a run-in with Caleb Hansen on the way home. Tell you about it when I get out." Would Dad bring up the footprints? Should I? Not an ounce of me wanted to deliver Jaxon's message because Dad would freak over the fact I approached him, and that would ruin all other conversations.

Dad was nearly asleep in his recliner with the newspaper on his lap when I entered the living room in my pajamas, wet hair rolled up in a towel. I glanced at the mantle clock. Almost midnight.

"You didn't need to wait up for me." I sat across from him on the fireplace hearth and unwound the towel.

He yawned, stretched, and put the footrest down. "Caleb's home?"

"For the summer, I guess. Not sure. He passed me on the road and accidently drenched me. I'm meeting him for coffee tomorrow evening." I cringed. "Is that bad?"

"Just be smart. Keep an open mind."

"A part of me wants to punch him again."

Dad's smile was short-lived. "I advise against that. It didn't work out well last time."

I had sprained my wrist when I hit him in the jaw after he accused my mom of being intimate with Bigfoot. He'd called her a furry and added a few vulgar words for emphasis. All while he laughed at me for being a prim. Hitting him had been worth it. Until Doc reminded me how I allowed people to control me when I reacted to their behavior. And he was right. It would take a miracle to change what people thought of Mom.

"Caleb looks better."

"Best thing Hansen did was get him away from the McGraffs."

"I wonder if he'll stay away."

"Hope so. How's the calf?"

"Looked real good. Did you know Jake's family raises cattle on an organic farm? A calf birth was nothing new to him."

"Didn't know that."

"How well did you know his mom?"

"Not too well. We grew up in the same town, but Kim kept to herself. Gertie homeschooled her."

"What was she like?"

"Truth?"

"I won't tell Jake if that's what you're thinking." I set the towel aside and worked my fingers through my hair.

"Always seemed a little too big for her britches."

"Seems strange, doesn't it, given how friendly Doc is?"

"Gertie was the same way. Until Kim left home, she didn't associate with the community. Always went all the way to Lexington to shop and go to church."

I hadn't seen that side of Gertie. Long as I could remember, she and Doc went to church in Hush Briar. "Is that why no one ever talks about Doc's daughter and her family?"

"He gave Kim the world, and she wouldn't have anything to do with him." I detected a hint of bitterness in his voice.

"Do you know why?"

"No."

"Do you think Jake's mom would've talked to him about our family? About Mom?" I gently broached the topic, hoping it might lead Dad into talking about her.

Dad folded the newspaper and laid it on the table beside him. "Doubt Doc or Gertie ever talked to Kim about us. Besides, I have a feeling Jake will form his own opinions." Dad stood, a sure sign we were about to end our conversation. I stood too, afraid of losing my opportunity. *Where were you today, Dad? Why didn't you come back? Why did you leave me alone?* The words were right there, but I couldn't speak them. Why couldn't I spit them out with the same anger I'd felt earlier today?

Because I knew how it would end. We'd been down this road before. I looked at him, pleading for answers, but his passive, tired eyes said he wasn't up for an argument. If I started in, he'd simply walk away. Fine, I'd wait. But I wasn't brushing his evasiveness under the rug. Once I discovered where those footprints led, I'd somehow make him talk to me, even if it meant bringing up my visit with Jaxon.

"I'm showing Jake around tomorrow if that's okay. I'll get the morning chores done and be home by early afternoon to help finish the mowing or whatever." I couldn't help my clipped tone, but Dad let it roll off.

"If you're not home, Sarah will feed and walk the dogs. But I wouldn't go too deep into the wilderness. Jake's not used to this."

"Jake'll be fine. He's no pansy."

"I just want you to be careful. Extra careful."

"Why?"

"We don't know who's stealing." He pointed at the lock on the fireplace mantle. "But they're desperate. Going after easy money. I don't want you to get between them and their stupidity."

Dad's protective side warmed me to the core. He'd waited up, concerned. That counted for something. He loved me.

We stared at one another for a couple seconds. A battle waged inside me. Hug him goodnight as I'd done every night of my life, or avoid him because I was still peeved he'd disappeared on me? Generous and caring, he helped so many people. Yet he'd been totally unfair today. I wanted him to know that if he didn't talk to me about Mom, our relationship would never be the same.

"We'll be extra careful. Thanks for waiting up." I brushed past him and jogged up the stairs.

Chapter Seven

Early the next morning, despite fatigue from a night of fitful sleep and terrible dreams, I flew through my chores, excited to be tromping out in the hills on a beautiful day. I cautioned myself to be smart. This was about tracking an animal and the truth behind those footprints on Hansen land. Not spending time with a boy. After tossing biscuits, apples, and bottles of water in my backpack, I headed into town on the four-wheeler.

The sun barely skimmed the horizon when I stopped in front of Doc's place. Birds sang loudly from the large oak. Jake sat on the porch steps in jeans, hiking boots, and a blue-gray flannel that hung open to reveal a gray T-shirt with purple LSU letters across the front. I killed the engine as he removed his ear pods, stood, and shoved them in his pocket. Eyes hooded with fatigue, he lifted a corner of his mouth, causing my insides to race as if there were baby chicks running around with no speed control.

Ridiculous. *Get a grip, Ellie.*

"Morning. Just so you know, I'm more of a sunset versus

sunrise kind of guy." He tossed his backpack into the cargo bin.

I grinned, amused by his just-crawled-out-of-bed-and-into-clothes aura. "Lucky for you, we got both."

"Look at you, all witty at the crack of dawn. Do I need rain gear to keep the mud off, or do you think you'll be able to dodge the puddles in the daylight?"

I started to ask if he was trying to get a rise out me when the screen door eased open and Doc stepped out, coffee cup in hand, looking ready to start the day. "Morning, Ellie Mae."

This was new. I glanced at Jake, silently asking if he'd talked to Doc about last night. He ever-so-slightly shook his head.

"Morning, Doc. Whatcha doing up and about so early?"

"Oh, I'm putting in a couple hours at the free clinic in Hazard. Haven't been for a while, but they called the other day a little short-staffed, asking if I'd help out this morning. Fine morning for a hike, but you're looking tired. Dark circles under your eyes."

"Didn't sleep the greatest, but I'm all right."

He walked down the steps, forehead scrunched. "Ellie Mae . . ." Doc hem-hawed, looked me in the eye, then off down the street toward the edge of town. "Your grandma ever tell you about the time Dean Martin passed through town?"

My mouth fell open. Hadn't expected that. "No."

"He happened along one weekend back in the summer of . . . guess it would have been '63 or '64. Big deal for a mud puddle like Hush Briar. Sang one Friday night and generated some interest in swing and jazz. I want you to ask your grandma about it. See if she remembers that night." Grandma rarely shared her life history. Sad and unimportant, she'd say. After several failed attempts, I stopped trying to convince her it was important to me.

"Why don't you ask her?"

Jake touched my arm. I narrowed my eyes at a total loss. He smiled. "She'll ask her. We better get going."

Doc lifted a hand. "I'll be home by lunch. Have a good time, and be careful." Doc climbed the steps and went back into the house.

"What was that about? Why don't you think he should ask her?"

"Because that would be too obvious. He wants someone else to plant the seed. Jog a memory or something." Jake pointed at the helmet in my hands. "That for me?"

I thrust it toward him. "Brought you this so you could protect your hair."

He rolled his eyes and climbed on behind me, placing his hands on my waist. Those chicks in my belly picked up speed. I popped the clutch, and he slammed against the cargo bin. Again.

"Sorry!"

Once he repositioned, I drove out of town and back up Dillard Hollow to the deserted coal mine road. We hid the four-wheeler in a tree line past Hansen land then back-tracked about a quarter mile to where we left off last night. I honestly hoped there'd be no trail and the footprints would look totally different in the daylight, but that wasn't the case. Those footprints hadn't been faked. And Dad didn't want me poking around them, but Jaxon did.

The trail was easy to pick up. Impressions in the wet ground trailed up to the ridge. Leaves and pine needles obscured some prints, but where the brush thickened, we found plenty of trampled foliage. Another day, and the ferns and grasses would lift into place, briars would bounce back with the breeze, and the trail as we saw it now would mostly disappear.

A mile from where we started, we crested a ridge overlooking the outlying hills. The footprints weren't as obvious on the harder ground, and the trail would've gone cold except for droplets of blood on scrub brush leaves or the occasional stone.

"My guess is the blood dripped from the nose or mouth of the cow, the result of a broken neck." I grabbed hold of a tree for balance as I stepped down the rocky slope.

"Have you ever seen a cow with a broken neck?" An edge of challenge laced his tone, but I didn't care. He was sifting for truth, and I could respect that.

"Couple years ago, a cow went headfirst over a cliff. I went along with Dad to see if we could save her."

"What happened?"

"We helped the owner dress it out and carry the meat back."

"I once saw a cow taken down by an alligator."

"Seriously?"

"It was mating season. We were out in the pickup checking on the herd. Found them grazing near the river. This male gator had wandered upstream. He was huge. I saw him grab hold of a cow's leg and then roll. Flipped her around like a rag doll. They shot the alligator, but not before it killed the cow. We also lost a dog to a gator that same year."

"From a different alligator?"

He shrugged. "That's the thought."

"That's wild. I've never seen an alligator outside a zoo." We walked side by side. At two large maples, we passed through at the same time and bumped shoulders. Laughing, I pushed him. He pushed back. It felt good to be out in the woods. Simple, serene. I think Jake felt it, too. The fact he didn't need to ramble on and talk all the time added relief. Nearly two hours in, we sat on a large boulder and shared the biscuits and water.

"These from last night?" Jake pulled open the baggie.

"Yeah, I saw you put strawberry jam on yours, so I fixed a few for ya."

"Thanks."

I shrugged.

He smiled and held my gaze until he looked like he wasn't sure what should happen next. He refocused on his biscuit and cleared his throat. "Do you think the sheriff will be out here today?"

"No."

"You sound sure. Cows were stolen. Why wouldn't he be?"

"Because no one's gonna want to admit the truth."

"Which is?"

I rolled my eyes at him because he was well aware of what I was tracking. "This is some kind of big animal."

"You mean a Bigfoot?"

"Yeah, no one, except cryptid researchers or crazy trophy hunters, will care about those footprints. The people who matter–the sheriff, the town–they'll continue to believe this is a theft or an animal attack. You heard my dad. Fake footprints? Did the same pranksters travel this far just to break twigs and drop blood?"

He unscrewed the lid off a water bottle then took a drink. "Why do you care?"

I sucked in a deep breath, remembering I hadn't shared my secret. "Because my mom died out here. At her funeral, I overheard the sheriff tell my dad that Mom died chasing legends. Her own stupidity got her killed. People made fun of her and called her crazy. No one, not even Dad, defended her. She wasn't crazy, Jake. I never believed she studied Bigfoot, until last night. So now, if this oversized beast is out there, I aim to prove it and clear her name. But I also understand if you don't want to be a part of this."

"Why would you say that? I'm here." He stuffed a second biscuit in his mouth.

"I'm sure what I'm doing seems idiotic. You don't really even know me. It's not your problem."

He swallowed. "You're right. It's not my problem, but I don't think it's idiotic for a girl to search for answers so she can defend her mom. As for not knowing you, maybe that's true, but I've been waiting years to meet you." He half-smiled.

"Now that's idiotic." Secretly, I tucked those words in a safe place to ponder another time. "What was all that with Doc earlier today?"

"What? Dean Martin and your Grandma or working at the clinic?"

"All of it, I guess. It's been a while since I've seen him do anything more than read the Hazard Herald before noon. Grandma has sort of made it her mission to see he's been kept in baked goods since Gertie died, but when would they have ever been together? She married at sixteen."

Jake lifted a shoulder. "I don't know. How old were they in '64?"

I glanced at the sky, counting. "Teens. Fifteen or sixteen." I tipped my head, intrigued by thoughts of years gone by. "Grandma has a secret. Guess I'll just have to ask."

We stowed our trash and continued to follow blood spots and broken-down forest. Along a cliff edge, I walked with my head down, scanning the ground until I realized

Jake wasn't behind me. I walked back to where he stood and followed his gaze to the smokiness embedded in the trees and knolls left over from the cool night. The sun inched upward behind us, burning the mist that danced among the hills.

He crossed his arms. "Don't think I've seen anything so beautiful."

I sat down, legs dangling over the edge and patted the earth beside me.

Jake sat. A mourning dove cooed a peaceful song as other birds chattered away with more urgency.

"How do you not come out here every morning just to watch this?"

"Sometimes I do, especially in the summer." I leaned back with my palms on the ground behind me. In the wilderness, I walked and talked with Mom, embracing the peace where nothing but nature existed.

"I could get used to this." He inhaled deeply and assumed my pose, resting his palm on the ground next to mine, eyes closed. The breeze lightly tossed his hair. When he opened his eyes, he noticed me watching him.

I smiled, a little embarrassed at being caught. My turn to shift my gaze.

Jake pulled up one knee and wrapped his arms around it, leaving the other foot to dangle over the drop-off. "What was your mom like?"

I picked up a pebble and tossed it into the expanse before us. "She was tough. Both of her parents died when she was young. The Simms' family took her in when she was around five or six. They might have been her foster parents, but I think these hills raised my mom, if that makes any sense. She really didn't talk much about her childhood, but she lived most of it outdoors. When she was nineteen, she earned her GED and enlisted in the army. Then she worked for the University of Kentucky and the Department of Fish and Wildlife. She was an expert tracker, worked with search and rescue, and conducted wildlife research."

"Which explains a lot about you."

"She used to bring me out here all the time. Sometimes with Jeanine and Caleb. This was our entertainment."

"What about your dad? Does he believe in the Bigfoot?"

I shrugged. "He's never talked about it."

A red-shouldered hawk flew overhead. I pointed. "Coolest thing about my dad . . . he specializes in wild birds. There aren't many vets around with his expertise."

"You like 'em, too. I can tell by your smile."

I nodded. "Just look at him. Isn't he gorgeous? I have his mate over at the bird sanctuary." The hawk cried out the typical *kee-ah*. "He's calling for her. Kind of sad and wonderful at the same time."

Jake lifted a brow as if in question.

"Red-shouldered hawks mate for life. He'll wait forever for her return. Lucky for him, she'll be back in a few weeks. I'll take you over to see her if you want."

"Yeah." Jake and I watched the bird circle then disappear into the trees.

Brushing his hand over the earth, smoothing out the dirt and grit between us, Jake cast me a side glance. "How did your mom die?"

I tossed another pebble. "At the coroner's office, the records say she died from injuries sustained in a fall."

"But you say . . ."

"That maybe she did, but someone pushed her over a cliff or placed her there." Focusing on those kind eyes, Jake's compassion relaxed the anger that wanted to surface every time I thought of the injustice.

"You think the Bigfoot are responsible?"

I shrugged. "I never thought that. Until last night, I would have said no way. Thing is, I can't prove how Mom died, but I might be able to prove the Bigfoot are real. I owe her that. Dad barely talks about her. In fact, he keeps her office locked up. I'd been okay leaving well enough alone until yesterday. Now, his avoidance feels like a betrayal. We have a chance to vindicate Mom, so why doesn't he jump at it?"

"Maybe he doesn't feel she needs it."

I blew out a breath and glanced away. Jake touched my hand. "Hey, I'm sorry about your mom. I think you're right. She doesn't seem like a person who'd accidentally fall."

Those words meant more than the moon and stars on a clear night. Especially after yesterday. I smiled. "Thank you."

"And I kind of get what you're feeling. I wish my dad had stood up for me and let me visit Pappy, but he wanted to keep the peace. Still, to deny us for the sake of keeping peace with my mom seems unfair. Selfish." Jake pressed his mouth into a firm line. "I needed this." He opened his arms, encompassing the wilderness.

Enjoying the serenity, we sat for a few more minutes. Then, break over, we stood, walked a short distance along the crag, and entered another section of dense forest that descended before taking us back up a steep hill. Jake watched the scenery while I inspected every branch, rock, and leaf, looking for anything out of place. A good mile or two past the limits of where I normally traveled, we crested a hill and abruptly came to another cliff that dropped at least thirty feet into a lush gorge where limestone walls bordered three sides of a canyon.

Pine trees, a couple fallen logs, and scrub brush lined a

creek that I suspected branched off North Fork River. Ferns and wildflowers dotted the area, and a thin fog hung over the water that flowed south, rippling around huge boulders, widening as the gorge flattened into a thicket of new saplings. Three buzzards circled overhead, and near the water, a blue heron skimmed the surface, landing on the far edge.

I scanned the hill behind us, but the scrub pines and wild roses looked untouched. "I think I missed something. I don't see any more trail."

"Ellie!" Jake jabbed me with an elbow then pointed at the rock wall to the right. "Look down there. What is that?"

Chapter Eight

"What? Did you see something?"

"I don't know. But look over there on that ledge. Is that an opening of some sort?"

I placed a hand on his bicep, my cheek next to his shoulder as I followed his outstretched arm to a flat piece of rock jutting out from the cliff wall. The smell of cotton, cologne, and the warmth of his body messed with my concentration.

I squinted, forcing away the distraction. "Um . . . yeah . . . looks like it." I pulled away, faked a smile, and turned. "Let's go back." I pointed the way we had come. "I want to see if there's a way down there. I'm sure they didn't climb down right here. It's way too steep."

"You sure we should go down there?"

"Let's at least see if they went that way. We won't get too close." A good rule to keep with Jake, too, if I wanted to think clearly.

We retraced our path all the while watching the garage-door-size cave opening. After a good half-mile hike, the cliff descended to where jutting rocks and brush made it an easy climb into the gorge. There were no footprints, just plenty of broken twigs with stripped-off leaves. We walked to where we had an unobstructed view of the cave opening still several hundred feet away.

"Wish I'd brought binoculars. Look over there on the ground at the base of the ledge." I pointed toward the water's edge, near the monstrous limestone wall. "See the pine tree jutting out of the cliff? There's a slew of kudzu that way, but it hasn't quite reached the tree."

"You think those are cow remains?"

"Maybe." I pointed at the buzzards. "They're after something."

We stood silent, brows furrowed, trying to decide our next move. We didn't dare go closer in case something was in the cave, and there was no way to know if the animal remains were cows or random deer.

I hated to leave, but I had no idea how to proceed. We couldn't just march up to the cave entrance of a wild animal, let alone one that was possibly large enough to snap the neck of a cow. But I needed to get video or decent pictures. Then the sheriff would have to acknowledge their existence. The whole world didn't need to know. I understood the locals not wanting a bunch of strangers roaming these hills, but our neighbors and those who thought mom was chasing legends had to see and believe Mom had been right. I hadn't been able to support her as a kid, but I could now. I owed it to her.

"I'm searching Mom's office tonight after Dad's in bed. See if I can find out how to best approach the cave. You want to help?"

Jake raised his brows. "Closer? Are you crazy?"

Every ounce of warmth I had for him drained into the rocky soil around us. I clamped my mouth shut, brushed past him, and stormed back up the rocks and broken trail. I didn't need his help. I would be perfectly fine on my own.

Back on the crest, I moved at a fast pace, ignoring Jake when he called my name. I retraced our steps through the weeds and trees. Mom documented all her findings. She'd never brought me into the woods without also bringing one of her journals. The one I had contained animal sketches with factual details, stories about search and rescue, and details on tracking. I'd read and reread those entries. Many had footnotes that cross-referenced other journals. She had to have kept more secret. I was sure of it.

When I reached the big rock where we had eaten biscuits, I dropped my backpack and sat down with a thud. I pulled out my water, took several gulps, and lowered my elbows to my knees as I caught my breath. Jake wasn't even winded. Stupid jock.

"Why are you mad?" He opened his water and lowered himself next to me.

Really? He needed to ask? "You insisted on coming along, and then you insulted me."

"Insulted you? Yesterday you thought I looked down on you. Now, what, because I don't agree with you, I'm insulting?"

"No, you said I'm crazy because I want to get closer."

He made a face, indicating I sounded absurd. "Poor word choice. Sorry. I only meant to say it seemed dangerous. I don't think you're literally crazy." His face and words softened.

I took another long drink and forced my temper to relax. "After she died, I took a lot of ribbing because of my mom's work. And when kids made fun, Dad wouldn't help me understand if her work had been fact or fiction, so I've learned to stand up for myself. When someone calls me or my mom a name, well . . ."

It hurt. I didn't say it aloud because I didn't want to sound any more dramatic. Jake didn't know about Caleb and the wounds he'd carved in my heart, making sensitive topics difficult to traverse.

Jake reached over and brushed off my shoulder. Then he lightly touched the tiny L-shaped scar on the left side of my chin, smiling a scant bit.

"Why'd you do that?" I asked, conscience of the warmth that lingered from his touch.

"Chip on your shoulder. Checking if it's still there."

I could have told him to tag along this evening and watch as I flung that chip of insult at Caleb, but, again, too much drama for someone I'd only known a little over twenty-four hours. Such behavior would push me over into the slightly unbalanced personality column. If I wasn't already there. Instead, I allowed Jake's easygoing nature to relax my own.

"Not much affects you, does it?"

"I'm a little freaked that a very large animal might be living in that gorge, but I'm a realist. I'll wait until I see it."

"So . . . does that mean you'll help me go through Mom's journals tonight?"

"You really think your mom has journals on the Bigfoot?"

"Maybe. She wrote a lot of stuff down." I stood and slipped on my backpack. "The only thing I know is what I've overheard, been told about the legend, or what other people gossiped about the last five years. Dad and Grandma wanted to protect me. I get it. Now, I'm not only old enough to handle the truth, but I think I'm entitled to it. I'm guessing you understand."

He heaved a sigh and followed as I started to walk. "I do, and because I want to see where this goes, I'll help you. As long as I don't have to be back out here at six tomorrow morning."

"City boy." I elbowed him.

He shoved back. "Thought we established I didn't live in the city."

"You didn't say that. You said you lived next to the farm. For all I know it's an urban farm." We walked on, talking about the different folklore in the mountains and witchcraft practices around New Orleans. They had their own legendary monster called the Rougarou, something like a bloodsucking werewolf.

"Hey"—Jake swiped at me with the back of his hand—"is it true that when you were little, you broke three fingers after you crashed your bike then rode all the way home before your dad took you to see Pappy?"

"Doc told you that?"

Jake pulled a leaf off the knee-high weeds we tramped through. "In the emails."

I glanced his way. "*Why?*"

He shrugged and glanced away. I let it go not wanting to embarrass him.

"What else did he tell you?"

"He said when you were like twelve, your parents made you wear a dress to church on Easter. You were so mad, you stripped it off in the parking lot to reveal shorts and a T-shirt."

I grimaced. "I remember. Not the first time I was sent to my room for being disrespectful. Jake, I am so sorry. Reading those emails must've been painfully boring."

"No. It wasn't. Any news from Hush Briar fascinated

me. And now, it's sort of fun seeing the real-life you in action."

"You lead a boring life if my stories entertain you that much."

"Over the years, I imagined Hush Briar as a sort of magical world where parents didn't fight or manipulate, where my expectations for myself were good enough, and I could be happy. When Pappy wrote about you, I imagined us friends, and you liked me for me. Not because of my name or who my parents were." He bumped my shoulder again. "And being around you less than a day has far exceeded my expectations. I've already been covered in mud, almost fell over a cliff in the dark, tracked Bigfoot, and told you more about my family than I've shared with anyone. Ever."

His words tugged on a string of emotion bundled deep inside me. How could anyone not like Jake as is? His smile alone could bring about world peace. "I find it hard to believe you don't have a ton of friends who care about you."

"You might be surprised. There're plenty of people who want to party, but that gets old. I'm so ready to move on and do something meaningful with my life." He picked a cluster of small wild daisies and began pulling off petals.

I understood his need for a friend who listened and wasn't out to fulfill their own agenda. How long had it been since I'd had that? Jeanine and Caleb had been my closest friends since birth, but thanks to the fantastical stories told by Rodney McGraff and his posse, I had lost Caleb and most likely Jeanine.

I wasn't quite sure how to accept Jake's words because it wasn't me—the backward tomboy—he desired as a friend. He wanted the girl from Doc's embellished stories. Surely, Jake could see the difference. I'd already proven myself judgmental and rude. Given enough time, I'd no doubt crush his fantasy.

At the four-wheeler, Jake jumped on first. "Care if I drive this time?" He motioned for me to hand him the key.

"Can I trust you?" I slowly climbed on behind him and placed my hands on his waist.

"We'll find out." He took off, driving and maneuvering the ATV like he'd been doing it his entire life. I'd told myself I didn't care what he thought of me, but at some point in the day, my mindset shifted, and something deep inside made me care quite a bit. I relaxed, moved in close, and pretended for a second that I was everything Jake imagined, and that, like his experience so far in Hush Briar, I far exceeded his expectations.

All too soon we pulled to a stop in Doc's drive. Jake climbed off the four-wheeler, stashed the helmet in the cargo bin, and pulled out his backpack.

He paused next to me as he ran a hand through his hair. "Ellie, I don't mind helping out, but if Pappy suspects and asks questions, I won't lie to him."

I nodded. "That's fair. I wouldn't want you to lie. I'll come pick you up later tonight. Dad goes to bed around ten."

"Cool. See you then."

Chapter Nine

The café's pink neon open sign sputtered and strobed like it might die at any moment. Formally known as The Sweet Shoppe, the owners used to serve only ice cream and malts but later turned it into a full-service restaurant. As a kid, Mom, Dad, and I would eat here once a week. The smell of the grill and greasy fries always took me back, and it was no different this time when I opened the glass door. But with memories of Mom close to the surface, the bell jingle and greasy aroma met me with overwhelming melancholy.

The place was full. Caleb sat in a booth near the back, fiddling with an unopened packet of sugar. By the way curious eyes followed me, I should have thought better about time and location. I sucked in a deep breath that morphed into a yawn as I slid onto the black vinyl seat across from Caleb. My eyes watered, and the heaviness in my shoulders returned. I had to keep reminding myself it wasn't his presence, but my reaction, dictating the outcome of this evening.

"You cut your hair."

Because Caleb liked my long hair, I'd cut off twenty inches last year and donated it to an organization making wigs for kids with cancer. It had seemed like the right thing to do until Doc asked me who got credit for the donation, Caleb or me. Still, it was just hair, and since it'd grown out a bit, I preferred it shorter.

Looking Caleb in the eye, I swallowed my emotions and didn't let the sight of him cause chaos like it did last night. He averted his gaze back to the sugar packet. I wasn't letting him off easy. If he wanted to talk, fine.

He lifted his eyes and spoke quietly. "You can stop it with the intimidating glare. I come in peace."

"I haven't decided if I come in peace or not. Don't tell me how I should act." I matched his volume, keeping it down so I didn't attract attention.

He slowly shook his head. "Wondered last night if it was really you."

Gritting my teeth, I remained silent as Eleanor set water and menus on the table. She worked the diner a couple evenings a week but spent most days down at the mission. Any overheard word would find its way to Grandma's ears, and I sure didn't want that. Once she walked away, I met Caleb's gaze, refusing to let his concerned stare whittle away at my resentment. "What do you want to talk about?"

He let out a deep breath and leaned back. "Guess I want to say I'm sorry and prove I mean it. I want to know how, and what, you're doing. Can you even forgive me?" He held eye contact.

Talk about getting hit with both barrels. I could barely comprehend I sat across from him, let alone civilly discuss how I felt. The weight of his words sapped my logic and cracked the dam inside me that held back emotion. I went on the attack because it was easier than trying to reason or decipher the swirl of pain threating to break my resolve.

"I want to forgive you, but it wasn't only about you cheating with Megan. It's what you implied when you called my mom names. You knew where to throw the punch so it would cause the most damage. You've made me question our entire childhood. At times, I thought you were my only friend. Now, I wonder if I even had that. You want to know how I'm doing?" This was my opportunity. I sucked in a deep breath, ready to fling a year's load of emotionally charged venom at him. Doc's voice lectured in my head as I glanced around the crowded restaurant. *One of these days, they'll move on, and you'll be left with how you reacted.*

My tension unwound into exhaustion.

Caleb flexed his jaw as if bracing for my worst.

"Why didn't you come back sooner?" I whispered and hated how the pain in my voice mirrored my feelings.

Caleb blinked twice, obviously surprised I hadn't attacked him. "I felt ashamed. I still feel ashamed. You're the last person in the world I wanted to hurt."

"I don't believe you."

"I'm not the same person I was a year ago. The drugs and alcohol aren't speaking for me anymore."

We stared at one another in silence, and I saw the clarity in his eyes, the healthy color in his face. "I heard you were in rehab."

"Losing you made me realize I needed help."

"Your parents made you realize you needed help."

"I hurt them, too."

"The McGraff's are still in town. How are you gonna keep away from them?"

"I'm only here for a week. I'm still working at the quarry in Knoxville."

"Oh." One corner of my mouth slightly lifted. Then I frowned, sad his life moved on outside Hush Briar. But it was a good thing.

"How are you?" he asked again and leaned across the table on folded arms. I looked away, unable to recapture the vehemence of a few minutes ago. I didn't want to punch him anymore. I wanted to crawl under the table, slink to the door, and race into the night where I could hide from the sting of the past.

I looked at him and lifted my shoulders. "I'm good. Working for dad and helping out, same as always. Getting ready for college."

"You'll do great. I never would have graduated if it hadn't been for you."

I didn't want to reminisce. I'd cried a river over Caleb, over our lost friendship, over the boy who'd been my first kiss, my confidant, and at times, my protector. He'd been a safe place, a stronghold after Mom died and Dad stopped talking. Then he found more satisfaction getting drunk with Rodney and Todd. He chose to sleep in on Saturday mornings instead of traipsing through the woods, and he preferred Megan and her sex appeal over me.

I thought I hated him, but in his eyes, I saw the Caleb from long ago, and it stirred the pot of mixed emotions. My insides grew hot as my control slipped. I needed to get away and sort this out before the dam burst in front of all these people.

I tried to pull up Doc's words of wisdom, but my mind tangled in a mess of confused memories. "I need to go. I don't want to be here."

"Wait, Ellie. I need to tell you—"

Without another word, I slipped out of the booth, brushed past Eleanor, and exited the restaurant. I climbed into my dad's truck and slammed the door before Caleb could stop me. Tears came quickly as I raced to the edge of town.

I didn't want to go home where Grandma would worry over me. So, at the roadside park off North Peak Road, I shut off the engine and lights, and cried.

Grandma said tears cleansed emotional wounds and spoke to God when we couldn't find words to explain how we felt. I sat in the semidarkness for a long time, forehead against the steering wheel, letting my emotions speak as I thought about Caleb. We could never go back and be the carefree kids who rode bikes down Dillard Hollow so fast not even the dogs could keep up, and I wasn't sure I wanted him in my future to constantly remind me of the pain. I needed to move on, put Caleb out of my mind, and look toward a time not riddled with someone else's dysfunctional drama. I had enough of my own.

It was nine-thirty when I finally pulled it together and headed back to town. I stopped at the Marathon, put gas in the truck, and went into the bathroom to wash my face. My eyes and nose were a little red, but not too noticeable with my darker complexion. I smoothed down the green sleeveless blouse, covering the top of my jeans, and walked out, stopping at the cooler to get two bottles of sweet tea for this evening's work with Jake.

I heard Jeanine's unmistakable laugh from around the corner in the small Subway shop. I peeked and saw her sitting with Rodney McGraff. My heart fell to my toes. She looked up, meeting my dumbfounded gaze, smirked, and took Rodney's hand.

Straightening my shoulders, I walked over. "Hey, guys."

"Hey, Ellie. Thought you were with Caleb tonight." Jeanine offered a coy smile.

"I was. Why are you hanging out with him?" I said it with disgust as I glanced at their hands.

"I can do what I want. Now be nice."

So this is why she avoided me. She knew how I felt about Rodney. "I can't. After what he did to Caleb? What are you thinking?" Entwined with anger, my nasally tone from crying was barely noticeable.

Rodney scowled, but I didn't care. He could scowl at the end of my shotgun if he wanted to.

"Ellie, don't be rude." Jeanine narrowed her eyes at me. "What you did to Caleb was much worse."

I opened my mouth to argue but why waste my time. Instead, I shifted my gaze to Rodney. "Caleb won't play with you anymore. You need to drag down Jeanine?" I looked back to Jeanine. "What do you see in him? He's only gonna get you in trouble."

Rodney stood, but I wasn't about to back down. Let him hit me. Let him do whatever he needed to do. No way would I allow him or his lowlife brother to hurt more of my friends without a fight.

"You need to go, Indian girl."

"You don't scare me. I see the real you."

"And just what do you see?" He stood close enough I could smell his soured tobacco breath.

"The lowest form of white trash these hills have ever known. So broken and dysfunctional, the only time you feel good about yourself is when you hurt someone else."

The door to Subway opened. Rodney looked over and then scoffed at me. He sat back down and motioned for Jeanine to scoot over. "We have company."

Following his gaze, my jaw dropped. Todd McGraff approached with Caleb in tow.

Anger bubbled to the point of overflowing as I made

eye contact with Caleb. Heat flooded my chest and neck as a jumble of venomous words threatened to fly off my tongue, but I was so over this drama. If they wanted to ruin their lives, I couldn't stop it. I turned and walked away.

How stupid could he be? My hands shook as I fumbled in my pocket for the twenty-dollar bill. I slapped it on the counter. The cashier looked at me but kept quiet. After stuffing the change in my pocket, I stormed outside without a backward glance.

Caleb must've ran back out the door he entered because he stood by my truck, blocking the entrance to the driver's side door.

I shook my head. "Move out of the way, and do not speak to me!"

"It's not what you think, Ellie."

"Move." I spoke through gritted teeth.

Caleb stepped away from the door and circled around me. "Jeanine's in trouble. I'm trying to stop this. That's the real reason I came home."

Pausing, I looked at his face to see if he was telling the truth. "What?"

"If you'd calm down and let me explain . . ."

Anger rushed out of me. A chill swept over my skin. Wrapping my arms around my stomach, I slumped with my backside against the truck.

"Why'd you run out of the diner? I was going to tell you."

"Because I am sick of this emotional roller coaster. You shouldn't have sucked me back in. I'm glad you're helping Jeanine, but I'm done. I'm saying goodbye to you and to all of this. I can't take it anymore." Exhausted, I motioned toward the store where the other three watched out a window. Then I said with as much sincerity as my heart could muster, "Caleb, be careful. This is not good."

I climbed in the truck, started it, and pulled away. In the rearview mirror, Caleb stood watching until I drove out of sight.

At least the tears stayed away. I felt slightly empowered as if I'd come to a forked path and chose the right direction for a change.

At the edge of town, I stopped in front of Doc's house. Lights burned in the window. I sat for a full ten minutes just breathing before I pulled out my phone and texted Jake. Within seconds he joined me in the truck.

"Hey, how's it going?" Jake hopped in and pulled the door shut. Another sporty T-shirt, this one a dark blue Kentucky University baseball shirt. How could his smile so easily lift my spirits? And if he noticed any remnants from my emotionally charged evening, he didn't say anything. I appreciated that.

"Haven't eaten." I told him and tried to sound enthused. "Care if we get a pizza and take it back with us?"

"I'm always open to pizza."

We ordered from Willie's then drove over and parked in the lot, listening to country hits on the radio. I shared with Jake how my mom's office occupied one of Dad's examining rooms, but he always kept it locked. I'd spent the afternoon trying keys he kept in various places. In the end, an unlabeled key hanging in the storage room worked.

"Weren't you curious about her stuff before?"

"I never wanted to believe Mom studied Bigfoot. I just wanted it to go away, but I can't ignore it anymore. And I keep thinking that if the Bigfoot are the reason Mom died, then that's probably why Dad's lying about the footprints. For some reason, he doesn't want me to know they're real."

"If that's true, why'd he let you go out last night? We were gone for hours. Don't you think by now he's figured out we went and looked at them?"

"Why, did Doc say something?"

"No. We didn't talk about it, which was kind of weird. After seeing the lock at supper, talking about tracks, us going over to Hansen's. I expected questions, out of curiosity if nothing else."

Thinking back to Dad waiting up, I didn't pick up on anything out of the ordinary. Maybe that in itself was a clue. Why did he let us go? Hadn't he been afraid we'd get hurt?

Jake turned the radio knob, lowering the music. "You didn't say earlier today, but does your dad agree that your mom died in a fall?"

I blinked my thoughts away and focused on his question. "He does, and that's what confuses me. He found her body, but he wasn't there when she fell. How can he be so sure about what happened, unless he saw it?"

"You think he knows more than he's telling?"

"Yes, and I thought he was finally going to open up to me yesterday, but he bailed on me. That's why I was spittin' nails at dinner."

Jake lifted a corner of his mouth. "Pappy told me. I also overheard him talking to your Grandma on the phone earlier in the day. She was afraid you and your dad were gonna blow the roof off the house. That's why she invited us for supper, I think."

I winced. "Actually, it was kind of great you and Doc came over. Doc always has a way of neutralizing a situation." *And I got to meet you.* "Sorry you didn't get your coffee."

He shrugged. "We've got all summer."

A comfortable silence fell over us and we sat together,

listening to the radio until my phone buzzed. I held it up. "Pizza's ready."

Opening the bar's door, Toby Keith blared from a jukebox in the far corner. Pool balls smacked together, and the smell of alcohol surrounded us. We waited at the cash register. Laughter erupted from the corner as someone spilled a bowl of peanuts on the floor.

I paid for a medium pepperoni, and we walked out into the cool night.

"This isn't my favorite place, but they have great pizza."

"Bar pizza is the best. Why is that?"

"I have no id—" My last word died before it left my mouth. Caleb pulled into the lot and parked his truck right next to mine. Our eyes met briefly. His face went stoic behind the windshield. How was going to a bar with McGraff's and Jeanine helping anyone? Seemed more like enabling.

Jake glanced from me to the truck. "What's wrong? Who's that?"

"Tell you later. Let's get out of here."

Caleb. The McGraffs. Willie's. The sight was all too familiar and made me nauseous. I lifted my chin and steadied my shoulders, intending to ignore the group of four. Jake climbed in the passenger side, holding the pizza, as Rodney stepped out of Caleb's extended cab right next to my driver's door.

"Well, look who it is." Rodney grinned barbarically and slammed a hand on my door, forcing it shut. "The hellion with the mouth."

Chapter Ten

I wasn't a violent person, and I never started fights in school. Generally, I walked away when someone spoke unkindly. But on a day when my emotions had run the full gamut, tension wound tighter than a barbed wire fence strangling the life from a deer, my self-control slipped. Rodney McGraff was an idiot, taunting the wrong girl on the wrong day. With nothing in my hands, I generated solid momentum as I lifted a knee and dropped him to the ground like a sack of potatoes whose bottom ripped out.

"Ellie!" Jeanine screamed and ran around the rear of the truck. "What are you doing?" She pushed at me with her elbow to get to Rodney's side.

Caleb and Jake rounded the fronts of either truck, exchanged looks, then glanced from me to Rodney. Todd climbed out of the passenger's seat and glared. I glared back. His leader had fallen, so he didn't scare me.

"There." I jerked open my truck door and glanced at Caleb. "Simple resolution. Now he won't be bothering Jeanine tonight."

Jake climbed back in the truck. Gripping the steering wheel hard, I worked at steadying my breath. At the first bend on Dillard Hollow, I loosened my shoulders, tucked a piece of fly-away hair behind my ear, and looked over. Jake watched me.

I opened my mouth to explain, but no words came, so I closed it and fidgeted with the steering wheel until we stopped in front of Dad's clinic.

Brow furrowed, I shot a quick glance at Jake. "I probably shouldn't have done that." Quietly, I exited the truck.

As soon as I opened the clinic door, the beagles fired to life, barking. I left Jake holding the pizza and tea while I carried a flashlight and gave the dogs bully sticks to keep them occupied and quiet for the next hour. On the way back, I slipped my fingers into the cage of two cats that had come in toward the end of the day, offering a couple soothing words while touching their noses. They'd be staying for a week while their owner went on vacation.

Back in the front, I motioned for Jake to follow me down the hall to the last room on the right. We entered Mom's office, greeted by the smell of cardboard and fake pine from a wall-outlet deodorizer. I avoided the overhead light. Even though I didn't think the window was visible from the house, the illumination on the ground outside might be. I turned on the desk lamp. Shadows draped boxes stacked two high along one wall. Mom's desk, untouched, still displayed the pencil holder I'd made her out of clay in the third grade. Beside it sat a family picture and a vintage Swingline stapler.

Growing up, I'd spent more time following Dad around his part of the clinic, so I felt no nostalgia in mom's office. At least not what I felt standing under a weeping willow or when I held a monarch butterfly and remembered the time Mom and I hatched and released hundreds one year.

I grabbed a box of tissues for napkins, and we sat on the cool tile floor, the pizza between us. Picking up a slice, I inhaled with longing and bit off the pointed end. Jake slowly took a slice and studied it like he might have lost his appetite.

I swallowed. "I'm not sure how to explain what happened back at Willie's. So why don't you just say what's on your mind?"

"Besides Jeanine, who were the others?"

"The one I hit was Rodney McGraff. The other two were Todd McGraff and Caleb Hansen, Jeanine's brother."

"The Caleb she mentioned last night?"

"One in the same."

"Not a boyfriend?"

"Ex."

"When did you break up?"

"A year ago."

"Why did you hit Rodney?"

I stopped chewing and set down my slice. "The obvious reason is because he held my door shut. The not so obvious is . . ." The excuses in my head sounded lame. If I told Jake anything but the truth, he'd know I was lying. But if I told him the real reason, he'd see how close Caleb and I had been, and I wasn't sure I wanted to share those details or allow my emotions to get the best of me again. "He'll hurt Jeanine. He's a louse, and she can't see it."

He narrowed his eyes. "Her mistake to make, isn't it?"

I sighed and looked at Jake sadly. If I wanted him to truly understand, I needed to tell the full truth, but he didn't deserve to be victimized by the stupidity in my life.

That was not why he came to Hush Briar. "Jake, you need to know that being friends with me is probably going to ruin your summer. I have too much going on."

"Impossible. You don't determine my happiness. Besides, it's too late. We're already friends, right? And we have this agreement to speak bluntly, so spill it."

I chuckled half-heartedly. "Why are you so nice?"

He wiped his hands on a tissue and opened his tea. "You don't have to tell me anything. But if you want, why don't you start at the beginning?"

I picked two pepperonis off a slice of pizza and ate them as I thought of where to start. I had a lifetime of memories.

"Caleb, Jeanine, and I grew up doing everything together, but Caleb and I were best friends. We began dating my freshman year. I thought we were close, maybe even in love, but the summer before my junior year, his senior year, he started hanging out with Todd and Rodney. Pretty soon he was partying heavy and getting drunk. He cheated, sobered up, cheated again. Finally, near the end of my junior year, I broke up with him. That was a little over a year ago. He went off to a tech school in Knoxville. His parents put him in rehab, and I guess he's stayed sober. I hadn't talked to him at all this past year, until earlier tonight, right before I picked you up. I didn't handle our first encounter very well.

"Come to find out, Caleb's only here for a week to try and convince Jeanine to stay away from Rodney."

"I don't think that'll happen."

"Me either. It's not the first time I've seen her with him."

"So you have it in for these brothers because of what they did to your relationship with Caleb?"

"No. Caleb ruined the relationship. It's what the McGraff's *did* to Caleb. What they'll do to anyone who crosses their path. They have no conscience or moral code. They're bad people, and I won't let them bully me. You said it. I determine my own happiness, not some thug who takes whatever he wants."

Jake narrowed his eyes. "If you truly believe you determine your happiness, then why are we sitting here?"

I picked up the slice with no pepperonis. "This is different. This is to vindicate my mom. Solid proof will do that."

"What if you don't find the Bigfoot? What if what we saw this morning was something else? Then what?"

I didn't have an answer for *then what?* "At least I'll know I tried."

When we finished eating, I set the pizza box and tea bottles by the door and handed Jake the flashlight. I went to work on the two standing file cabinets near the desk, using the light on my phone while Jake rooted through the boxes along the opposite wall.

"What exactly am I searching for?" He peered over the flap of a cardboard box.

"Anything related to Bigfoot."

The bulk of her files were full of research and informational articles, covering every species of animal known to Kentucky. I searched through unimportant graphs, charts, and topography maps but found nothing out of the ordinary.

I plopped down in her desk chair and stared at the picture of us. If Mom were here, what would she be doing?

Journaling.

But any recent journal would have been with her in the field. Maybe lost or with belongings Dad found or brought from the funeral home. I vaguely remembered the funeral director handing him a box. Still, I opened the top right drawer. Nothing. The left. Same. The bottom file drawers were locked. Then I remembered the center tray door often unlocked the others. I pulled it out an inch then tugged on the right file drawer. It opened.

Manila folders lined the drawer, each labeled with information about an animal she called Nun'Yunu'Wi. I picked up my phone and googled the foreign words. A monster of Cherokee origin. The Stone Man. Giant apelike creature.

My head swam. I dropped my elbows to my knees. A piece of me had held out hope this was all a twisted prank. But it wasn't.

Mom kept files with articles covering food sources, hunting techniques, communication. More maps. My mind wanted to reject this stuff. It wasn't normal, but I'd followed a trail that couldn't have been faked. Saw the blood.

The left drawer held newspaper clippings on Bigfoot. Sightings listed by county in the mountainous states. I rolled my eyes. Did she really believe this stuff?

I scanned the office. Where would I stash a box of mom's belongings? Could be any of the half-dozen boxes along the wall, except the two Jake was rooting through. My gaze stopped at the closet. I stood and crossed the room. Please don't be locked.

The knob turned. I pulled it open and stared at Mom's tan corduroy coat, a denim shirt jacket, and a UK hoodie. A musty smell overpowered the pine. At my feet were two stacked boxes with mom's hiking boots on top. Why did he keep those? I carefully removed the boots, still crusted with dirt. Swallowing hard, I opened the top box.

Her journal rested on top of a green ball cap and khaki

shirt jacket. I picked up the book with the baggie holding her watch, a cracked phone, and a wedding ring. An image of the phone cracking the same time her body hit stone flashed through my mind. I dropped the baggie and quickly closed the closet door, my breaths coming fast and heavy.

"Check this out." Jake wiggled the light over what appeared to be a scrapbook. A little shaken, I sat beside him on the floor and scanned the picture . . . of me.

"What were you, like, five?"

"Why are you looking at this?" My throat clogged. I cleared it, forcing myself to focus on the picture and not the images in my head.

"I'm curious. Is this your mom?" The picture on the opposite page showed us sitting together on a log, me in her lap.

"Yeah."

"You look a lot like her."

Mom's hair had been short and hung to a length between her shoulder and chin. Like mine now. Her hair was a mite darker, and mine tended to fall forward into my eyes. I tucked a wayward strand behind my ear, self-conscious as Jake studied my face and my eyes.

"Uh, moving on." I reached down and turned the page for him. My grade school artwork covered both pages.

"Pappy didn't tell me you were an artist."

"Probably for a good reason. Those are awful."

"Nothing is awful to a mom. Unless you move out against her wishes." He mumbled the last sentence.

Next page showed an award I won for the science fair and an essay award my senior year. Those came after Mom died.

"I have a hard time believing Dad put this together." I

tapped the page. "But he must have. Who else would have done it?"

"You're quite the overachiever, aren't you?" Jake looked at several pages of 4-H awards.

"I'm an only child." I shrugged and opened the journal but stayed on the floor next to Jake so I could sneak glances at the photos. Why hadn't Dad shown me this stuff?

"You find anything?" Jake pulled another album out of a different box.

"Her most recent journal. I haven't read any of it yet."

He looked at me with those friendly eyes and a half-smile like he could see the battle playing out in my head. Truth or Ignorance. At this point, there was no better option.

"Want me to read it?"

I shook my head and opened the book, allowing the papers to ruffle through my fingers until I landed on her last entry. Three days before she died. I touched the words written in her handwriting.

June 12

I've seen three hunters on the Western ridge, lighting fires and making a general nuisance of themselves. The police are aware, and they're watching. I guess that's as much as I can ask for. I hate delaying my approach, but I need to throw them off. I'll make sure they see me, then I'll head south, away from the gorge.

June 11

Today, I saw the Nun'Yunu'Wi in the gorge. I didn't

let them see me for fear they would mistake my identity. This appears to be a family of three. Parents and an infant. They may be my family, but I couldn't tell from the distance. Tomorrow I'll prepare for my approach (8). If all goes well, I think Ellie is old enough to know. I hope it works out. She'll be amazed.

I put a hand to my heart. My head swam with a million thoughts. Mom was studying the Bigfoot. *My family?* What did she mean? Were there others? She was going to tell me. How long had it been since I heard her say my name? I reread the entry. Life would have been so different if she had told me. Possibly for the worse if I would've had to constantly defend their existence. Then again, Mom would've been here to help.

June 10

It was a beautiful climb. I found downed trees, roots pulled up, the tops of wild onions discarded. They're close.

"Hey, you." Jake shined his light in my face. "Earth to Ellie. You didn't tell me you were Valedictorian."

I sat there dazed. These were Mom's last words, last thoughts. "Yeah, so?"

"So, that's a pretty big deal. What?" He frowned. "Did you find something?"

"Yeah, I think I did." I read the entries aloud and waited for his comment.

He was quiet.

"Are you okay?"

"Yeah, but are you sure you know what you're getting yourself into?"

"Not at all." I swallowed a lump of sadness and regret. "What do you think this number eight is?" I showed him the page. "You think that's just another journal?"

I started to stand when the overhead lights snapped on, and Dad's frame filled the doorway.

Chapter Eleven

I tensed, sitting motionless next to Jake, feeling the same as I did the day Dad caught Caleb and me smoking behind the barn when we were ten. Holding Mom's book, I readied myself to fight, if that's what it came to. Dad had no right to keep this information from me. Not when Mom wanted to tell me. I met his gaze, surprised he looked more defeated than angry.

Heaving a sigh, Dad walked over to the wall, sorted through the boxes until he found several black hardcover books. He placed them on the floor in front of me.

"I figure if I don't help you, you'll . . ." He sat on the floor in front of me and stared with such intensity it almost frightened me. "I don't want anything to happen to you. But Ellie Mae, you need to understand, this is a sensitive topic that can stir up a lot of trouble and chaos. Your mom went to great lengths to keep peace."

He looked haggard, and I hated it. My intent wasn't to worry him or dredge up haunting memories, but it was his fault I had to dig. Nothing would stop me.

"Yeah, and it cost her her life, so was it really worth it?"

I said softly. "Her name is tainted in this town, and I aim to fix it. It's the least we can do for her. Don't you want that?"

"Is being right so important? If your mom was content keeping the truth to herself and knowing the people she loved believed in her, isn't that enough? In reality, will people care if your mom was right?"

"So you believed her?"

"Of course." Dad looked over at Jake. "You okay, son?"

Jake had paled a shade or two but nodded. "I just have a question." He waited for Dad to nod then held up the album. "Why didn't Mrs. Schmitt show anyone her pictures?"

My mouth fell open when I saw the Polaroids and the 35 mm shots. I grabbed the book from Jake's hands. Like something out of a tabloid, the pictures displayed a family of three oversized primate-like animals. Male, female, and toddler. Not exactly like gorillas, more naturally erect, taller.

Their skin looked dark, but not black—the color of cinnamon and cocoa mixed and leathery. The obvious female with protruding breasts was a lighter shade of cocoa, and the young one a lighter cinnamon. Their fur matched their skin tone but carried a reddish tint and hung straight, maybe three to four inches in length. Their noses were flat, head a conical shape, and eyes larger than any primate I'd ever seen. Each face offered an expression, making them look humanlike.

Dad shifted toward Jake. "Such a loaded and yet very simple question. The short answer is no one believes a picture. They can be staged as easily as photoshopped, and belief never mattered to Jodi. Her intent was to protect the Nun'Yunu'Wi and help them survive as naturally as possible. Not bring people in to disturb them. If livestock mysteriously disappeared, she knew what to look for. She set out to find them and to make sure they hunted wild game. She detoured hunters and warned the Nun'Yunu'Wi when it was time to move on. They're peaceful animals who've survived too long. They're caught in a time when fanatics are hungry for monsters and beasts. You'll see, if you study Jodi's work, that the only way for the Nun'Yunu'Wi to survive is for humans to protect their anonymity."

"So the footprints over at the Hansen's belong to them? They're not fake?"

Dad nodded at me.

"They twisted the lock?" I swallowed hard, a chill snaking up my spine. My voice hitched up a couple notches. "Do you have any idea how strong they would have to be to do that?" I traced a finger over the enormous arms of the male. "Why did you let us go out there? Why did you lie about the footprints?"

"Ellie." Jake laid a hand on my arm. I jerked it away.

"Of course I know how strong they are. I also knew they wouldn't hurt you last night or even this morning," Dad said firmly. "They don't approach humans. They find easy prey. You were in no danger because those cows were meant to be taken."

"What?"

Dad sucked in another deep breath. "Diversion. Those cows will keep the Nun'Yunu'Wi fed for several days. Don Hansen knows they exist. I'm not sure the rest of his family knows."

"Wait. So you, Mr. Hansen"—I huffed—"JT. Who else knows?"

Dad clenched and loosened his jaw. "Doc, Travis. I don't know. Plenty of others who will hurt them if we aren't careful."

Jaxon Reid.

I pressed my fingertips to my temples and lowered my head, elbows braced on either side of the photo album. "She communicated with them?" I stared at the pictures in my lap. A family of three eating fish, sitting on their haunches using rocks and sticks, sleeping huddled as one. As tall as humans, maybe taller. Hard to tell with no comparison.

"Yes. They're intelligent. They don't speak words, but they understand them. They appear to have a complete language using sounds, growl-like noises, and even sign language. They seem to understand intent and don't act purely on instinct like most animals. You'll find details in her journals and other notebooks." He nodded toward the wall.

"Have you seen them?" Jake pulled another album out of a box.

"From a distance, but they didn't let me get close. If you see them, stay back. Both of you." He looked pointedly at me. "I'm sure they could become violent if they felt threatened."

Dad groaned as he stood up, knees popping.

"Why didn't you just tell me about them?" I blurted out. Dad wouldn't ignore me in front of Jake.

He lifted his arms. "And say what?"

"Anything. But don't lie to me."

He shook his head. "You don't understand, Ellie. This" —he motioned to everything in the room—"is so much more complicated than you realize."

"So I have to find out everything on my own?" I quipped.

"It's the easiest way, and believe it or not, it's the safest."

"Why didn't the police, or anyone, help her?" I lifted

the journal. "She told them hunters were in the area causing trouble."

"If the police stopped every yahoo out there hunting Bigfoot, they'd get nothing else done. And Ellie . . ." Life drained from his voice as he picked up the pizza box and stood in the doorway. "You have to understand our neighbors get scared. They want to believe men or wild animals steal their livestock. It's not easy to accept legend as reality. What you're remembering about the way people treated her is from the perspective of a young girl who lost her momma. Our neighbors weren't mean to her. They didn't understand and didn't want to talk about it."

"She died because no one helped her."

He winced. "No. She died because of an accident. She fell."

"Really, Dad?" My volume increased. "She was a soldier who grew up in these mountains. The only way she went over a cliff was if someone pushed her. And if the police had been doing their job instead of appeasing the neighbors, it probably wouldn't have happened!"

I regretted the biting words and should have apologized, but I didn't want to let Dad off the hook. It didn't make sense that Mom fell. I couldn't accept it, and his easy surrender hurt.

Dad blinked rapidly and looked away. "Maybe, but we'll never know. Turn out the lights when you're finished, and now that you've stirred up the dogs, why don't you let them out for a bit." He started to close the door but stopped. His broad shoulders heaved before he turned back.

"They hunt at night, but they start to rouse late afternoon. You might catch a glimpse then." He frowned as he made eye contact with me. "Keep your distance and you'll be fine."

The door clicked shut. Frustrated, I lifted a hand. "See what I mean by Dad closing me out?"

Color had returned to Jake's cheeks, and his eyes lit with some kind of excitement even though he offered a grim smile. "Maybe this will open the door for more talk." He bumped my knee with the back of his hand. "Is this you?"

The album was open to a newspaper clipping of a young girl with thick dark hair pulled off to one side with a comb.

"No." I watched as he flipped through articles about unexplained missing livestock, downed trees, missing dogs, and even a child. "You think these are all true?" I said it skeptically. Even with proof that Bigfoot carried off a couple of cows from our neighbor, the reality was hard to digest.

"I doubt your mom would've kept anything she didn't feel was relevant. Don't you?"

A folded piece of paper slipped out of the book onto the floor between us. It was old, yellowed, and threatened to fall apart at the heavy creases as I carefully unfolded it. Heads nearly touching, Jake and I stared at a sketch of Native Americans interacting with several large creatures resembling those in Mom's pictures. Jake splayed his fingers across the bottom of the page, holding it flat and tapping his index finger near the signature. "Simms? Who is that again?"

"People who fostered my mom." I stared at the name. "Simsy's the only one still around these parts. She was my mom's foster mother." Simsy knew about the Bigfoot? Was that how Mom became involved?

I glanced at Jake, sensing I'd stumbled upon a clue as to why Dad barely tolerated the older woman.

I run scared, pull my legs as if they are caught in mud. Move. Right leg. Left leg. I look over my shoulder. Trees sway under a moonlit sky as the creature gains on me. Willow Tree. I hoist myself up to hide in the weeping ropes of leaves, but lead fills my body. I grope at the branch above my head, throw one heavy leg over and then the other.

"Ellie Mae-fly." Mom's endearment chases after me, but it's not her. She's dead. The creatures learned to mimic her. "Ellie Mae-fly." They want to hurt me like they hurt Momma.

I hold my breath. The creature is directly beneath me, its snort-like breath circles the tree. Branches move. I tuck my knees up under my chin, trying to meld into the trunk.

The shadow below shifts. Everything stills. Looking down, I see nothing. Out of nowhere, round, yellow orbs appear in the darkness.

I opened my eyes, breathing heavy. Moonlight sifted through the curtain and illuminated my bedroom enough to put me at ease.

Another dream. The second one in as many days.

Chapter Twelve

I latched the door on the cage and offered the cats a few reassuring words to help them survive an afternoon of barking dogs. Dad came out of the storage room, carrying a small brown box.

"Ellie, can you please deliver this antibiotic cream to Rebecca? I planned to take it over after work, but Rick Matthews called. He sold a couple Thoroughbreds and wants me to check them out before the buyer gets there in the morning."

"Sure. I want to take Jake over there anyways. Did you get the brakes fixed on the Jeep?"

"Did that while you were out yesterday. Tell Rebecca I'll call later and that I want to see her new hawk's fecal samples in the morning."

"Okay." I paused next to a stainless-steel table occupying the center of the surgical and lab room. "Jake and I are gonna hike out to the gorge afterward. Is that all right? Or do you need me in here?"

He narrowed his eyes. "You and Jake have been

spending a lot of time together. He's only been here a couple days. Something brewing between you two?"

Heat crept over my face. "No. Dad, he's . . ." I couldn't find a description that didn't include embarrassing words like amazing, nice, or genuine. "He's . . ."

Dad waited, a slow smile creeping across his face.

"He's too perfect for someone like me."

His smile slipped away. "No one is perfect. And while he might have his hands full with someone like you, he'll always know where he stands. You're a good person. You either settle for the best or nothing, hear?"

This conversation needed to end. "So you're good with us hiking out there?"

Sarah waved a file folder, making sure Dad saw it, then placed it in a tray on the backside of an exam room door.

Dad walked that direction. "Just keep your distance." He turned around like he wanted to add a thought. Instead, he offered a tight smile, grabbed the folder, and disappeared to take care of his next patient.

After I washed up and changed into jeans and hiking boots, Grandma loaded me down with containers of smothered steak, mashed potatoes, and chocolate chip cookies. She felt certain Jake missed home cooking and wanted to ease him into Doc's frozen dinners and fish sticks.

It was just after one o'clock when I knocked and, out of habit, barreled through Doc's front door without waiting for an answer. I stopped cold before I'd taken two steps.

"Oops." Today, I should have definitely hesitated. From the overstuffed brown chair, angled toward the baseball game on the TV, Jake sat in only a pair of black basketball shorts. He glanced up, spoon stopping midair between his mouth and the bowl he held. A slow grin spread across his face.

"Morning, Ellie Mae."

My eyes fixed on his wet hair and moved down to his arms, bare chest, abs, long legs.

I'd seen Caleb in less a million times. Granted, most of those times had been during sleepovers or impromptu swimming adventures as kids. During football season, Caleb looked good, but not this good. Jake had the body of a guy who worked out regularly, not only when he was forced to.

"Uh . . ." I wasn't at a loss for words, but it was hard to concentrate on his body and focus on what I wanted to say. The moment was growing awkward, so I pretended indifference and returned his smile. "More like afternoon. Are you just now eating your breakfast?" I lifted the plastic container. "Grandma sent lunch. Where's Doc?" I passed through to the kitchen.

"Don't know. He was gone when I got up." Jake hollered around a full mouth.

"Which was what? Ten minutes ago?" I resisted the urge to peek back into the living room.

"Yeah, something like that. Hey, I'll be right back. Don't go anywhere." The stairs squeaked as he trotted up them. I took that opportunity to look around the corner and glance up the stairs. I expelled a heavy breath. They sure knew how to grow 'em down in New Orleans. Holy cow.

Two ceramic mugs and a plate sat in the sink. Otherwise, the kitchen was spotless. I scanned the living room. Aside from Jake's cereal bowl, it also looked neat. Impressive. Doc and Jake were getting along fine. I placed the cookies on the table and the steak in the fridge. Eggs, fruit, rotisserie chicken. Looked like Doc was finally eating better.

I retraced my steps out to the front porch. Jake joined me a few minutes later, fully dressed in jeans and a light blue T-shirt that made his eyes appear more blue than gray.

"Sorry about that. I was moving kind of slow this morning." He dropped his shoes and socks on the porch and sat in the opposite chair.

I waved him off in an effort to hide my attraction. "I'm on my way out of town. Delivering medicine to the Raptor Rescue. You want to tag along? I can show you the hawk. Afterward, I thought maybe we could head out to the gorge."

He put on a sock. "You planning to visit the Simms? Ask about that drawing?"

"No, Simsy can be a little high-strung. I don't want to bring her into it."

"Yeah, but she might have some insight. Aren't you curious if there's some truth to that drawing? I could hardly sleep. I kept wondering how much we don't know about this world."

"I don't think we'll have time. Maybe another day."

He slipped his foot into a tennis shoe. "So you're just going to ignore a piece of valuable evidence?"

"It's not evidence. It's just a drawing." Truth was I didn't want to reminisce about the Bigfoot and however Mom became involved with them. Get the video, show the sheriff and people at the next township meeting, and be done with it. Last night had been fun poking through old photos with Jake, but all the Nun'Yunu'Wi stuff left me feeling weirded out. I just wanted it to be over.

Jake shrugged. "I'd go, but I'm not sure where Pappy went."

Was he blowing me off because of my refusal to talk to Simsy or just offering up an excuse to put some distance between us? I hoped neither, because I wanted a chance to show him the girl who simply loved animals, the mountains, and her family, minus the secrets and monstrous creatures.

"You know"—I leaned forward conspiratorially, placing my elbows on my knees—"we have these things in Kentucky called cell phones. You could call Doc right up and ask him where he went and when he might return. You could even tell him where you're headed out to."

Jake finished tying his second shoe and let his foot fall to the porch. He leaned in close, matching my pose with a cheeky grin. "You know, if I were a person who wanted someone else's help, I wouldn't be so sassy."

"Good thing I don't need anyone's help. I'm here 'cause I wanna be."

He rolled his eyes, pushed my knee, and went into the house.

Twenty minutes later, Jake and I pulled into Raptor Rescue, a one-story brick structure where they worked on the birds and housed food and equipment. I reached back, picked up the medicine off the rear floor of the Jeep Cherokee, and led the way.

Rebecca and her assistant volunteer, Connie, arched over a table in the far corner near a window. The older, thin woman held a piece of cloth over the bird's head and wings while Rebecca worked to unwind the fishing line from its legs and feet.

My mouth twisted in sympathy. Poor thing. Looked like a red-tailed hawk by the rusty-colored tail feathers and larger size.

The women looked up as we approached. "Hi, Ellie Mae." Rebecca glanced from me to Jake and nodded.

"Hi, Rebecca. Hi, Connie. This is my friend Jake. We brought your medicine."

"Wonderful. You can set it on the counter over there." Rebecca cut at the fishing line and placed it in a bowl.

"Dad said he'd call you later. He has some instructions for your new birds and said he needs fecal samples."

"He's not coming over?" She straightened and stretched her back, brow furrowed.

"I think he's figuring on tomorrow morning. Needs to see about some horses after work."

"Oh, okay." She wiped her brow with her shirt sleeve and flipped her single blonde braid over her shoulder.

"Is this one of the new birds?" I pointed at the exam table.

"This one came in a couple of hours ago. We've been working on him the entire morning. Poor guy has been tied up for quite a while."

I stepped forward and examined the fishing line, wound so tight the string wasn't even visible through the blood and broken flesh of his upper legs and feet. "Fought hard against it, didn't he?"

"Yes, and the harder he fought, the tighter the line."

"Anything I can do?"

"You did a lot by bringing down the medicine. Why don't you show Jake your girl, and I'll be out in a bit?"

I led Jake out the back door that opened into the woods. Several pens and shelters of various sizes lined a gravel path that stretched away from the main building. Resident bald eagle, Jerry, sat atop a perch about eye level in the nearest pen.

"Hey, Jerry." I slowly stepped over the knee-high barrier and motioned for Jake to follow. "I want you to meet a friend of mine." Jerry turned his head as we moved closer, blinking his light-golden eyes.

Jake scanned the bird with a wide-eyed smile. "Wow. He's big. What's his story?"

"Probably about eight years ago, he was hit by a semi. Broke both wings, a slew of other bones, and nearly died. He can't fly anymore. Best he can do is hop up on that perch. Because he was handled so much, he imprinted. Now he believes he's a human. Except he will bite if you try and pet him. Admire but don't touch."

Jake stuffed his hands in his pocket. I smiled, impressed by his interest as he rounded the bird, taking in every inch. Caleb hadn't once stepped over the barrier.

The next, much larger, enclosed lean-to was surrounded completely by trees and stretched up high to a roost in the treetops. I pointed to the ground where four fledglings, still sporting a little fuzz between light brown feathers, hopped around. "Know what these are?"

"Owls."

"Yeah, but what kind?" I knelt for a better look as three of the four fledglings pranced with wings outstretched, practicing balance, squawking a little as they awkwardly played with their newfound abilities. I looked up. Jake tapped on his phone. "Are you googling it?" I stood and grabbed his phone.

"You asked."

"You were supposed to guess. They're great horned owls, goofus." I put his phone in my back pocket. "You'll get this back later. Around here we learn on the job."

"So why are they here?"

"Some guy cutting down a tree found the eggs. I've been watching them since they hatched."

"You and your dad spend a lot of time here?"

One of the strutting teenage birds tripped, and we laughed. "My dad volunteered even before Rebecca moved to the area. She and my parents worked on different conservation projects. After Mom died, Rebecca helped me with some 4-H stuff, and Dad and I helped her build several of these outdoor pens. Rebecca's incredible. Every year she hikes to the crest of the Smoky Mountains to study birds migrating down from Canada. I went with her last year after everything that happened with Caleb."

Jake entwined his fingers with the fence and faced me. "Think she knows about the Bigfoot?"

I shrugged. "Sorta feels like I'm the only one who didn't know about them." But I couldn't imagine Rebecca would keep anything from me. The big sister I never had, she'd shared about her divorce and the messiness of romance, but she believed in love. She encouraged me not to give up.

Jake and I stood and walked down the stone lane to the red-shouldered hawk I had rescued. She perched on a tree-limb-sized wooden rod that stretched across the shelter. "I found this girl about a mile from home, limping and dragging her wing. We think she might have been pushed from her nest. Probably by an owl." I pointed back toward the fledglings.

"Man, nature can be brutal, can't it?"

I nodded. "So can humans. Have you talked to any of your family? Are they speaking to you?"

He let out a single chuckle at my comparison. "Mom's not, but I talked to my dad yesterday. He listened but doesn't understand why I left. The only one who grasps why I came here is my brother, Ty. Speaking of which"—he crooked his hand—"give me my phone."

I handed it over. Jake leaned in close, hand on my shoulder, and captured us both in the picture with the hawk in the background.

"Are you sending this to him? Let me see that."

He gave me the phone, and I stared at us standing side by side in front of the wire mesh, surrounded by tall trees. Both smiling. "We look good." My eyes widened. I really said that. I shoved the phone into his chest.

Jake laughed and snapped more of the hawk and me with the hawk. "You don't take many pictures, do you?"

"Phones are annoying." I motioned to the bird. "You miss half the action messing with it. Besides, I'm too busy."

"You aren't busy now."

"Yes, I am. I'm talking to you." But I pulled my phone out and snapped a couple pictures of the two of us. Mainly because I liked standing close and feeling his hand on my shoulder.

Rebecca approached, smiling. She wrapped me in a big hug. "Sorry about that." She held her hand out to Jake. "Been an intense morning. Nice to meet you. You're not from around here, are you?"

Jake explained where he moved from and fit in as Ethan Dillard's grandson. "You found a good one to keep you company." She nodded my way. "You won't get bored."

Hard to believe he wanted to spend any time with me after my stunt with Rodney last night and then the forceful way I talked to my dad. Focused and mad, manners hadn't even been a secondary thought. I needed to get a grip if I simply wanted to keep Jake as a friend.

"How's your side?" Rebecca nodded toward my belly. "Can I see? Your dad bragged about his stitching job."

"You discussed my cut?" I lifted my shirt tail to expose the four-inch, nearly healed wound that came from the hawk. Heat crept up my neck and over my face as I tried to ignore the tilt of Jake's head and his gaze, fastened on my belly.

Rebecca bent over. "We discussed his ability to stitch. Look at that. Not too bad. I was concerned he'd only put in a few stitches and leave you with a nasty scar like he did on your leg." She nodded toward the two-inch scar on my calf, courtesy of a hidden barbed wire fence. "The man doesn't realize you might want to show off some skin."

I jerked my shirt down. "Could be he's tired of wasting thread on me."

"Not likely. When you're in college, he'll drive all the way to Lexington to patch you up if he needs to."

We talked for a bit more while checking in on Simsy's owl, then Jake and I headed back to the car.

"Well, that was amazing." He sat and pulled his door shut. "Wouldn't it be cool to have a bald eagle like Jerry in your front yard?"

"I know where you can find one carved from a tree." I joked, sensing he wasn't the lawn ornament type of person.

He laughed. "That'd be a great gift for my mom. Or maybe I could send her one of a Bigfoot."

I snorted a laugh. "If she knew what you were doing today, you'd be disowned."

"I'm probably disowned anyways. Hey, thanks for bringing me here. I really enjoyed it."

"You're welcome." I smiled. Caleb tolerated my love for the sanctuary, but he wasn't into it. He never thanked me. I started down the winding lane, annoyed that Caleb kept popping into my thoughts when I wanted to dwell on Jake. Caleb was the past. Jake was right here, and there was a connection between us, different from what I had with Caleb.

But why would Jake settle for a hillbilly girl? I was definitely more Caleb's type.

"You got quiet all the sudden. Sure you're up for a hike? Pappy was right. You look tired."

"I'm fine." I flipped my gaze to his. "We need to do this before they move on."

After I'd turned onto the main road toward Hush Briar, Jake tapped the back of a finger next to my belly. "Tell me more about how you got cut."

I touched my side, still slightly tender. "Nothing to tell. I used my shirt to cover the bird's head and wings, but it wasn't big enough for the entire body. She caught me with one of her talons while I carried her out of the woods."

He grimaced, then his eyes grew wide. "Wait. You took off your shirt to wrap around the hawk?"

"She never would have settled if I didn't cover her eyes, but after carrying her for nearly a mile, my arms got tired and her foot slipped out of my hand."

"Okay. So let me visualize this correctly. If the hawk was wearing your flannel, then what were you . . ."

I swung at him to stop his line of thinking, but he caught my arm and shifted toward me, laughing. "It's only fair, isn't it, after the way you ogled me earlier?"

"Oh, please. Don't flatter yourself. I was caught off guard." I put both hands back on the wheel.

"Yeah, I know. You already told me you're not impressed, but we're talking about you, and I'm very impressed. Tell me the whole story."

I ignored my flaming face and focused on facts as I recounted how I lost control of the hawk and trapped her next to my body so she wouldn't further injure herself.

"When her talon laid me open, I almost dropped her. She flapped her wings and splattered blood everywhere.

We left a trail of blood anyone could follow. By the time I got her into a cage, I was soaked and in a lot of pain. How's that? Enough detail?"

"We really need to work on your presentation. Covered in mud or sweat, fine, but the blood and pain sort of ruins the image."

I rolled my eyes. "You asked."

Chapter Thirteen

By late afternoon, Jake and I had made our way to the same cliff overlooking the beautiful gorge. With eyes on the cave entrance, we backed our way into a stand of fragrant pine trees and hid while we ate a cold, fairly odorless meal of nuts, apples, and butter bread.

"I'm thinking we should end this evening with another cheese-dripping pizza," Jake whispered.

"Great idea. Extra cheese."

"Yes! And extra pepperoni." Jake tossed a couple peanuts in his mouth.

Earlier, on the trek out, we talked about college, Jake's relationship with his siblings, or about nothing at all. But from the moment Jake snapped the picture of us together at the rescue, I had wanted to ask a single question. Now, sitting close enough that every movement forced us to touch, I had to know.

"Jake, don't you have a girlfriend who'll be jealous when she sees pictures of us online together?" I imagined a southern belle with long curls and a beautiful dress sipping iced tea and playing croquet while she waited for his return.

"No." He tipped the baggie, dumping the rest of the nuts in his mouth.

"I find that hard to believe. You're like . . ."—I lifted a hand up and down—"every girl's dream."

He looked at me with a sarcastic, are-you-serious look.

"Who is she?"

"Who?"

"The girl you left behind."

He stashed the baggie in the backpack, giving me his full attention. "Hard to have a girlfriend back home when I have no intention of returning."

"But there was someone?"

He hem-hawed. "We went out a few times, but there wasn't enough to make me want to stay."

"Do you miss her?"

He rolled his eyes. "Are we doing this?"

I nodded once. "Tell me."

"I liked her. We were friends, but I'm not a mess over leaving. I certainly wasn't in love with her. She was more of a . . . family expectation."

I twisted up a corner of my mouth, feeling a little sorry for the girl. "What's her name?"

"Mary Beth. We broke up over a month ago."

Mary Beth. Sounded like a southern belle.

Jake rooted through the backpack, pulled out two apples, and handed me one. "We grew up together. Our parents made sure we attended all the appropriate social functions at the same time. We went through the motions of a couple, but there was no spark. Not like . . ." He held my gaze, his eyes twitched, barely, holding onto the unspoken words. A tingle raced through me. Go on.

"Not like when you find that dream person." He said the last two words with cheesy exaggeration.

"So how long were you and Mary Beth a couple?"

"Two years."

I paused, apple midair. "Two years!" I whispered louder than I should have. "That's more than a few dates."

"Not as many as you and Caleb."

"Yeah, but . . ." I wanted to argue how different my relationship with Caleb was, but then I thought maybe it wasn't so different after all. We grew up together. The line between romance and friendship blurred. There weren't family expectations, but when I saw him with Megan for the second time, I settled on higher expectations for myself.

"But what?"

"Nothing."

We sat in silence for at least an hour playing tic-tac-toe, hangman, and other stupid games before we saw movement near the cave. I slowly and quietly fished in my backpack, found the binoculars, and handed them to Jake, not sure I wanted to see up close.

When a large Bigfoot stepped into the clearing, we gasped in unison and scooched back into the brush close enough we could have melded into one person. Binoculars were not needed to see this creature was at least eight feet tall. It hunched at the edge of the shelf and looked out over the gorge. Could it see us? Smell us? A smaller one exited the cave and jumped on the larger Bigfoot's back with a high-pitched growl.

"No way." Jake breathed the words and pulled out his phone.

I leaned forward, certain my heart thundered out of my chest, and rolled over the cliff. A child. Jake scooted onto his belly and shimmied to the edge of the drop-off. I lingered back and watched the monster of my dreams reach over its shoulder to grab at the youngster. The little one maneuvered out of the way, playing.

Examining footprints was a whole lot different than seeing the real-life creature. If I had stumbled upon a cougar or a bear, I would've been excited to see them in their habitat, known what behaviors to anticipate. These creatures were foreign, and not knowing what to expect frightened me. Guess I was more like our neighbors than I thought because I wasn't enjoying the reality of their existence or the idea they might be the source of Mom's death.

Jake looked back with a grin and motioned for me to join him. I stayed rooted beside a pine tree, nearly folded into a ball with my knees pulled up and arms wrapped around them. He tipped his head and patted the earth at his side.

To come all this way and not take advantage of the discovery would bring massive regret, so I unfolded myself and scooted on my belly until I reached Jake's side, fully encroaching on his space.

The large Bigfoot reached up and flipped the youth over its shoulder and held it in its arms. Then emitting a low, rumbling sound, it jumped down into the knee-high water in one effortless yet powerful movement. I flinched and inched a tiny bit closer to Jake, pulling my phone from my pocket. Jake kept his camera rolling but leaned over and whispered, "This is the most incredible thing I've ever seen."

He glanced my way, did a double take, then gave a reassuring smile. "They won't come up here. Remember what your dad said. They'll run before they attack."

The two splashed in the water as I fumbled to turn on my phone. In one swoop of its hand, the adult held a fish. Jake handed me the binoculars. I set my phone aside and watched with clarity as the big one tore the fish in two and gave one half to the child. They sat on their haunches at the edge of the water and ate.

Resembling Mom's pictures, both had reddish-brown hair, but the child's fur was lighter, more of dark strawberry blond. Their faces were a dark tan, leathery with flat noses and protruding foreheads. The large, almond-shaped eyes offered expression even though their mouths didn't smile. Their arms and legs were long and powerful looking. Defined muscles laced the larger creature's body, even with the fur coat. They both jumped and moved with ease.

Jake began filming again as another significantly shorter Bigfoot emerged carrying an even smaller child. It sat on the ledge outside the cave entrance with its feet dangling three feet above the water. The small child nursed in the most natural and easy manner. The mother stroked the baby's face and plucked at its fur with her fingers.

"Do you think this is a family?" The longer I watched the more at ease I felt.

"Sure looks like it."

The older child climbed onto the ledge, and the nursing mother stretched out a hand, touching her palm to the child's cheek. The child did the same. I sucked in a sharp breath, an ache forming deep inside me.

We watched until the sun touched the trees across the gorge. I whispered to Jake. "We need to get away from here before it gets dark."

He looked at the sky. "Now? Seriously?"

"It's a three-mile hike. They hunt at night."

"But they've eaten."

"It'll get dark in the woods soon."

We watched for several more minutes. When it appeared the family was preoccupied with something on the opposite side of the cave entrance, Jake and I scooched our way out of sight then took off at a fast walk and entered the woods without being seen, although we might have been heard.

Back at the large rock, we stopped for a breather. "Ellie, that was incredible! To be honest, I was skeptical right up until I saw them. I can't believe they're real! And they were so . . . normal-like. They were a family. Did your mom write anything about where they came from . . . originally?"

My mind reeled with possibilities as I opened my water bottle. "You know about as much as I do, but in her journals, Mom mentioned a family of three. I wonder if this is the same family with a new baby?"

Last night we became so caught up in pictures, we didn't make it through more than one journal, and there were volumes of content.

Jake stashed his water. "Do you remember seeing any labs or bloodwork to show DNA? They're huge. Did you see the size of the male?"

"I did."

"And you were scared." He pointed at me.

I grabbed his finger and twisted. "I wasn't scared."

"Yeah, right." He laughed and used his other hand to break free, then grabbed my water and splashed it on me.

"You. Did. Not." I reached for the bottle, but he pulled it out of reach and stood.

"Admit it." He held the bottle over my head. "You were scared."

Careful to avoid the sticker bushes off to the left, I braced a foot against the boulder and lunged forward, ramming my shoulder into his thighs. With a grunt, he stumbled and fell to his bottom. I hopped up, straddled his waist, and grabbed my bottle out of his hand, emptying the contents on his face before he realized a girl had just tackled him. Bounding to my feet, I laughed and stowed my trash.

He laid there, shock on his face. "So you weren't scared?"

I extended a hand and pulled as he stood. "Maybe I was a little scared. You weren't?"

He vigorously shook his head, sending water everywhere. I ducked away, laughing, and started walking again.

"I think I was too shocked to even think. You know what I found incredible?"

I smiled at his enthusiasm. "What?"

"The way they played—a happy family enjoying one another. Simple and carefree. What was your favorite part? Oh, wait . . . the mother and baby, right?"

"Did you see the way the mother touched the older child on the face?"

"Yeah." He ran hands through his semi-wet hair.

"I think it means something different than when we do it." I turned and stepped in front of him, backing up a step so he didn't plow me over. I placed a hand next to his cheek, and we came to a halt. A bold move, but I was making a point. "For us, it's a gesture or an endearment, but for them . . ." My brain stuttered at the intensity of Jake's gaze, proving I was right. All I could do was stare back, my thoughts jumbled. He was so close, and even though darkness edged in, it didn't disguise how mind-crushingly handsome he was. "I-I think it communicates something deeper. A mother-love."

His eyes held mine. It'd be so easy to slip my hand around his neck and pull him closer. Everything within me wanted to. Except the tiny voice of fear. The one that reminded me how much it would hurt to lose someone again.

Why did I always act before thinking? I stepped away, scared by how much I liked touching him. How much I enjoyed being with him. Pushing a strand of hair out of my face, I refocused on the point of our conversation. "My mom used to do the same to me. It's one of my first memories."

He cleared his throat, eyes roaming over my face. "No wonder that was your favorite moment."

"You took a video. Will you send me a copy?"

"Why didn't you record anything?"

I cast him a sideways glance. "I tried, but I couldn't do that and hold the binoculars. Besides, you were. And I guess I was in a bit of shock."

He draped an arm over my shoulders. "I get it. What do you plan to do with this information?" He held up his phone and wiggled it.

"Take it to the township meeting next week. People don't believe in pictures or word of mouth, but an unedited video that isn't a bit blurry—"

"No, you can't take this there."

"Why not? Chances are they'll laugh at me and ignore it."

"Why take the risk?" He looked confused which confused me.

"Because my mom deserves for someone to prove she was right."

He dropped his arm and stuffed the phone in his back pocket. "Then I'm not giving it to you. You're not thinking clearly. Your mom would not want you to expose those peaceful animals or . . . whatever they are."

I frowned at him. "You don't know anything about my mom. And I care more about her than I do the Bigfoot."

"Seriously? Say you prove to these people that your

mom was right—the Bigfoot exists—then what? They're killed, captured, studied—"

"Not my problem." I hardened my heart. Dad taught me that no matter how special an animal is, people always came first.

"What do you mean?" He scowled at me. "If you expose them, the consequences should be your problem."

"I'll deal with it as it happens."

"If that's how you feel, you're not the person I thought you were."

I threw up my hands. "And you just proved you're no different than anyone else. Sweep it under the rug and avoid the truth. Allow my mom's memory to be desecrated."

"What the heck!" Jake laced both hands on top of his head. "That's not true, Ellie, and you know it! I came out here with you. I trusted and believed you. But I won't help you destroy something magnificent so you can be right when it won't make a single bit of difference."

I felt the heat rise into my face. My nostrils flared. "Fine! I'll get my own pictures tomorrow."

"Not with my help."

I shrugged and stepped around him.

We rode back in silence. At his house, he slipped off the four-wheeler and, without a word, walked inside.

Chapter Fourteen

I stared at Jake's back, baffled. I thought he understood my point of view and the importance of setting the record straight. The whole reason we ventured out was to prove Mom right, so people would know she hadn't been just some crazy mountain-woman chasing legends.

Frustrated, I backed out of the drive then gunned the throttle, switching gears with more force than necessary. I blew through the last stop sign, but at the edge of town, heaviness fell over me, and I slowed until I came to a halt. A knot formed in my chest, and I dropped my head forward, arms stretched out on the handlebars.

Was I wrong? Was my perception completely off again? Confused, I turned around and made my way back to Main Street and the police station. Inside, JT sat at his desk sawing a piece of meat on a dinner plate. Two other desks, one by the door and one across the room, sat empty. The place was as still as the American flag situated in the far corner. JT looked up, chewing, a paper towel tucked in his shirt. Fluorescents flickered overhead, and the light glinted off the linoleum floor.

He pointed to his mouth, indicating he couldn't greet me. Tired and heavy-hearted, I plopped down in the chair beside his desk and tipped my head from side to side, working out the stiffness, fighting the burn of tears.

He swallowed his bite. "Ellie Mae. Whose tail have you yanked today?"

I bit the corner of my lip, weighing my words. I lifted my shoulders and dropped them with force. Might as well be blunt. "I just saw Bigfoot in the woods."

His gaze darted around the office. I was grateful we were alone in case I lost the battle with the anger and betrayal twisting inside me. Jake, Doc, Dad. Grandma. Even Mom, and she wasn't here. They all lied, and for what?

"Y-you saw what?"

"Bigfoot, Nun'Yunu'Wi, Sasquatch. You heard me. Is it worth it for me to make people aware, or am I setting myself up for ridicule and disappointment?" I was tired and frustrated and didn't care if my approach was a bit rude.

He shook his head as if to clear his thoughts. "Ellie Mae, I told you, those footprints are fake. Your daddy said so. They was planted there by some thief to throw off suspicion. There's no way it was some legendary Bigfoot."

"Really, JT, on a night when the ground was so wet and soft my four-wheeler left ruts, you expect some thief backed his truck up to Hansen's pasture and herded two cows out without leaving tire tracks? Or do you think they hefted them right up over the fence and trotted down the hill with 'em?"

"I don't know how they did it, but that's what happened."

"Well, Dad admitted to me they were real and that he

told you about them. I wish everybody would stop lying to me." I swiped at my cheek as an angry tear leaked out.

JT let his eyes fall shut for an extra second before reaching into his back pocket and pulling out a hanky. He shook it out and handed it to me. "It's clean."

I snatched it out of his hand and wiped my eyes. "Thanks."

"Ellie Mae, I'm caught between a rock and a hard spot. I'm sorry I wasn't up and front with you, but, well, I respect your daddy."

"JT, you remember back in school how the kids used to make fun of me because of the suspicions surrounding my mom's work?" I looked down and pulled at the edges of the hanky. "You probably don't because you'd graduated by then, but it happened, and it's nagged me ever since. I can't seem to get the image people have of my mom out of my mind. I never really thought the Bigfoot were real either, but they are. People need to know that she wasn't crazy. She was right! I need to prove her right. I owe her that. Am I wrong?"

He leaned back in his office chair. "Listen, kid. What you say, what others say, it don't matter none. Only the truth matters. Your momma didn't cower under pressure. She knew who she was, and wasn't no one else gonna tell her otherwise. Some folks, including my daddy, knew she was telling the truth. That's all she needed—to be understood and heard by the people that mattered. Everyone else around here remembers her search-and-rescue work and that her name is on the Veteran's monument over in Jackson."

"You know that?"

"Everyone knows that, and everyone's right proud. So

why do you want to stir up this Bigfoot issue and ruin the good image people have of her?"

His words doused me with cold awareness. I studied my hiking boots. "I never thought of it that way."

Was I the one who had a tainted image of Mom? I twisted the hanky, thinking about what Dad had said: *What you're remembering is from the perspective of a child who lost her momma.*

Had my childish mind distorted the truth? "At her funeral, the sheriff said Mom was chasing legends."

JT squinted and stared at the drop ceiling panels of the office. "Don't exactly remember everything from that day, but I'm guessing that's what he thought."

"Why didn't anyone set him straight? Right then and there." I had wanted to, but I was torn not knowing whether or not to believe him.

"I don't know, but I remember my daddy praying for your family every evening. We all did."

My anger dissipated into exhaustion, and I let my shoulders fall. I was so tired.

"Listen, you're a right good assistant to your daddy, helping out people all over the place. Just keep being that person. The bitterness . . . It don't look so good on you, and I'm guessing it don't feel good neither."

"It's exhausting." Sensing I'd stumbled upon a small light of awareness in a dark and confusing cave, I stood up. "Thanks, JT. You've been a big help."

"Yer welcome."

I stopped halfway to the door. "I have something else to talk to you about."

He paused, knife and fork midair. "Go right ahead."

"I think Rodney's aiming to stir up trouble with Jeanine and Caleb."

"Saw Caleb in town. You two back together?"

"No, but my fear is if Caleb doesn't cower to those McGraff's and do what they want, it'll give those boys a reason to hurt Jeanine."

"I'll keep an eye out, but you keep your distance."

"I'm headed to Willie's for pizza . . ." I cocked my head, silently asking if that was a bad idea.

"Todd's there, but Rodney hasn't made an appearance yet. Nursing a recent injury to his ego, I think. Best be watching out for him." JT lifted only his eyes toward me as he sawed his meat.

I chewed at my lower lip. Small towns. "Right. I, uh, have one more thing."

JT set his fork on his plate and gave me his full attention. With his patience, he'd make a great dad one day.

"Jaxon gave me a padlock the Bigfoot supposedly twisted off a barn door, but my dad said Mr. Hansen's cows were planted as a diversion because the Bigfoot go after easy game. Also, the footprints start near the back of the pasture and head west. They aren't even near the barn, so the lock makes no sense to me. I'm also wondering why Mr. Hansen roped off those tracks."

"You thinking Hansen and Reid are in cahoots to do something with the Bigfoot?"

"I think Jaxon might be, but Dad said Mr. Hansen's known about them for years."

"Only takes a whisper about Bigfoot to bring roaches out of the wall. And temptation makes men ornerier than the devil. You be careful with whatever you're doing out there."

"I will. Is it okay if I leave the four-wheeler here? It's a nice night for walking."

"Sure thing."

I headed down to Willie's tavern, ordered a large pizza, and waited at the bar. Memory of the Bigfoot gently playing with his kid drowned out Shania Twain and the loud chatter of customers. The way he flipped the child over his shoulder and swooped a fish out of the creek had been spectacular. The two sat as a family sharing a meal. Then I imagined I heard the crack of a rifle. The big male staggered. Blood soaked his broad chest. The child ran scared into the wilderness. The mother emerged from the cave and was also shot, her baby captured by cruel men. Then I saw my mom's horrified expression and felt her pain, her disappointment. And it was all my fault.

Tears pooled in my eyes as a coldness rippled down my spine.

What did I almost do?

Someone whooped from behind me. I quickly wiped the moisture off my face with JT's hanky and looked over my shoulder. Todd McGraff, pool stick in hand, grinned and took a drink of his beer. Whoever Todd bested threw money on the pool table and turned toward the corner where three more strangers sat drinking.

"You all right, kid?"

Travis laid the pizza on the bar. "Yeah, thanks, Travis."

"Hey." He leaned forward, resting his elbows on the bar, a big-brotherly gesture. "If you or your pa need help, you let me know, okay?"

I narrowed my eyes as I fished the cash out of my pocket. He nodded once. An affirmation someone had bent his ear about the Nun'Yunu'Wi. I grabbed the box and walked out into the dusky, evening air, welcoming the silence as each step brought me closer to Doc's.

Moving slowly, I took my time to sort through the uneasiness in my gut. I'd rationalized a need to prove Mom right because I thought it would erase my pain, but I was only making things worse. I was no more equipped to delve out justice than I was to approach the Bigfoot.

Heat built beneath my flannel as I sucked in a deep breath and climbed Doc's porch steps. Would Jake even talk to me? Give me a chance to explain? I rapped on the screen door in sore need of a friend. Hopefully, I still had one. Jake appeared on the other side. When he saw me, he turned away.

"Jake, wait. Let me apologize. I'm not sure why, but I have this tendency to act terribly when I'm mad."

He halted and turned, crossing his arms. His wet hair had been combed to one side, and he wore black basketball shorts and a red T-shirt. "You mean you throw a fit when you don't get your way."

I winced. "I wasn't carrying a chip on my shoulder. It was more like a giant oak. I'm sorry for being rude to you. Will you forgive me?"

"Which time? When you assumed I was a hypercritical jerk the first day we met, or when you nearly killed us driving an impossible hill in the dark, or when you actually thought I called you crazy? You know, I'm not sure I'm cut out to stand in your line of fire. It's exhausting."

I bit the inside of my lip. What could I say to fix this?

I decided to be honest. "Look, confronting Caleb and Rodney, along with the return of the Bigfoot, dad's refusal to talk much about it—" I lifted my free arm in a hopeless gesture. "My emotions have been all over the place. Today, when you refused to give me the video . . . I felt broken.

"I went down and talked to a friend at the police station. He helped me see that no matter what others think, it doesn't make Mom wrong. She had been strong and secure enough to not care what other people thought. If I'd been thinking clearly, instead of wanting to satisfy a childish need, I would have realized you, and my dad, were trying to tell me the same thing." I swallowed hard as I watched him process my explanation. He didn't look like he believed me.

"I'm not always rude. Will you give me another chance to prove I can be a friend? I promise I won't backlash at you anymore. Please?"

He studied my face for a long moment. Was he processing or thinking of locking the door? His cold gaze warmed, he shrugged, and he said in a resigned, bored tone, "What's on the pizza?"

"Extra pepperoni."

"Extra cheese?"

"Yes."

"All right. Come on in, but don't even think about stealing my phone." There was no smile in his eyes, and I hated that I was the one responsible.

I gave a tight smile and hesitantly followed.

Doc sat in the oversized chair, watching the Reds on TV. Didn't matter he overheard everything. He already understood how rotten I could be. Opening the box, I offered him a piece before placing it on the coffee table and sitting on the floor. Jake brought napkins and cans of Coke from the kitchen. After he sat on the sofa across from me, I filled them in on my conversation with JT.

"Good people had tried to help Mom protect the Bigfoot by allowing her to talk about them. There were only a few cruel people, mainly kids, who didn't know better." Which is why it hurt when Caleb said what he did last year. He knew better.

Doc swiveled our way. "Your daddy has been waiting for the perfect time to tell you about your mom's relationship with the Nun'Yunu'Wi, Ellie Mae. With their return, the timing made sense, but with it being the anniversary of your momma's passing, remembering has been harder than Neil expected."

"Did he tell you that? Why doesn't he talk to me about it?"

"I don't know, but I suspect he's suspicious of people who might do almost anything to earn a buck. Word gets out and there'll be yahoos crawling all over this place looking for a trophy and prize money. He doesn't want you getting caught in the middle."

"Dad could have told me all of this, and I would have kept quiet."

Jake snorted. "You wouldn't have listened unless it fit your agenda."

My gaze met his, not unfriendly, but unyielding. I deserved it. He'd been nothing but kind, and I treated him badly. "Well, my agenda's changed now. I want to help protect the Bigfoot." If he couldn't hear the sincerity in my tone then there was nothing more I could do.

He stared at me like he was mulling over some great decision. When he spoke his voice was the friendly Jake whose opinion mattered more to me than I realized. "What exactly changed your mind?"

"The fear of disappointing my mom. Especially after what we saw today." I glanced at Doc, his face impassive as he listened in. "Did Jake show you the video?"

"Not yet. Jake had a few other things on his mind." Doc fought a smile as he stood. "Think I'll head on upstairs. Jake, make sure she gets home safe and sound. Ellie Mae, you get some rest."

"Okay, 'night, Doc."

"G'night, Pappy."

I watched Doc climb the stairs. How long had he known

the Bigfoot existed? The other night at dinner, he listened to everything about the footprints and the lock but didn't let on he knew more. Did Grandma know, too?

"Want to sit outside?" Jake interrupted my thoughts.

"Sure."

It was a gorgeous night. Warmer than it had been but not balmy. Almost nine o'clock, I was tired but too wired to even think of sleeping. I still wore the flannel, sleeves rolled up to my elbows, and hiking boots that were feeling heavier by the moment. My hair, pulled back in the short ponytail was falling loose around my face. Jake softly closed the screen door, and we sat in the two wicker chairs, our Coke cans on the table between us.

I texted Dad to tell him I was at Doc's then leaned my head back. "Did we really see Bigfoot today?"

"I can show you the video. I won't give you my phone, though. C'mon, sit with me on the steps."

Chapter Fifteen

"I promise I won't steal your phone."

"No offense. I would trust you, but I've seen how determined you can be."

We sat side by side, shoulders and legs touching as we stared at the screen of his phone.

"This is amazing." I replayed it over and over. Without intrusive thoughts of revenge, I picked up movements, gestures, and subtle grunts and whines I'd missed before.

"They whine like you do." I pushed my leg against Jake's in a playful gesture.

"I only whine when I have to get up before the rest of civilization."

"And when you get a little dirty."

"A little dirty?"

"And with the whoop of a wild animal."

"If I think it'll rip me to shreds."

"Always an excuse."

"Do you think your mom would be proud of you right now?" he said as we faced off with grins and locked eyes.

"She'd thank you for not giving me the video and for giving me a second chance."

He sucked in a deep breath, holding my gaze. "I've never met anyone quite like you, Ellie Mae. You're a mixed bag of brains, grit, and sweetness. And as Pappy says, you have just enough sass to spark a fire."

"I sparked something earlier, didn't I?"

"I can be stubborn, too. Hence, my living situation." He lifted his hands to encompass the house.

"We're quite a pair, aren't we?" Heat washed over my face. I hadn't meant to insinuate we were a couple, but I think I liked the idea, so I didn't correct myself.

"You think your mom would like me?"

Mom and I had never discussed boys. Caleb had been present since infancy, and there'd been no other guys. The only piece of advice Mom offered after Caleb tried to kiss me in grade school was not to give in until I was ready. Jake was about as honest and sincere as they came. She'd have liked him for many reasons.

Jake leaned forward and brushed at a pebble in between his feet. "You weren't supposed to hesitate. Now, I feel insecure."

I leaned against him and spoke softly. "Her approval isn't important. Mine is. And you shouldn't feel insecure."

His eyes found mine and focused in the same way they had in the woods when I had touched his face. Fear edged in again. Did I want to go down this path? Open myself to potentially get hurt when summer ended? I swallowed hard, curious what it would feel like to kiss a big-city football jock. He leaned in, and I met him halfway. Our lips touched, at first soft and mesmerizing. He pressed closer and placed a hand on my hip as his mouth stole my breath, leaving me more dazed than when I'd first seen a picture of the Bigfoot.

Headlights and then a familiar truck rolled into view. I pulled back and watched as Caleb slowed and looked directly at us as he went on by. Awkward didn't begin to describe the mixed glob of happiness and uncertainty whirling inside me. I didn't want to hurt Caleb, but I couldn't regret kissing Jake. Caleb braked at the stop sign and sat a full thirty seconds before he went on his way.

Jake leaned back, placing his hands on the porch behind him. "Did I just mess something up for you?"

"No." I lifted a corner of my mouth. "There was a brief moment I considered getting back with him, but at the same time, I dreaded the thought." I chuckled. "I'm pretty sure being with someone isn't supposed to feel dreadful."

I shifted on the step so I partially faced Jake. "Besides, I have no desire to share with Caleb my earliest memory with my mom or the details of her work, and I don't trust him. I mean, I'm thankful for the friendship we had as kids, but that's over now."

"You do seem a whole lot better tonight. Definitely more at peace. I can see it in your face." He reached up and tucked a few stray hairs behind my ear.

"I feel better. I had this epiphany after I talked to JT. When my actions are motivated by bitterness, I give away my control. I'm dependent on others for my happiness. You, Doc, and probably my grandma told me that, but it didn't register until I talked to JT."

"So how do you not let bitterness control you?"

"By forgiving, I guess, or at least realizing we can't change the past."

"Wish my mom could hear you. She can't seem to get

over the past. She called right before you came over. Instead of talking to me she yelled at Pappy."

"Why is she so bitter?"

Jake hesitated, furrowing his brow like an internal battle erupted. "I don't know if I should tell you."

"Why?"

"I don't want to hurt your feelings."

I straightened and leaned back a little. "How would you hurt my feelings?"

"It has to do with your family."

Fear hit the pit of my stomach.

"Ellie, just because my mom has issues with your family doesn't mean I do. Understand?"

I frowned. "No."

"You want me to be blunt?"

I nodded, intimidated by the secrets. My face must have shown it because he took my hand and laced his fingers through mine. The chicks in my belly ran wild as if they feared being stomped on.

"According to my mom, Pappy and your grandma had an affair."

Over the years, I'd learned Grandma's marriage had been strategically arranged, meant to benefit the family farm and the town as a whole, but an affair with Doc seemed out of character for either of them. "According to your mom . . . How does she know?"

"Gertie told her. Gertie was pregnant before she married Pappy. Doc isn't my mom's biological dad. According to Mom, Doc married Gertie because he felt sorry for her and thought he could learn to love her."

"So Gertie and Doc were never in love. He loved my grandma instead?"

Jake nodded. "And Gertie—out of jealousy, I assume—wouldn't allow Pappy to adopt my mom."

"Your poor Mom. Do you know anything about the affair? When it happened?"

"No, but I've kind of wondered if your dad is Pappy's son."

"No way!" I pulled my hand free and squinted into the night. "Wait. How old is your mom?"

"Almost 50."

"My dad's 52. If you're right then the affair had to have been before Doc and Gertie married. Why would that be a big deal?"

"Because he never got over her."

"You know, it's all my great-grandfather's fault. He basically sold Grandma to a wealthy logger when she was sixteen." I stared at the houses across the street. Poor Grandma. So much pain and loss. Bits of life fell together—Dad's calm demeanor, the time he and Doc enjoyed ranting over medical stuff, and the way Doc doted on me. Not to mention the time Doc chose to spend with us.

"Did you ask your grandma about Dean Martin yet?"

"No. Haven't really had a chance."

I braced my forearms on my knees and watched as bats swooped around the streetlight until a horrifying thought hit. I snapped my gaze toward Jake. "Does this make us related?"

A laugh burst out of him. "No. Doc's not really my grandpa. At least not by blood. He might be yours, though."

"This is too much." I dropped my head between my knees, breathing heavy. The loose strand of hair fell in front of my face.

"But it makes sense, right?" Jake leaned forward and tipped his head to make eye contact. "You okay?"

"Can I ask you a question?"

"Sure."

"Why are you so close to Doc if no one else in your family is?"

He shifted his gaze toward the bats. "On the few occasions he visited, Gertie would go off with my mom and the girls, leaving Pappy to fend for himself. I felt sorry for him, so I kept him company. Now I realize how lucky I was to have his full attention. I was like seven when we went fishing for the first time. I'd listen to his stories about doctoring the hill people and what it was like growing up in the mountains. Everything, right down to his accent, fascinated me." His face moved from happy to disgusted in the beat of a heart. I sat up, listening to his pain.

"Mom made it obvious she didn't want me calling or visiting him. But my brother Ty—he's the rebel. He's seven years older than me even though he doesn't act like it." Jake chuckled. "Anyway, he set me up with an email account on his computer and taught me how to use it. The rest you know."

I leaned into Jake. "Even if Doc isn't your relation by blood, you're like him in so many ways. Does your mom know who her real dad is?"

"No. Gertie wouldn't tell her. I think she preferred to villainize Pappy and your grandma instead of herself."

"Doc should never have married her."

"He should have rescued your grandma. Taken her away from that logger."

"He would've been shot."

"Would have been worth it. If he truly loved her."

I looked up at the oak leaves, rattling in the breeze, and tried to imagine a relationship between Doc and Grandma. They might've sat on these very steps as young teenagers.

"You ever thought about what your dad's childhood must've been like? Were he and his other dad close?" Jake asked.

"I don't think they were. Grandma's husband was an alcoholic. Mean. Dad went off to college and didn't move back until after Grandpa died, and guess what? That's all the information I have because no one talks about it." I was about to say more when a red truck squealed around the stop sign at the corner and barreled toward us. Loud country music spilled out the windows. My body tensed.

"McGraff's." Rodney's ego must have recovered. I picked up my phone and searched for JT's number just in case.

The truck slowed as it passed. I didn't know the driver, but Rodney stood in the truck bed with Todd and cupped his hands around his mouth. "Heard there was a party down here. Brought you a gift." He and Todd flung bottles.

I threw my arms up as a bottle smashed against the handrail next to my face. Several more exploded at our feet. Tires squealed as the truck did a U-turn and sped back toward town.

"Idiots!" I sprang to my feet, and Jake did the same. My heart raced, more out of anger than fear. "What jerks!" I shook the beer off my arms and winced at the sting.

"You okay?" Jake spit out the words.

I grimaced. "No, I have some glass in my arm."

Jake grabbed my wrist and elevated my hand. Blood oozed around a brown jagged piece of glass, dripped down to my elbow, and onto the porch. He immediately pulled me into the house, keeping my arm raised. "C'mon. Let's clean that. Are you cut anywhere else?"

"No. Are you?"

"No."

After pulling the glass out and cleaning it with warm water, Jake applied a four-by-four gauze pad and wrapped the cut tight.

"It's deep. We should get you to the ER."

"No, take me home. Dad'll take care of it. But let's clean up first. Doc'll think we had some kind of freakish party if he comes downstairs."

"I'll leave him a note." Jake wrote on a small tablet on the kitchen table. "And I'll clean this and the glass up later. You should call your dad."

I waved my phone at him. "Done. I texted. He's headed out to the clinic now."

Chapter Sixteen

Jake grabbed a set of keys out of the basket on the microwave, and we drove out of town in Doc's truck.

Blood seeped through the gauze pad. "Hope I don't get blood on his seat."

"That's what you're thinking about!?" Jake jerked his head my way. "Why don't you dial 9-1-1 instead?"

"Because the emergency is over. This is nothing. The cut on my stomach was much worse."

"What about the fact those guys threw bottles at us, meaning you? The police need to know."

And force JT to confront them because of my impulsivity. "I provoked Rodney. Calling the police would just make those boys retaliate harder. And, despite your striking and incredibly humble personality, they threw them at you, too."

Jake scoffed at the poorly slung insult I meant as a joke. "Even worse since they don't know me. Will they get over what you did or keep this up?"

I glanced at Jake's perturbed expression but didn't have an answer. The only certainty was I had no intention of retaliating against the McGraffs. "Try not to worry about it. We'll steer clear of them."

Jake pulled into our driveway and stopped in front of the clinic. "Never thought I'd bring a person to the vet," he said with a hint of disgust in his voice and exited the truck.

I wanted to quip that he'd never tracked Bigfoot either, but why remind him of how far he'd tumbled down the societal ladder? Besides, I was more concerned Caleb had ratted me out to the McGraffs. Why would he do that?

Jake jogged around the front as I unsuccessfully fumbled with my door. He pulled it open, and I hopped out, gritting my teeth as my feet hit the stone drive.

"Sure you wouldn't prefer the ER?" Jake held the clinic door. The dogs barked over Jake's words. He spoke louder. "Smells like a wet dog!"

"It is an animal clinic. No need to be rude." I pointed my head toward the exam room where we could see Dad setting up supplies. Jake's steely expression didn't hint at an apology.

"Hey, Dad." We entered, and I slipped up on the exam table while Jake sat in a metal folding chair, facing me.

"What happened? Jake . . ." Dad flipped on a free-standing surgical lamp as he unwound the bandage.

Leaning back, Jake crossed his arms. One leg bounced up and down as he locked eyes with me. "A truckload of party crashers wanted to share their beer. They tossed it from the street, and the bottles shattered."

Dad looked into my eyes. "McGraff's?"

I nodded then winced as he stuck a needle in my cut to numb it.

"Are you hurt anywhere else?"

"No."

"How about you, Jake? You okay?"

"I'm not cut if that's what you mean." Jake's tone teetered somewhere between majorly annoyed and fighting mad.

"That's what I meant. But if there's something you'd like to say, I'm listening." Dad's voice was kind, almost sympathetic.

Jake clenched and unclenched his jaw. When he chose to stay silent, Dad focused on me. "Okay, why don't you scoot your back against the wall and prop your elbow up on your knee." Dad moved the lamp as I shifted. Sitting on the edge of the table, facing me, he placed a basin beneath my arm.

Catching a hint of cologne, I noticed he wore a plaid button-down shirt and his good jeans under the white lab coat. "You look nice. Did you go out tonight?" I sucked in a sharp breath as he poured the antiseptic wash into my wound.

"I did."

"With who?" I studied his face for some resemblance to Doc. It was there in the shape and color of his eyes, the bushy eyebrows, and in his mouth. Did he know the truth?

"Where's the four-wheeler?" Dad examined the cut, ignoring my question.

"At the police station. I walked a pizza down to Doc's after talking to JT."

"I can bring it out tomorrow." Jake leaned forward, elbows on his knees.

"Thank you." Dad lifted his eyes to mine. "Did you call JT about this?"

"No." I furrowed my brow. "Do you think I should've?"

"Not sure calling the police would be the best option after the judge told you to stay away from Rodney."

"Kinda what I thought." I winced and not because Dad

punched through my skin with a needle and string, but my gaze had flitted to Jake who stared with a furrowed brow. He didn't know the extent of last year's trouble. I swallowed hard.

Dad turned slightly to include Jake. "From here on out, I'd like it if neither of you were out alone, especially after dark. And Ellie, you keep your distance from Rodney. There should be no reason for your paths to cross."

"But I thought Jeanine—"

"You let Hansen handle Jeanine!"

I snapped my mouth shut and nodded.

When he finished, I had six stitches. Legs a little shaky, I sat in the waiting area while Dad and Jake cleaned the exam room. I heard Jake apologize for his rude "wet dog" comment. Then Dad took him on a tour of the place.

My eyelids bobbed as my body relaxed and my mind drifted. I reeled at the thought of Dad being Doc's son. Only surefire way to know would be to ask Grandma. Jake only knew because Gertie speculated. But unless Grandma told her directly, then Gertie's conclusion was still nothing more than gossip.

Poor Jake. I closed my eyes. He understood his mom's grief but remained strong enough to stand alone and support Doc. Do what's right. Even if the truth hurt. I could get behind that motto. I laced my fingers and held my hands on my lap, recalling his touch and the thrill that had hugged my entire body. Then my heart broke a little. After what the McGraffs did tonight, he'd likely avoid me. And for a good reason. He deserved to be with someone who didn't put him in danger every few minutes.

Pitch black.

I can't see my feet or anything around me. I shimmy slowly over solid ground, but tiny pieces of rock shift as I move. I grab at the air for branches or tree trunks, anything to give me some bearing.

I move an inch, then another until my foot slips off the edge of a precipice and hangs midair.

I back up quickly and sit on my bottom. Behind me the forest stretches for miles. I can't go that way. I'll get lost. Why did I leave the backpack behind?

I woke, trembling. Relief instantly edged in, knowing I'd never go anywhere without my supplies. I'd always have a flashlight and my phone.

Stupid dream.

Sunlight filtered in through the white curtains surrounding my bedroom window. I pulled the sheet up under my chin, closed my eyes, and relaxed into the softness of my pillow and the flowery scent of fabric softener. Details of last night's dream dissipated behind memories of yesterday. The Bigfoot. The argument with Jake. His kiss. Doc, Gertie, and Grandma. I thought about all of it.

I could've slept all day, but my stomach growled, and I was anxious to get through my chores and out to Mom's office so I could learn more about the Nun'Yunu'Wi. My arm pulled as I lifted myself into a sitting position. Blood had saturated the bandage and leaked onto my bed, leaving a brown, quarter-sized ring.

Coffee first. New bandage second. Then change my sheets.

Stiff from two days of extreme hiking, I carefully thumped down each step, the hardwood cool under my bare feet. I shuffled into the kitchen and rubbed my eyes, tipping my head side to side to work out the kinks. My hair fell into my eyes, but I didn't care.

"Morning," I mumbled. Grandma sat behind a newspaper at the kitchen table. I pulled a cup from the cupboard, but the remaining coffee was cold. Odd. I poured it and placed the cup in the microwave. When I turned, all grogginess disappeared. A smile worked its way across my warming face.

"More like afternoon." Jake set the paper aside as his eyes took in the whole of me then settled on my face with a grin. "Nice shirt."

Running a hand through my hair, I shook out a few tangles while pulling it out of my eyes. I glanced down at my favorite, worn-out, friends-in-high-places nightshirt. A red-tailed hawk soared above the lettering.

"What are you doing here? Where's Grandma?"

"I brought the four-wheeler back. Pappy followed me out and then took your grandma in to the mission. I guess a shipment of stuff came in, and she wanted to help sort it. She wasn't crazy about leaving you here alone after last night, so I offered to stay. Thought maybe we could go through some of your mom's research, if you aren't busy."

The microwave dinged. I pulled the cup out and winced as pain shot through my arm. "First, I've got to take care of this cut." I set down the coffee. "Bled on my sheets."

He stood. "I can help. Where're your first aid supplies?"

From the cupboard I pulled out a basket full of gauzes, tapes, and bandages, trying to make sense of why he'd want to stay. I honestly hadn't been sure I'd see Jake again. How many strikes did he allow a girl?

"What happened last night? I don't know how I got to bed." With my left hand, I touched my chest. "I don't know how I got into this."

Crossing the kitchen, Jake brought with him a heady scent of wood and spice. "You fell asleep in the clinic, and your dad couldn't wake you, so he carried you inside. From there, I don't know." He took the basket in one hand, and with the other, moved a wild piece of hair that refused to stay out of my eyes. "How do you feel today?"

"I-uh . . . I'll be right back." I rushed out of the kitchen. If he planned to get that close, I needed to prepare. Upstairs, I quickly dressed in denim shorts and a blue tank top, brushed my hair and teeth, not perfectly since I had to use my left hand, but passable. On the way down, I glanced at the mantle clock. One o'clock! Holy cow.

"Grandma probably left some lunch," I said, reentering the kitchen.

Jake turned from the window over the sink. "She did." He pointed to a pot on the back of the stove.

"Mind helping me out? Then we can eat." I was capable of changing my own bandage, but now that I was decent, I welcomed the opportunity to get closer after last night's disaster.

"Any idea where your dad is?" Jake unwound the bandage until it stuck with dried blood.

"Over at the Rescue, checking fecal samples."

Jake scrunched up half his face, turned on the faucet, and stuck his hand underneath. "Not your typical Saturday."

"It is for him."

"Think Rebecca's quizzing him about this stitching job?" Holding my wrist, Jake guided my forearm under the warm water to loosen the remaining gauze. He leaned down and gently rubbed at the blood with his opposite thumb, causing a shiver to pass through me.

"I'm wondering if there's something going on between them."

"Yeah?"

"He's been going over there more than usual. Without me."

"You okay with that?"

"Yeah, Rebecca's great. But I wish he'd clue me in."

Turning off the water, Jake searched the kitchen. "Where're your towels?"

Instead of pointing, I reached around and opened the drawer just behind him. My cheek brushed his shoulder. Our bodies nearly touched, and I thought about lingering there as I imagined his arms wrapping around me. But that didn't happen, so I stepped back and held up the towel.

While he focused on drying and redressing my arm, I studied his face and those bright blue-gray eyes. The square jaw that had carried a rigidity last night now appeared optimistic and kind. Like his touch.

What was this attraction? Our friendship, or whatever it was, existed in a whirlwind of disturbing occurrences. What did I hope for? What did Jake want?

"What do you expect from me?" I blurted out.

His eyes snapped to mine and he furrowed his brow. "What do you mean?"

"I understand why you're here for Doc and the relationship you have, but what do you want from me?"

He held my arm up and applied the tape. "Friendship, but . . . I don't know. You're like a magnet I've been drawn to since I was a kid. I couldn't wait to meet you in person. Turns out, I like being with you. I don't expect anything."

I locked eyes with him, then with my hands on his upper arms, I pushed up on my toes. He met me with a sweet kiss that only made me crave more. I slipped a hand behind his neck and kissed him harder, every inch of my body responding to his touch as he pressed his hands into my lower back and pulled me close.

When I dropped down flat to my feet, he kept a hold on my hips and tipped his head. "Why do you keep asking me to hang out with you? Am I a distraction, a rebound, or is there something else?" He lifted his eyebrows.

How could he be so calm after that kiss? My insides were as skittery as a bug walking on water. And the warmth of his hands on my waist muddled my thoughts, but I wasn't moving away. What was the question? Oh yeah, why did I keep asking him to hang out?

He'd known about me for most of his life, so wanting to hang out made sense from his perspective. But I hadn't given him more than a passing thought before last week, and he knew it. So, what exactly was I hoping for?

I grinned up at him. "You are a distraction but in a good way. And I'll be honest, I've never rebounded before. I'm not exactly sure what that's supposed to feel like, but I wasn't looking for you or anyone else. You landed in my world on a really bad day and should've ran, but you didn't. You haven't even flinched with all the crap going on. Well, until yesterday."

He folded his arms and leaned back against the kitchen sink. "I'd be lying if I said the McGraff's didn't intimidate me."

"They don't worry me. When I said you flinched, I was referring to you getting mad at me for wanting to expose the Bigfoot, putting you in danger, and accusing you of thinking I was crazy." I picked up my cold coffee and took a drink, overwhelmed at how rotten I'd been.

"That stuff's history, but McGraff's aren't, are they?"

"You want to talk about Rodney and Todd?"

He shrugged. "A little perspective would be nice."

I opened the fridge and pulled out supplies for ham sandwiches. "I was probably ten or eleven when Rodney and Todd moved to town. Their momma left them with their uncle and ran off." After placing the food on the table, I grabbed a loaf of bread off the counter. Jake stirred the black bean soup.

"Caleb, Jeanine, and I included them whenever we went fishing or swimming. One day after school, I caught Rodney torturing a bird, and we got into a fight. At that time, he was shorter than me, and I beat him up. He slashed my bicycle tires. I didn't retaliate, but when he wanted to hang out with Caleb, I convinced Caleb to ignore him."

I handed Jake two bowls and set the table with plates and glasses of water as I continued. "I also stood up for anyone else he bullied and didn't miss an opportunity to call him out. So, as we got older, Rodney's goal wasn't to simply break my relationship with Caleb, he set out to ruin Caleb. The ultimate revenge."

Jake offered a tight-lipped smile, but his eyes held concern as he placed the bowls of soup on the table. "How'd he go about that?"

We sat down, and I pulled up a knee, placing my bare foot on the chair. "Offered an endless supply of drugs, alcohol, and partying. At prom, my junior year, Rodney persuaded Caleb to leave me at the dance. I would have been okay if Caleb had told me he was leaving." I swirled a spoon through my black bean soup. "I had to call Dad to pick me up. Later that night, I drove out to McGraff's. Every light in the house was on, and I could see Caleb in the bedroom with a girl from school. Same girl I'd caught him with a month earlier." With the windows open, the music had been loud, the smell of weed so strong I could've sworn a family of skunks lived under the place.

I fixed my eyes on Jake. For the first time, I felt remorse for how I acted that night. He would never have stooped to my level. His manners and behavior were impeccable compared to mine, but he showed no judgment as he layered ham and cheese on bread.

I continued. "Rodney's truck is the only thing he cares about, so I shot his tires. I was about to shoot Caleb's next, but everyone came running out of the house. Rodney pressed charges, but we had a good lawyer and JT vouched for me. I paid Rodney back and apologized, tried to explain why I'd done it, but it didn't matter because he knew I wasn't sorry."

Jake sliced his sandwich into perfect halves. "And that's why the judge told you to keep your distance from him?"

"Yeah, Rodney was pretty mad I got off so easy."

"So how do you stop him from doing something else?"

I swallowed my bite of soup. "I can't stop it. I can't change the mindset of someone like Rodney. He has nothing to lose. Even if I back down and cower to his bullying, he won't stop. Besides, I'm not wired that way. I think I'd hate myself if I let him control me."

"But isn't he controlling things when you react to him?"

"Not if I'm defending myself."

"The other night outside the bar, you didn't need to fight. Caleb and I were right there. What would Rodney have done if you stepped away?"

My mouth opened, but I had no words. I was used to watching my own back. Relying on others hadn't crossed my mind. But Jake was right. I could've turned and walked away. I didn't need to hit Rodney then, or provoke him earlier at Subway.

Pushing the bowl aside, I forced myself to make eye contact. "Guess I enjoyed seeing him look stupid. I don't know if I have what it takes to walk away. I'm not like you. I wasn't gifted with an endless supply of nice-guy."

Jake moved his soup bowl to the side and leaned forward, resting his forearms on the table. "One reason I keep hanging out with you is because your heart is in the right place. You're a good person."

"What's the other reason? Cheap entertainment?"

He burst out, laughing, and I joined in. We both knew it was true.

After lunch, we cleaned up the kitchen and went out to the clinic. Jake helped me clean the cages, then we carried the two boarding cats into Mom's office where we spent the afternoon playing with them and learning about the Nun'Yunu'Wi.

Chapter Seventeen

Later that evening, I walked out to the barn where Dad was preparing for three new calves. At supper, he'd mentioned they would be arriving tomorrow afternoon. I felt bad for not helping prepare, but Jake and I had spent the entire afternoon and the past two hours since dinner studying. Mom's office floor was currently covered with open journals and newspaper articles. We'd tacked a map to the wall and began pinpointing sightings, the Nun'Yunu'Wi's travel patterns, and where the people who seemed to be contacts lived, including Simsy's two sons.

I passed through the open barn door. "Hey, Dad."

Daisy bleated and hopped up on the bottom rung of her gate. I patted the goat's nose. Lulu joined her, expecting her share of attention. I scratched her head.

Dad looked up from where he was fastening the gate hinge along the wall. "Hi Ellie. Jake go home?"

"Yeah. Need some help?"

"Can you hand me one of those pins?" He nodded to

the long, round pieces of metal on the ladder that led up to the loft. I passed one over and held on to the other until he lined up the bottom hinge and held out his hand.

"Jake and I thought you should know we found the Nun'Yunu'Wi yesterday. I didn't say anything at supper because I wasn't sure what Grandma knew."

Remaining quiet, I hoped Dad would ask a question or at least show a little interest in our discovery, but he simply walked to the other end of the gate, made sure the latch worked, then climbed the ladder.

"Watch out." He tossed a bale of straw out of the mow. It smacked the floor in a puff of dust. I pulled the bale into the pen as he climbed down. "Careful you don't pop those stitches."

My arm throbbed a tiny bit, barely noticeable. "In her notebooks, Mom talked about how she prepared the Nun'Yunu'Wi for her approach. She had a sort of ritual to help them feel comfortable with her presence."

"I'm aware."

"Well, I'm thinking about doing the same by circling their cave this week. I want to see if they'll acknowledge me and let me get close."

With one knee against the bale of straw, he pulled off a circle of twine. He grabbed the second string and gave it a shake, causing the straw to spill across the floor in flakes, making my nose itch with all the dust. He handed me the twine, offering the same straight, no-nonsense expression I'd seen every time I presented him with a quandary.

"What are you thinking?"

"That I told you not to go out alone."

"At night." I crossed the barn, hung the twine on a nail with several other pieces. "This'll be during the day. I'll take my phone and the GPS and be home long before dark. There's absolutely no way either of the McGraffs have the stamina to follow me out there. And I have to do this. I never got the chance to support Mom. I want to do this for her. Besides, it's the right thing." I reentered the pen. "I'll be careful. I promise."

"Is there any way I can talk you out of this?" He picked up a flake of straw in each hand and shook them in one corner to create a nice bedding.

"No. My heart's sort of set on doing it."

"When?"

"Beginning Monday." That gave me one more day to prepare. We worked silently, shaking out the entire bale at one end of the pen. Then I followed Dad outside. He pulled the barn door shut and secured the padlock. "Promise you won't take any unnecessary risks."

Bats swooped in the overhead light that cast our shadows across the gravel. "I won't."

"Keep the GPS on and take the extra battery chargers for your phone." He turned and walked toward the clinic. I hurried to keep up. "Tomorrow, I'll show you how to map a route in the GPS. You'll need to memorize it in case you lose reception or your battery dies. It won't be an easy hike."

"Which is why no one will follow."

When we reached the clinic, Dad unlocked the door and allowed me to enter first. "I'll let you take the tranquilizer gun. It'll be easier to carry than your shotgun. Don't tell anyone." He said the last few words sternly, frowning.

"I won't." Tranquilizer guns were illegal to carry without a permit but effective in stopping a rogue animal. I was as much grateful for his concern as his trust. "Thank you."

I wanted to say more about the Bigfoot, discuss their interactions and behaviors, tell him how the mother touched her child and nursed her baby, but I feared pushing the issue would ultimately cause a disagreement.

In his office, Dad pulled the gray ten-by-ten case off the top of a cupboard, opened it, and examined the three prepared darts.

He snapped the case shut and handed it to me.

I tucked thoughts of Bigfoot away and followed him out of the clinic. "Dad, can I ask you a personal question?" One that had been nagging me since he sewed me up last night.

He cocked his head my way. "You can ask. Doesn't mean I'll answer."

"Have you ever thought of remarrying?"

He narrowed his eyes. "Where did that come from?"

I shrugged. "Just curious. You've never talked about it. If dating someone would make you happy, it's okay with me."

We stopped at the pole barn, and he checked the locks. "I think about it."

"Is there someone?"

"Maybe."

My excitement grew. It had to be Rebecca. We entered the house through the back. Dad washed in the kitchen sink while I leaned against the counter, facing him. "Who is it?"

He dried his hands on a towel and kissed the top of my head. "I'm going to bed. See you in the morning."

Chimes sounded in the bell tower of the Hush Briar Methodist Church at ten in the morning and had done so every Sunday since they were added in 1968 by the generous contribution of my deceased grandpa. It wasn't uncommon to see folks step out of their homes and begin the short trek down the hill to the little white, coal-stained building sitting across from Grady's Market near the end of Main Street.

The place filled up quickly. Folding chairs lined the back corners for overflow. There'd been talk awhile back about building a new place, and I was all for it. Even though we'd been attending since long before I could remember, this building was a link that shackled my family to past hypocrisy. My grandpa gave to the church all while abusing his family. I'd overheard Dad and Grandma talk about attending church in Jackson, but nothing ever came of it. Probably because leaving would raise more questions than ignoring the disillusioned past that Grandma said was more our hindrance than anyone else's.

Today was a special day, the one hundredth anniversary of the church. Several members and former attendees stood outside, chatting amongst a couple dozen round tables set up for the potluck while cars passed by slowly. The aroma of ham and beans wafted from the church's open basement door as we walked inside.

Dodging a number of familiar faces and visitors, I walked down the center aisle toward our usual pew but stopped when a hand captured mine. I turned toward a smiling Simsy and her two sons, both slightly younger than my dad. Last I'd seen them was at Mom's funeral.

They were only foster brothers to my mom, and holiday get-togethers had been rare, but I liked to think of these guys as go-to uncles. They always sent gifts and cards and used to call Mom quite a bit. On occasions when they had come home, we all went out four-wheeling, and I hung out with their kids. But that had been before Mom died.

After Mom died, everything changed. They hadn't been home once, until now. At least Simsy hadn't said anything if they had. I supposed changes like that were true for everyone who lost family. Even if you weren't blood related.

"'Morning." I bent down and hugged Simsy then touched the floral hair barrette encircling her salt-and-pepper bun. "I love this." Hair sticks with chipmunks on the ends crisscrossed through the middle. Kyle, the older of the two and a little on the heavy side with a closely shaved head and goatee, extended his hand and spoke over the chatter in the room. "Ellie Mae, good to see you. Man"—he shook hands with Dad—"she was knee high to a grasshopper last I saw her. Now she's full grown. Looks just like Jodi, don't she?"

Steve offered me a fist bump and nodded at Dad. "Good to see you. How are ya?" Steve was thin and resembled Simsy with brown eyes and high cheekbones. Only his hair was dark and hadn't started to gray yet.

"I'm good," I said. "You guys haven't changed a bit. Where're your families?"

"Too much going on with sports and summer programs," Kyle said.

Steve lifted a hand. "Same. We'll be up for an extended stay later in the summer."

"Can we eat lunch together? I want to hear all about your families." Feeling a need to move out of the influx of traffic, I glanced at my usual seat and did a double take. Curiosity tugged me away. "I'll see you guys later."

Caleb sat stiffly, facing forward. I smoothed down my black ribbed shirt, tucked tightly in my tan capris. Dad slipped an arm around my waist. "Sit next to me."

By his set jaw, he looked tempted to toss Caleb out on his ear. Over breakfast, I'd filled him in on my meeting with

Caleb and the details behind my confrontation with Rodney, but I didn't have time to tell him how I'd talked to JT and worked through some issues. I wasn't angry anymore, and I wasn't afraid to sit next to Caleb.

I slid into the pew next to him. "Hi."

"Hey." Expressionless, Caleb handed me a sealed envelope with my name on the front. Our eyes met, and I felt years of friendship balance precariously on a precipice as if one wrong move might destroy any of the good we had shared.

"What's this?"

"Nothing much. Just . . ." He rubbed his hands on the thighs of jeans. "See you around, Ellie Mae." He stood and walked out. I shifted and watched him weave through the crowd, my heart a little heavy even as Jake and his Pappy came through the door.

With a spring in his step, Jake filed in and took Caleb's seat. On the opposite end, Doc slipped into the pew beside Grandma. I folded the envelope and shoved it into the back pocket of my capris to save for another time.

"Quite the buzz happening here." Jake looked around at the happy, chattering crowd. "I like the bells. Felt like a holiday walking to church."

"It is a holiday." I leaned close and spoke in a soft conspiratorial tone. "This is your first Sunday in church, and you're everyone's new gift. People came from all over just to see you."

Jake grinned. "I happen to know that isn't true, but even if it was, you were much scarier. They'll be a piece of cake."

Dad snorted a chuckle. I elbowed him. "Hey!"

"Truth is truth."

My spirit lightened as the worship minister came out and began the service. The hour passed quickly; in part because I enjoyed the rush of excitement that came whenever my hand or knee touched Jake's. But, in truth, Pastor Long knew to keep the sermon short or he'd loose his congregation to the smell of food and the sounds of preparation that happened beyond the sanctuary doors.

After the final prayer, Doc snagged Jake to introduce him to a few people while I followed Simsy and her boys outside. Songbirds chattered loudly under the brilliant blue sky until someone turned up the music, and "In The Sweet By and By" took off, drowning them out.

We jumped into the food line off to one side of the church. My mouth watered as I forked ham onto my plate followed by cheesy scalloped potatoes and fresh green beans. I updated the guys on my future plans and heard the latest about their kids.

In her journals, Mom wrote about visiting these guys routinely. She mentioned their part in documenting the Nun'Yunu'Wi's travel behaviors and helped to isolate migration patterns—one reason a map was easy for Jake and me to mark up. All of this made me reluctant to believe Simsy's boys came up from North Carolina and Virginia just for the church potluck.

We secured a table that would sit both our families and where I intended to ask Simsy about the Native American/Bigfoot drawing. She might not know anything, but her reaction would dictate my next move.

I placed my phone on the folded drawing next to my plate and was about to tip five chairs to save spots for my family when Jeanine flew into the chair next to me. She plopped her plate, a passel of napkins, and her scarf on the table. Several pieces of raw cauliflower rolled off her plate, and she giggled, chasing them. I recoiled and pinched my mouth closed, the whole ordeal way overdramatic. But that was Jeanine.

"Hey, Lills, room for two more? Sorry, everyone." She moved her junk to her lap.

I opened my mouth to tell her no, there wasn't room, when Rodney dropped a plate next to hers.

Chapter Eighteen

I froze, looked him up and down, then glanced away. What was he doing here? Church? Really? Heat moved through my veins. I peeked at him out of the corner of my eye, and Jeanine laughed, slapping my arm.

"Don't act so shocked. Everyone has a right to come to church. He actually came to say he was sorry. Right?" She leaned against Rodney's bicep.

Rodney met my gaze for only a second then lowered it along with his shoulders. "We were being stupid. I'm sorry you were hurt."

Music and the sounds of everyone milling around us faded out. The heat filled my body. I flicked a glance at Mom's foster family, conversing between themselves while they ate. They didn't notice me mentally grappling for a foothold in the shifting sands of my world. The pulsating heat intensified. I had trouble capturing my breath. I scooted my chair from the table. "I'll be right back."

I needed a minute. Two days ago, Rodney taunted me. Maybe he didn't mean for me to get hurt physically, but he meant to intimidate. And now he sat at my table. On the church lawn. People don't change that fast.

At the drink table, I grabbed a white Styrofoam cup and pushed the button on the red-and-yellow thermos. Lemonade splashed into the cup. I downed it and got another.

"Careful there. People might think you have a drinking problem."

I looked up into Jake's amused face, and my insides cooled considerably, the tightness in my gut loosened. Rolling my eyes, I finished the second cup and got a third.

"Saw you get ambushed. What's up with that?"

"Can you believe it? He came to apologize." I nodded at Rodney, who had stood up and now walked toward the church.

"Is he serious?"

"Can't tell." We watched as he disappeared inside the building.

Jake grabbed my hand and pulled me out of the drink line.

"Sorry," I said to Mr. Snyder. He smiled and stepped up to the table, guiding his five-year-old foster daughter, who sported a pretty yellow dress and a pair of bright red tennis shoes.

Jake spoke softly. "Should you mention something to your dad or JT?"

"And say what? I don't think Rodney should be at church."

"You can always move." Jake pointed to a table on the opposite side of the yard. "We saved you a spot. Come join us."

I waved at Doc and Grandma. "I brought the Simms'

picture with me. I want to show Simsy and see what she knows about it."

Jake jerked his gaze to the table. "So those are the sort-of uncles? The ones we put on the migration map?"

"Yeah. I need to talk to them and Simsy alone, but I don't know how long Rodney and Jeanine will stay."

"Even if Rodney did come to apologize, they'll probably take off soon. This isn't exactly their scene."

"Think if I yank his tail he'll move along quicker?"

"Might make things worse."

"I won't do anything I'll regret later." I hid a smile as I sipped the lemonade.

Jake stuffed his hands in his pocket. "Don't do anything I'll regret later, either."

I almost spit out my lemonade as I laughed.

Jake smiled and those eyes, in slight contrast to the sky, danced along. "Change of subject. After they eat, Pappy's going out to your place to watch a documentary or something with your dad. You want to walk home?"

My tension gave way a bit more. A two-mile trek on a beautiful day with a nice guy. How could I refuse? "Sounds fun. Come find me when Dad and Grandma leave?"

"Sure." Then he grinned and touched my arm. "Go easy. A church brawl won't help your record."

I snorted and bumped his shoulder with mine before making my way back to the table. I needed to be quick about getting rid of Rodney and Jeanine so I had time to talk with the Simms' before lunch ended. At least I had dirt, and I felt confident I knew how to fling it for the greatest effect without causing too much of an uproar.

I plopped down next to Jeanine and whispered in her ear. "You and Rodney need to leave now, or I'll tell JT it was you and McGraff's who tried to bust into Mr. Smith's place the other night."

"You don't know nothing about that." She sneered at me.

I lifted my eyebrows. "Oh yeah? Dad and I were driving home from an alpaca emergency at Hatley's. The boys hid when they saw us drive by, but not before we saw them with a crowbar at the back door. Dad honked long and loud before he called JT." Her face blanched. "I'm guessing you heard it since Rodney's truck was parked next door at the library and you were sitting inside the cab. Since y'all ran off, we didn't say anything because we didn't want *you* getting into trouble. But that on top of Friday night's assault, which I haven't mentioned yet, won't go over well with JT." I glanced at the food table, where my cop-friend stood talking to his dad and a few others. "Do you want me to make a scene?"

"I really hate you." She quietly ground out the words. I flinched internally but kept a straight face. Did I push too hard? Did I care? Rodney strutted across the lawn and weaved between tables like he owned the place.

"We're finishing our food," Jeanine snapped and shoved a carrot in her mouth.

I glanced at her raw vegetables. "You aren't here to eat or apologize, and you know it."

"Then why don't you tell me why you think we're here?" Her ponytail slapped side to side with each sassy word. Rodney plopped into his seat and lifted one corner of his mouth at Jeanine, oblivious to our conversation.

I honed in on him. "If you really want to say you're sorry to someone"—I jerked my head toward Jake—"apologize to Jake. He might actually believe you. As for me, I think you're here as Jaxon's tools, but you might as well move on because you aren't getting anything from me."

Jeanine stood, bumping the table and forcing everyone to grab their drinks. "You don't know what you're talking about. Let's go, Rodney. We're obviously not wanted here."

Without a word, he stood, grabbed his plate, and ate until they reached the trash can where he dumped the entire plate.

"Ellie Mae?" Simsy touched my arm. Kyle chuckled and looked at Steve. "Jodi all over again?"

"No kidding." Steve's eyes drilled mine. "Always had a way with words."

My tension completely unwound as the words to "Standing On the Promises" pulled me back into my comfort zone.

"I just needed to get you guys alone." I reached for the paper, but it was gone. Looking around, I found it on the ground with my phone, knocked off during Jeanine's ruckus. I passed it to Simsy then watched her face as she unfolded the paper. Her breath caught, and she leaned to the side so her boys could see. Kyle smiled while Steve focused on scanning the picture. "Who did this?" He glanced from me to his mom.

Simsy touched the signature. "I'm guessing Floyd Simms. Your daddy said he was always drawing. Bet he sketched this from a story told him by his granddaddy who was a full-blooded Cherokee from northern Virginia. Round about where you live, Steve. Floyd lived to be a 105. He must have given this to Jodi when she was a young girl."

"Who was Floyd Simms to you?" I asked, curious why he would have given Mom the drawing.

"Carl's grandpa." She smiled into my eyes. "And he would have accepted you as his great-great-granddaughter because he loved Jodi so much and her . . ." Simsy glanced beyond me.

I swung around and saw Dad watching. I turned back. Simsy folded the paper and handed it back. All three faces went stoic.

"He loved her what?"

"He loved her way with nature. It's just a fun picture." She smiled sadly, and I disliked my dad for making her feel like she needed to keep secrets from me. Sighing heavily, I propped my arms on the table and leaned in close.

"Listen. My dad would like to ignore what's happening around here for whatever reason." I tapped the drawing with my index finger. "But I've seen them. I know where they are. I want to get closer. Can you help me with that?"

"Why would you want to get closer?" Steve wiped his mouth and threw his napkin on his plate, giving it a little shove. "You don't know anything about them."

I narrowed my eyes, a little miffed by his reaction. He didn't own these creatures.

"That's not true. I've read a ton of Mom's research. Dad said they aren't violent. I'm intrigued. I want to see if I can interact with them. I want to continue mom's research if I can. And I want to help protect them since they're likely the last of their kind."

Simsy looked deep in thought while Steve shook his head. "No. Ellie, you don't understand what's at stake."

Kyle leaned forward. "What he means is that once you get involved, you can't go back. Whatever plans or dreams you have for your life now will be gone. Your dad doesn't want that for you."

"Well, he's not in charge of my life."

"If you were my daughter, I wouldn't allow it," Steve said.

Kyle skewed up a corner of his mouth. "Me either."

Simsy laid a hand over mine. "But you don't know Ellie Mae. She's different than your girls. This could be the life she's meant to live."

"Mom!" Steve glared at Simsy.

Simsy pulled her hands into her lap and stared at them, saying nothing more.

I huffed. How dare they be so rude? "I'll just figure it out on my own. And those goon heads that were sitting here —" I pointed at the chair beside me. "They're up to something. I need to make sure the Nun'Yunu'Wi stays safe."

Steve drilled me with a hard look. "This isn't a 4-H project or some kind of sideshow hobby." Steve glanced around then leaned in closer. "We need to move the Nun'Yunu'Wi now."

"Why? You think they're in danger from those two?" I nodded to the side and made a ridiculous face. "They'd get lost in their own backyard if it wasn't lit up."

"You said you thought they were Jaxon's tools," Steve said. "He's no joke and has gone after these creatures before. We need to move them before he gets wind of their location."

"Then I want to help."

"No." They both said it at the same time.

I slapped a hand on the table and shifted my gaze from one to the other. "I need to do this! This was my mom's life. I'm just starting to get to know her. Please! I've read most of her journals, and I've put together a plan that I believe will allow me to get close. All I need is three or four more days. Let me do this, then I can help you. Now and in the future."

"That's exactly what we're trying to prevent." Kyle ran a hand down his face while Steve adamantly shook his head. Simsy watched her hands with the barest hint of a smile. That was enough encouragement for me to push harder. Especially when Steve focused his gaze on a point behind me.

I jerked my head in his direction. "When did my dad call you? Last night or last week?"

The Bigfoot appeared sometime before Tuesday night, which was when Dad and Mr. Hansen planted the cows, but last night was when I had told him I'd found the Nun'Yunu'Wi. My breath caught. When Simsy brought the owl over Wednesday morning, she mentioned the boys were visiting. Had she actually come over to talk to Dad about the Nun'Yunu'Wi? I glanced at her face, fixed on her lap. She was biting her tongue; I'd bet my life on it.

I looked from one foster uncle to the next, not wanting to offend. "I'm the only one who knows their exact location." And I didn't tell Dad. He had only shown me how to map a route, but I programmed the GPS. "My guess is no one writes down exact coordinates." I nodded at Kyle. "You're on the map for the northwestern part of North Carolina." I glanced at Steve who fell back in his chair and tilted his head. "And you cover the western part of Virginia, which will be their next stop. But there are no coordinates, only names of people who live in those areas."

I leaned forward again, bouncing my gaze between them. "I know what's going on here. I know what's at stake and the importance of keeping a secret. Maybe it's a little dangerous, but you gotta let me do this. Outside our adventures and talks about wildlife and the forest, I didn't know my mom." I rested a hand on my chest. "Her goals, her dreams, her motivations. She didn't share any of that with me, but she was going to. The last entry in her journal said so. She was going to include me!" I pounded my hand once against my chest for emphasis. "Dad might not want this, but Mom did! And I do, too. Please don't take this away from me. I'll be careful. Just give me the four days! If I fail, I'll tell you exactly where they're at. I promise."

The chair moved beside me, and Jake sat down. "Okay for me to join you?"

I looked back at Dad and Doc, each carrying an armload of folding chairs toward the church, then introduced Jake to the Simms. An awkward silence ensued as people cleaned up around us.

Kyle drummed his fingers on the table. Steve clenched and unclenched his jaw, then in a miraculous gesture he lifted one shoulder while glancing at Kyle. "She is an adult, and she is her mother's daughter." He focused on me and stood. "You have until next weekend." His gaze shifted to Simsy. "That doesn't change our deal."

Simsy nodded. With a smile and glinting eyes, she stood and kissed me on the cheek. She squeezed Jake's shoulder and walked off in the direction of the parking lot.

Kyle came around the table and pulled me into a hug. "Always good to see you, kiddo. Almost like being with Jodi. Call me with updates, hear?"

"Can't you guys stick around for a while? You could come over and see what Jake and I have been doing with Mom's stuff."

"Not if I'm making a trip up next weekend. See ya." Kyle followed his mom.

"Same here." Steve gave me a fist bump. "No hard feelings?"

"Never."

"Then keep in mind your goal is to move them on. You can do whatever else you want to do at a different location, but since you have people watching you, it isn't safe for them here."

"I understand."

He scratched at a place above his eye and glanced my dad's direction. "He won't be happy."

"I know." I bit at the corner of my lip, hating the truth.

Steve draped an arm over my shoulder and spoke to Jake. "'Scuse us." Steve turned so we faced Grady's Market across the street, now visible since most of the cars had cleared out. "I just want to say one more thing. And I'm speaking as a dad. Be careful about your priorities. Your dad is here, and he cares about you. Your mom will always be a special part of who you are, but she's not the one losing sleep at night." He squeezed my shoulder in a side hug. "Understand?"

I nodded.

He ruffled my hair like I was ten. "See you in a week." Then he playfully backhanded Jake's shoulder. "Good luck with this one."

Horrified, my mouth fell open. "That was not okay!" I called after Steve. Without turning around, he raised a hand and waved.

Chapter Nineteen

Jake and I walked side by side away from the church, talking about my conversation with Steve and Kyle and how I'd convinced them to give me four days to establish contact. If I failed, I'd give them the coordinates and allow them to work their magic to move the Nun'Yunu'Wi on. If I made contact, then it would be my job to move them on.

We crossed the last intersection in town and headed down Dillard Hollow. The road had completely dried out, the trees lush and green. The air had grown warm and slightly humid, but in the woods, the early afternoon breeze felt cool. Birds sang while wood hyacinths and wild geraniums bobbed up and down in a rhythmic dance. An occasional car passed, and folks hollered greetings out their window or stopped to chat for a minute before they moved on.

"I love how friendly this place is. Mom made it sound like everyone was backward and rude." A maple seed twirled down, and he caught it between his palms.

"You talk to her recently?" I asked.

"She called again after I got home last night. She asked questions like: Are you getting enough to eat? Are you comfortable in the hot upstairs? Are people being kind? Every question assumed I wasn't happy. After talking about how things were at home, she warned me there would be terrible consequences for leaving. I asked her to tell me what those would be, but she wouldn't."

"I think how-to-effectively-sweep-the-truth-under-the-rug-so-you-don't-have-to-talk-to-your-kids-about-it is described in The Adult Handbook for Dealing with Conflict."

"And she wonders why I left." He ripped the seed apart and tossed half of it. "So, what's your plan? What day will you start circling the Bigfoot cave?"

I looked up into the canopy of frolicking leaves. "Weather looks good for the next few days. I should start tomorrow."

"You don't sound confident." He stopped and picked up a stone.

"Because I'm not. It's a major hike. I'm a little intimidated."

He pointed to a tree and threw the rock. It smacked against the bark. He picked up another and handed it to me with a challenging look. "Maybe there's another way. Do you have to do it exactly like your mom did?"

I threw the rock, hit the tree, and grinned, resisting the urge to jump up and down. "You've read as much as me. Seems like I need to. I'm just not sure I have what it takes."

"You have what it takes. You're the toughest person I know." Jake picked up a rock and tossed it up and down while he studied the trees. "But maybe you're putting too much pressure on yourself. You want to do it for your mom, but shouldn't it be what you want for yourself?"

"It's like I told Steve and Kyle. I'm just starting to understand Mom's motivation and, in some ways, her obsession. I don't want to give that up. But they're afraid I'll get sucked in and lose focus on everything else like college and a career, I guess."

"Why do they think that?" Jake pointed to a smaller tree nestled between two old oaks and pitched the stone as if he were throwing a baseball. It hit the tree with a clunk.

"I don't know." I picked up a stone. "We didn't have time to talk about it, but I'm guessing it's based on their own lives, maybe people they know. Maybe it's the enormity of the secret. It certainly consumed Mom, and I want to know why." I aimed and hit the sapling.

"Good shot." Jake retrieved another stone and furrowed his brow. "Sure you have to go alone?"

"You saw Mom's instructions. Too many human smells intimidate them, and half the plan is to convince them I'm her. I have my phone and GPS tracker. As long as I can get a signal, Dad'll know where I'm at."

"Still feels a little reckless."

"What other option do I have?"

"Don't go. Let your uncles handle it."

I rolled my eyes, having no desire to talk in circles. "I'm doing it, and I'll be careful. See that knot?" I picked up a stone and pointed to a tall silver maple where a rough spot protruded on the side nearest us.

Jake folded his arms and watched. I threw the stone and missed by a hair.

"Ooo...almost."

"It slipped. Let me try again." I reached for the stone in his hand, but he pulled it out of reach. "No way, Brandon Webb, you had your turn."

"Who's Brandon Webb?"

His eyes grew large. "What!? You call yourself a Kentuckian?"

I shrugged.

"Only one of the greatest Major League Baseball pitchers who happened to have graduated from the University of Kentucky. Don't tell me you dislike baseball, too?" He looked pained.

"I never said I disliked any sport."

"Just football jocks."

"Football, basketball, baseball . . . jock being the keyword." I grinned teasingly.

"Be prepared to lose. You should have asked what my scholarship is for." He pulled back his arm while lifting his left leg as if to pitch a fastball.

"Bear!" I teased and gave him a little shove as he threw the stone. I took off running as the stone missed its mark. He caught up with me in seconds. I squealed as he lifted me off the ground and threw me over his shoulder.

"By the way, I also wrestled. Don't fight me, or I'll fold you into a pretzel."

A car slowly rolled around a bend.

"Put me down you stupid jock." I laughed and slapped his back.

He squeezed my legs closer to his chest and lifted them upward. My head lunged downward toward the ground. I screamed. "Jake! I mean it. Those are the Hately's coming our way."

"Oh, yeah? I met them." Jake turned as they approached. "They're waving. In case you didn't notice."

I went limp as the car passed by. I would kill him.

"Say you're sorry." He walked on. I growled, sensing this would never end.

"Sorry," I mumbled.

"And that you'll never call me a stupid jock again."

"Just because I say it won't make it any less true."

He shifted. I shrieked, dropping closer to the stone road. "And I'll never call you a stupid jock again!"

He placed me on the ground with a cocky, but playful, grin. "You're not so tough."

Awkwardly bested, I walked on, feeling strangely feminine and, once again, sorely out of his league. My scholarship as a valedictorian from a tiny school was certainly no full ride. In my mind, I did a quick comparison and came up short financially, talent-wise, and certainly in world experience. A part of me couldn't fathom that he enjoyed this place and my backwoods company. His world was so much bigger than this tiny speck of poor hill country, and my world barely crossed the county line.

Still, I didn't argue when he dropped an arm over my shoulder and rattled on about his earliest memories of playing ball with his dad, brother and sisters, and a passel of aunts, uncles, and cousins. No surrogate anything.

Day One

I started out wearing Mom's jacket and her old boots, certain the mustiness would overpower her scent. But Dad said if the Bigfoot's nose was similar to an ape in any way, it'd probably smell the human. Possibly her scent, possibly mine. The coat was uncomfortable, but it protected me from the brush and wild roses.

I loved climbing over rocks, up and down, but hiking was more fun when someone else was along. Today's task was simply to create a barrier of my scent. I had no time to sit and enjoy the view if I wanted to get all the way around and back home before dark.

After looking at a topographic map, I learned it was Lucas Creek that separated the land. I'd have to cross it twice. What the GPS didn't show were impassable zones due to sticker bushes and kudzu patches or fallen rock, but even when I left the path, the GPS kept me headed in the right direction.

Since it was a long six- to eight-hour trek, Jake kept me company by text—his way of being involved while he spent time with Doc.

Jake: Learned some interesting news from Pappy.

Me: Let me guess . . . he wants to elope with my grandma.

Jake: Close.

Me: What!? I asked my grandma if Doc had ever been more than a friend.

Jake: What'd she say?

I stepped high through a patch of stinging nettles, lifting my hands to avoid the tiny stingers.

Me: Mind your business unless u want to get cozy with a forsythia switch.

Jake: Haha. Don't think you'll learn much from her.

Me: I know, but she blushed. What did you learn?

Jake: He's making dinner for her one evening next week.

Jake: I have to find somewhere else to be. Can u help me out?

I was at a loss for words. Doc was going to cook for my grandma?

Jake: You there?

Me: Sure. I can help you out.

Me: I think my dad looks like Doc.

Jake: Me too.

I tucked my phone in my back pocket and stepped carefully down a steep slope of loose rock and dirt. My feet slid, and I flailed slightly to keep my balance.

I still had trouble grasping Doc might be my grandpa. Part of me hoped it wasn't true, so I wouldn't be sad over the lost years. But would knowing have changed anything? Doc had always been there.

My phone buzzed, so I pulled it out once I hit level ground.

Jake: I think my mom believes a lie. Pappy was in Vietnam when your dad was born. He married Gertie after he returned home. Your grandma was married by then. He and your grandma never got together after that.

Me: You asked him?

Jake: Yes.

I stopped and stared ahead at the rocky hill in front of me and wiped the sweat from my brow with the coat sleeve.

Neither cheated, but both had married the wrong person. I felt sad for my grandma. My phone vibrated again.

Jake: U there?

Me: What else did u ask him?

Jake: Didn't have the nerve to ask about your dad.

Me: Yeah. The only one who knows the truth is Grandma, and she's a steel trap. Makes me feel better about Doc, though.

Me: He say anything more about Dean Martin?

Jake: No.

Me: Ask him if he'll tell u the story.

When I'd finally circled the river gorge, the sun was on the descent. I dropped my backpack and sat on the ledge where Jake and I had laid side by side watching the Nun'Yunu'Wi family. Lucas Creek Gorge settled in a remote piece of land that I wasn't sure was owned by anyone. Very few people ever wandered this deep into the forested hills. I watched the cave opening. With all my smell and romping around, they knew I was here.

This was how I would end the next two days in hopes the creatures would exit the cave and acknowledge me. I had no idea what that would look like or if I'd have the nerve to respond, but I felt reassured, after reading Mom's stuff, that I wasn't in danger unless they felt threatened by me.

After catching my breath, I dug out one of mom's sketchpads, allowed my feet to dangle over the cliff edge, and acted aloof to my surroundings as I attempted to draw. Like Mom would have done. Only my mother-daughter portrait was nothing compared to Mom's drawings.

When the sun reached the horizon, I walked back to where I'd hidden the four-wheeler, hurried home, showered, and collapsed into bed.

Day Two

It was hot. I trudged along a little slower. Sweat dripped into my eyes, burning until I wiped it away with the cooling cloth draped around my neck. My muscles hurt from yesterday. Sure could've used a few more hours sleep, but an early start, before the heat set in, was priority. The fatigue wore off as the sun began to clear the treetops. Around ten thirty, Jake texted.

Jake: Saw Jeanine at the grocery. She said you and Caleb were practically engaged.

I tripped over a tree root and paused once I caught my footing. I tapped out a return message harder than I should've.

Me: Not true! Why would she say that?

Jake: Any reason why Jeanine might have it in for u?

I came to the creek bed where I would make my second crossing. Water flowed over large, flat protruding boulders. This section of Lucas Creek was about as wide as the four-lane that ran along the edge of town and was the shallowest with banks easiest to climb in and out.

I removed the coat and slipped off Mom's boots and my socks. After rolling up my pants, I walked out into the water and sat on a dry stone, cooling my feet. Small rapids swirled around me. Large trees and brush loomed on either side. Above, the red-shouldered hawk circled. An entire choir of songbirds sang to one another.

I basked in the solitude and let Jeanine's nonsense roll off. What creature wouldn't love the simplicity of this? I felt refreshed already.

Me: U like to camp?

Jake: Haven't been. Most of our vacations were at resorts.

Me: Didn't your dad take u hunting, fishing?

Jake: No. Only fished when Pappy visited.

Me: U want to go camping sometime? Right here!

I recorded a video of the rippling water and the surrounding forest and sent it.

Jake: Bear? Snakes? Bigfoot?

I laughed out loud, my voice mingling with the river.

Me: Hahaha. Absolutely.

Jake: U didn't answer my question about Jeanine.

Me: And u didn't answer mine. But u asked first . . . I don't think she has it in for me. Nothing has changed.

Jake: R u sure? Caleb?

Me: That was a year ago. Doesn't make sense.

Except her attitude toward me had changed when I broke up with Caleb.

Me: Maybe you're right. We don't hang out as much. Might be Rodney's influence, too.

Jake: Or because you're smarter and prettier. Maybe she's jealous.

Me: The only thing she would be jealous of is you spending time with me and not her. You should've told her we've never gone out. That would've made her happy.

I attached an emoji with rolling eyes.

My phone chimed almost immediately as a video message came through. Reception was sketchy, and it took a few seconds to load. When it finished, I hit play. Jake smiled into the phone's video camera, his eyes alight with fun. My heart stuttered, and he wasn't even nearby. He wore a navy-blue T-shirt and a baseball cap set backwards on his head. Paint chips flecked his hat, face, and shirt. What was he doing? Look like he was scraping loose paint off Doc's house.

"Ellie Mae, we've been together almost every single day since I came to Hush Briar, but in case I don't see you this week, will you go out with me Friday night?"

I grinned as he moved to include Doc in the frame. Did nothing embarrass him? "Pappy, say hi to Ellie Mae." Doc stood by the chimney at the side of his house, wearing coveralls and holding a wire brush. "Morning, Ellie Mae."

Jake: Did the video come through?

Me: Yeah. Just watched it. Doc is scraping the house?"

Jake: Yeah . . . and?

Me: I will go out with u.

Jake: Awesome. I'll go camping with u after I finish Pappy's house.

Me: Before school starts.

Jake: Why?

I pondered that. We would be able to come home together and spend weekends with family, studying, maybe camping. Jake would easily make friends and probably go his own way after a while, but I'd have his company to start with.

Teasing Jake, I sent a lion head emoji.

Me: FYI Mountain lions come out in the fall.

Jake: Funny! Pappy asked if you're drinking plenty of water. It's warmer today, and you're wearing that heavy jacket.

Me: I'm fine. Took it off and I'm sitting in the middle of the creek.

Ten minutes later, I reluctantly gathered up my things, crossed to the opposite bank, and put on the blasted jacket.

Me: How'd u become so good at baseball?

Jake: My dad played for LSU and then in the majors.

Me: Seriously?

Jake: Yeah. He was injured soon after Andrea was born. Returned home to manage the farm. He coached my teams and taught me.

Me: Did LSU offer u a scholarship?

Jake: Yes.

Me: Not interested in LSU?

Jake: It's complicated.

It took me longer to reach the cliff site. The heat and humidity was oppressive and sapped every bit of my energy. I didn't dare take off the jacket in case the Nun'Yunu'Wi recognized the pattern. I pushed sweaty strands of hair back from my forehead, drank the last of my water, and sat motionless in a heat-induced stupor for about twenty minutes.

There was no movement from the cave's entrance. Mom noted the Nun'Yunu'Wi would stay out of sight until the fourth day, but they probably watched since my scent was undoubtedly everywhere. Based on her documentation, I believed she established this routine when she was about sixteen years old.

Mom detailed their communication—an intriguing use

of hand gestures, grunts, knocks, screams, and whines. I sort of thought this unique strategy of introducing herself was devised so they would recognize her specifically.

If this were the same group of animals, they hadn't seen her in over five years. Maybe they wouldn't even remember, but Mom indicated they had exceptional memories. They followed a pattern of movement throughout the mountains and returned to the same remote places year after year unless they felt threatened or one of the regional contacts moved them. Mom had moved them a couple of times over the years, and they remembered the change, with Lucas Creek Gorge apparently the most recent relocation.

So much to absorb, and I was too exhausted to think. My head and arm both throbbed, I was starved, and my feet hurt. I texted Dad, as I had been doing at various checkpoints, then I pushed back from the edge of the cliff and found Caleb's letter. Resting my head on the backpack, I opened the envelope. I'd put off reading it because I feared the contents, but he'd put himself out there by showing up at church. Least I could do was hear him out.

Dear Ellie Mae,

I'm not the best at writing so I hope you'll cut me some slack. I had to write you because it's too hard to say what I want to say in person. And you can get so fired up I forget what I need to say and end up making a mess of things. Like last Thursday at the restaurant. I should have come right out and told you I was home for Jeanine instead of opening old wounds.

Ellie, I'm glad you moved on and became friends with Doc's grandson. I'm sure he's a good person, and that's what you deserve. It caught me a little off guard when I saw you kissing him, but then I thought the guy would be a fool if he didn't want to kiss you.

It wasn't me who told Rodney and Todd where you were that night. Someone else saw you. Jaxon was spouting off about it in Willie's. Trying to get a rise out of me I guess—like he does. Yes, I went down to Willie's after I saw you. I felt sorry for myself and intended to drink a little. Then I received a text from a buddy—my sponsor from AA. Go figure. Talk about timing and divine intervention. I didn't drink a single drop that night, and it made me realize two things. One, someone out there cares about me (probably more than one person, but point is I'm not alone even when I feel it). Two, I'm stronger than I thought.

Rodney McGraff came into Willie's as I was leaving. Jeanine was with him. I took her home, and we had a long talk (once she stopped screaming at me).

Ellie, I can't say how sorry I am for what Rodney did to you—the beer and all. He's looking for a fight, and the drinking makes him dangerous. Be careful.

I can't go back and change the mistakes I made, and there are many. The biggest was hurting you. I didn't mean what I said about your mom. She was a great person, and I will always remember the times she took us out in the woods, played hide and seek, and taught us how she found us. Even up the willow tree. Remember? And you're like her.

I've chosen to forgive myself though because I think I'm a better person because of those mistakes. I hope you'll forgive me, too.

I'm leaving today. Headed back to Knoxville. It's where I need to be. Where I have the best shot ending up with a decent career doing something I enjoy. And there will be someone special. Different than you, I'm sure, because no one is quite like you.

So, I'm saying goodbye. I will always remember you as the best part of my childhood. Good luck at school. I hope you return to Hush Briar once you're finished. It's where you belong, and everyone here loves you (McGraffs and Reid excluded because they don't love anyone but themselves), and the people here need you. Say a prayer for me, and remember I'm only three hours away. If you ever need anything, give me a holler.

Your Friend Always,

Caleb

I swallowed hard and let the pages rest on my chest. A tear slipped down the side of my face and back into my hair.

"Good for you, Caleb." I stared at the sky. Clouds rolled across the blue, sending the first wisps of cotton seed across the gorge and scores of maple seeds twirling down to land around me. The wind was a blessing. My scent, mixed with Mom's, would travel.

Caleb seemed at peace, and it made me believe in our childhood again. I sat up and reread the letter. What a gift.

After finding my phone, I tapped out a message to him and hit send. A reply came back instantly.

> Caleb: You're welcome. Your friendship means the world to me, too.

Chapter Twenty

Day Three

By Wednesday morning, I could barely stand due to the knives gouging my heels. Mom's boots were a mite bigger than mine. I limped more than walked until my feet stretched and adjusted to my weight. It wasn't until after I had fed the animals and cleaned cages that I felt limber enough to start another day, but I wasn't confident I could make it the entire distance without collapsing.

After retrieving my supplies from the house, I shuffled to the pole barn, coat in hand. Hot and humid, the threat of rain hung in the air even though the forecast only predicted a twenty percent chance. Hopefully, it'd pass. In lightweight jeans and a tank top, I grimaced at the coat as I tossed it and my pack in the cargo bin.

I unscrewed the gas tank cap off the four-wheeler and hefted the red container, lulled by the glug, glug, glug of gas filling the tank. Jake jogged into the barn. I fumbled the can as a special kind of happiness bubbled inside me, drowning out my physical aches. Gasoline sloshed, but I saved the container from hitting the ground.

"Hey," I said as he bent over and placed his hands on his knees, sucking in deep gulps of air. "You okay?"

He stood up, cheeks flushed, and nodded as he slipped out of his backpack. Then he dazzled me with a smile. "That felt good."

"What are you doing here?" Felt like forever since I'd seen him.

"Wanted to see how you were doing, and I brought you a gift." He dug a Gatorade and two granola bars out of his backpack and placed them in mine. "Pappy's worried about you dehydrating."

"Yeah, wearing the coat is pretty intense."

"Last day circling the gorge. It's going to be a steamy one. You tired?"

"Yes."

"Wish I could go with you." He took the gas can out of my hand when I finished.

"Me, too." I dreaded the grueling hike.

"Kind of looks like rain. Maybe you should hold off a day."

"No way! That'd nullify the last two days. I can't take that chance."

"Better to play it safe, don't you think? If it rains much, it'll erase your scent anyways."

"I have to do this exactly like Mom. Besides, there's only a slight chance of rain, and a sprinkle or two won't hurt. Might feel good."

We both looked at the low white and gray clouds out the overhead door. "But I better get started just in case."

After closing the door, Jake climbed on the four-wheeler

behind me. "So what do you want to do Friday night? Go into Lexington? Stick around here? Or do something in between?"

I leaned back into his chest and tipped my head. "I don't care. As long as it doesn't involve hiking."

His arm slipped around my stomach, his breath warming my ear. "Okay, I have an idea then."

Maybe sit like this for forever. "What is it?"

"Hmmm . . . You'll have to wait and see. I have some details to work out."

Two days. I had plenty to keep me busy, but the wait would be as excruciating as today's hike.

I was planning to take Jake all the way into town, but as we neared the coal mine road, he reached up and placed a hand over mine on the gear shift and stretched his leg forward, shoving mine off the clutch. He did the same with the brake and shifted down until we stopped.

"What's going on?" Perplexed, I sat still. He killed the engine, dropped his hands to my midsection, and gently twisted my waist. Folding my right leg, I turned almost completely around and met his confident gaze. There was no doubt of intent as he smiled and placed a hand to the side of my face. My heart thundered, but I liked his train of thought and met his kiss with a breathtaking intensity that rivaled any mountaintop view. I suspected even the soaring hawk didn't feel this exhilarated. Right in the middle of Dillard Hollow. My happiness bubbled over. I was pretty sure I'd remember that moment for the rest of my life.

He grinned and hopped off the four-wheeler, slipping into the backpack. "Come back safe."

The first sprinkles hit as I crossed Lucas Creek the first time. Two hours would pass before I crossed again. I picked up my pace. At least I had a path somewhat cleared, and I knew my way. A little rain wouldn't completely wipe away my scent. Climbing the steep hill in front of me, I slipped on some wet leaves and went down on one knee. I took that opportunity to stash my phone in the waterproof bag, tucking it deeply inside the backpack.

Pushing back to my feet, I glanced behind me. Should I turn back? Save a few steps? Or should I keep moving forward? The rain could let up any minute, and I was almost halfway. Either way, I faced a long walk home. While the rain might erase my scent, it was only part of what I hoped to accomplish. The Nun'Yunu'Wi observed their surroundings. They knew I was out here and watched me from the hidden places. If I didn't finish what I started, I would lose all opportunity to get closer.

I pushed onward. Thunder rumbled, and the rain picked up speed. Traveling down the hill proved trickier than going up. Amazing how a little rain changed the landscape. Dry paths became small, rutted streams, and rocks once suitable hand holds were slippery because of the moss. Tree branches hung lower, and roots became more exposed. I had to nearly sit on my bottom to keep from sliding in places.

I looked up at the sky. Rain drizzled onto my face, soaking my hair and everything else. I probably should have listened to Jake or at least waited an hour or two to see what happened. If I'd stayed home, we might be sitting on the porch, watching the rain. Maybe eating Grandma's turnovers and mapping out plans for Friday night. Or kissing.

Was it possible to fall for someone after knowing them

for such a short time? Was it wise? This past week, I'd exposed about every inch of dirt in my life. Jake had seen me at my worst, literally, and he still wanted to spend time with me.

Holding on to such pleasant thoughts, I trudged forward, daydreaming about Friday night and what I would wear. Starting down the steepest bank this side of Lucas Creek, I held tight to small trees and bushes. Clothes never concerned me before, but I wanted to look nice for Jake. I rolled my eyes, remembering Grandma's words the first night he and Doc came over for supper. *One of these days you'll want to look nice for a boy . . .*

Grandma, this isn't that boy—

A rock gave way. My right foot slipped. The sapling ripped from my hand. Mud shifted underfoot as I slid, flailing my arms. I fought to stay upright and grabbed at a passing bush. It was too slick to keep hold of.

I was falling too fast. I had to stop this descent.

Just as I was about to sit on my bottom, my right foot caught on a tree root and pitched my upper body forward. My right hand hit the ground first, wedging between two rocks. Stinging flames shot through my arm. I shrieked at the ripping pain. My feet flew over my head, and I tumbled over rocks and tree roots. I tried to straighten my legs to slow myself, but the momentum forced me into the air. I flew a few feet before I landed on my chest, my right cheek smacking a rock. Air whooshed out of my lungs. I stayed still, afraid to move, but more because I couldn't breathe.

I'd fallen out of enough trees to know what it felt like to suffocate for about seven or eight seconds, but the air would come, and it did, making my eyes water. Or were those real tears from the pain in my right hand and forearm?

Gently, I shifted my body into a sitting position on the

mud and jagged rocks and sat still for a full minute as the rain pelted me. I moved my ankles and extended my legs. They were good, and my left hand, arm, and shoulder moved with ease, but my right shoulder hurt. I rounded it slowly and bent my elbow. Neither broken nor dislocated. But stiffness burned inside my trembling hand like a hot iron fused all the bone and tissue into one stinging mass. Broken for sure. Dad was going to kill me.

I slipped out of the coat and held up my arm. Four of the stitches had popped, and blood poured from the wound. My hand, wrist, and arm looked like something out of a horror movie. Trembling, I dug out my small first aid kit, wound the gauze tightly around the cut, and ripped it with my teeth. Water dripped down my face and into my eyes. I wiped it away and winced as my hand passed over my right cheekbone and eye. Blood dripped from my fingers. I gently probed around and felt nothing unusual beyond a small cut above my right eyebrow and swelling on my cheek.

I slid down the rest of the hillside on my bottom, careful not to use my right hand. Rain fell harder and turned into a downpour. Twenty-percent chance. How had Mom done this over and over again? I stood, bracing myself against a tree. My legs trembled, but they were strong enough to get me home.

The creek, no longer the trickly picturesque campsite, had morphed into a darker, faster-moving version. Not much deeper yet. I removed my shoes and socks and clipped them to my backpack. Awkwardly, I rolled up my pants using one hand and waded out.

Once I crossed, I knew it wasn't far to a small overhang where I could hole up until the rain let up. Then I would start the assent up to the ridge and travel for another two miles to the Bigfoot's gorge.

The current turned up mud, making it difficult to see where I stepped, but there were plenty of rocks to hang on to. I stepped with caution, water splashing up over my knees and soaking my pants. I had to let go of the last large boulder and walk about ten feet to shore. I took two steps and felt my ankle go sideways in a hole. I fell to my knees, my good arm stopping my fall on the creek's rocky bottom.

"Why!?" I yelled at the sky. My hand screamed in burning pain.

I stood and took baby steps to the shore and sat in the mud on the creek bank. I ripped off the coat, crying out when it brushed against my cut arm. I looked up into the gray expanse. *Please, help me get home.* After two minutes of self-pity, I stood, put the backpack on, and carried the coat over my right arm while I used my left to grab hold of trees to help me climb.

The overhang—a cave of sorts—was dry except for a few places where water seeped through cracks and dripped in puddles. I dropped Mom's coat in the dirt, eased myself down beside it, and opened my pack. I placed the Gatorade bottle between my knees, opened it with my left hand, and guzzled down half. *Thank you, Doc. I hope you won't be mad at me, too.* After I dried my pruny hands, I found my phone.

Dad: Turn around and come back.
Heavy rain coming in.

Jake: You okay?

Jake: ?

Dad: Give us a text as soon as you
can. Keep moving!

> Jake: Your dad said he told u to turn around. Did U?

It took some effort with my shaky left hand, but I replied to both stating I was okay and taking shelter for a little bit. I plugged the phone into a charger and left the power on in hopes my messages would send once I wandered into an area with service.

Dad's voice to keep moving rang through my head. Two hours to home on a good day. I shivered and slipped on Mom's coat. While it was heavy and mostly wet, it offered a little warmth and was easier to carry on my back than over my injured arm. I stored my phone, grabbed my pack, and slipped it over my right shoulder first, wincing as I jerked it into position.

One handed, I struggled up the hillside. No way I'd make it in two hours. I walked for an hour and came to another alcove offering a small amount of dry ground. I took out my phone.

> Dad: How far out are you? I expect to see you in two hours! Keep moving!

> Me: Moving slower than expected. May take longer. I should be home in three hours.

I put the phone away and kept walking.

All my hard work, washed away.

I slipped and fell to my knees as tears dripped off my face in rainwater trails. "I'm sorry, Mom. I thought I could do this. I thought I was supposed to do this."

The downpour intensified. Maybe, despite what Simsy thought, I wasn't meant to work with the Nun'Yunu'Wi.

Keep moving! Dad's voice rang through my head.

I wanted to stop. My head throbbed. My shoulder and wrist burned. I had no energy. But Dad would be angry if I gave up now and stopped moving forward. Not because he would have to come after me, but because he taught me not to give up. He taught me to work hard and put forth my best effort. That's why I excelled in school. That's why I didn't give in to Caleb when he crossed my moral boundaries. Dad's voice in my head pushed me to excel and be better than I thought possible. He believed in me . . . that I could do anything I put a mind to.

A memory replayed from when I was about ten. Dad took Mom and me kayaking. We came across some rapids and my kayak tipped. I was a decent swimmer but not strong enough to keep my feet under me. Whenever I stood up in the waist-high water, the undertow knocked me over. I had grabbed onto a rock and tried to climb up on it, but I couldn't pull myself out. Dad waded out to me. I cried and told him I couldn't hang on. He yelled at me to stop crying because I was strong enough.

I'm not sure I'm strong enough now. I stopped and leaned against a hundred-year-old oak, resting my head on my good arm.

Doesn't matter, Ellie Mae. Keep moving!

One foot in front of the other, I climbed the final bluff. The one where Jake had stopped the first time out and admired the mist rolling through the hills. Today, the colors were a mixture of browns and greens but mostly gray. Lots of gray fog, interspersed between the trees, hanging heavy.

When I finally arrived at the four-wheeler, I didn't take time to remove my backpack. I climbed on and went home.

Dad and Jake stood in the pole barn with the door open.

Both of Jake's hands went to the top of his head as I pulled in. Dad stood motionless until I stopped. Then he came at me like a hound on a coon.

He tipped my face, inspecting the right side.

"My right arm is worse."

"Okay. Clinic. Now." He walked away and looked madder than when he'd been quilled by a porcupine.

Jake stood to my left where I stepped off. Humiliated, miserable, and fatigued, I couldn't look at him. My knees buckled.

"Whoa." He grabbed me before I hit the gravel and scooped me up in his arms. My head rolled against his shoulder. I thought I might cry, it felt so good.

We followed Dad into the clinic. This time Jake sat next to me on the exam table with his arm around my waist. Guess he thought he needed to hold me steady. I didn't protest because his support eased the intimidation of my looming Dad.

Dad winced when he saw my hand–slightly swollen and bruised, shaking as I tried to hold it steady.

"Your wrist needs to be x-rayed for sure. I'll re-stitch your arm. What else hurts?"

"My shoulder."

He poked around. "I think that'll be okay, but we'll have it looked at anyway. Let's take care of the cut, then I'll clean up your cheek and eye. Your legs okay?"

"Just weak. Can I take a shower before we go to the ER?"

"Grandma will help you wash up."

"What happened?" Jake sounded like he was the one in pain. I still couldn't look at him.

"I fell. A couple times."

"Why didn't you turn around when your dad said to?"

"I'd already stashed my phone away to keep it dry. I thought I could make it. Dad, do you think I'll need to start over?"

Wrong question. His gaze scalded. A full minute passed before he spoke.

"Shortly after your mom and I married, she came in all beat up and soaked, looking half-dead." He sounded disgusted. "She'd fallen into a ravine and found herself wedged between rocks and mud. It had rained hard, shifting things around to where she could break free, but she was hurt. Find that in her journals and see what she said. Then decide if you should go out again."

I hadn't heard that story. "I'm sorry I worried you."

Jake kept his arm around me as we walked around the back of the house onto the deck. "Just a warning, your grandma's pretty upset."

I stopped outside the door. My body hurt, but not as much as my heart. I disappointed my family, Jake, and probably even Doc.

"Thanks for being here . . . again." I still couldn't look at him.

"I'll see you Friday. Six o'clock, okay?"

I cocked my head to the right, exposing my good side. "You still want to go out with me? Why? Look at me."

He shrugged and with a featherlight touch, tipped my chin to the side, examining the cut and my face. Then he made eye contact and smiled. "I've never gone out with a girl who had a black eye. This one'll be a doozy. You fell on your face?"

"Don't laugh at me."

He bent down, kissed my good cheek, and whispered,

"You're more beautiful than you realize. I can't wait to go out with you." He walked down the steps and turned. "Would you tell Pappy I'm waiting in the truck? But no rush."

I nodded as I watched him go. Unbelievable. I offered him an easy out, a chance to get away from the girl who'd surely embarrass him in public, but he rejected it. The corners of my mouth lifted into a slow smile as I turned and entered the house, ready to face the rest of my clan.

After a trip to the ER confirmed a broken wrist and sprained shoulder, I eased into bed around midnight . . . wide awake. Too much on my mind to sleep. I let down my family and called my judgment into question. I needed to reexamine my impulsiveness to avoid putting myself in danger, but I also had to make sure I didn't give up too soon. Jaxon, Mr. Hansen, and maybe even Rodney and Jeanine were up to something. *If* fate led me to this time and place, I didn't feel like I could ignore it.

Laughter. Mom. But it isn't mom. "Ellie-Maefly?"

I climb higher and higher in the willow tree.

"You can't go anywhere."

I'm going to fall, and it's going to hurt. I'm afraid, but there is no way down. Ever.

"Jump, Ellie." I say it to myself. "You can jump and run."

From the tree, I see the male Nun'Yunu'Wi, plain as day,

standing in the creek, blood soaking his chest. The mother sits on the ledge. She falls to her side and drops the baby.

"Ellie-Maefly."

Don't listen to it. Ignore the mimic and you'll be okay.

Jump.

Run.

Chapter Twenty-One

Friday evening, I gingerly walked down the stairs, carrying navy blue flip-flops that matched my cast cover. Smooth jazz played quietly in the background as I stared down at my polished toenails, also blue.

"There's a girl who wants to make a statement." Grandma sat in her glider near the bottom of the stairs and pulled on a string that disappeared into the basket at her feet. Her fingers worked the yarn and knitting needles as she watched me.

"Do I look okay? It's not too much, is it?" I fought the urge to run back to my room. It felt like I was trying too hard to be something I wasn't. The fact Jake was a rich boy with hugely successful parents didn't mean I needed to change my appearance.

"You look perfect." Rebecca followed me downstairs. At the bottom, she wrapped an arm around my shoulders and very lightly squeezed. "Sometimes you have to step out of your comfort zone and experience new things. How else will you know if *you* like it or not?"

She was right. This wasn't just about impressing Jake. I

tucked a piece of wavy hair behind my ear. With a little effort, and a headband, a ponytail wasn't needed to keep the hair out of my eyes. A good-to-know alternative, but not as a daily habit.

"You look nice and appropriate. It's not a bit too much." Grandma smiled at me then fastened her gaze on Rebecca. "Thank you for going to Lexington with her and helping her get around. I'm as useless as a slug on salt when it comes to shopping these days."

Grandma was grateful, but I knew from Rebecca that Dad had orchestrated the outing. While we shopped, she told me everything about their growing relationship and Dad's fear of hurting my feelings since memories of Mom were so strong right now. I understood. He cared, but why was it so hard for him to talk to me? Rebecca didn't have an answer, but she promised to work on it.

Shopping for a dress had been a chore worse than cleaning cages, but Rebecca had made it fun, and I settled on a silky navy-blue skirt that flowed to mid-calf in the back and below the knee if front. Just long enough to hide an ugly scar. I paired it with a sleeveless white blouse with buttons and scalloped edges. Pretty simple but practical.

"Not even this is too much?" I held up my foot and wiggled my toes. "This is so not me."

"It looks nice. Maybe you should consider making it a part of you." Grandma winked at Rebecca.

I set the flip-flops on the floor and retrieved Mom's journal from the dining room table.

"Problem with dresses"—I lifted my phone—"no pockets."

"Slip it in your bra," Grandma said matter-of-factly like she did this every day.

"Where?" I said, amused.

"Right here." She indicated under her arm. "Or carry a purse."

I wrinkled my nose. "I'm gonna wait outside. He'll be here any minute."

"Have a nice time." Rebecca settled on the end of the couch nearest grandma. I had a feeling those two would soon be swapping stories.

"And stay away from that McGraff riff-raff." Grandma yanked on her yarn again.

"We will." I escaped out the door and sat on the porch swing. Jake pulled in five minutes later. He parked in front of the garage and hopped out of Doc's truck, looking like a bona fide city boy in his khaki shorts and a neatly pressed silky blue button-up he left untucked. Tossing a pair of sunglasses back in the truck, his eyes danced over my outfit, and his smile threatened to hog-tie my thinking. I learned something about myself in that moment: Although it made me nervous, I liked feeling feminine.

I descended the steps and twirled. "It's not often you'll see this."

He put a hand on his chest. "You look great. I guess that hike is out of the question then?"

"I'll be happy to change." Teasing, I half turned, and he grabbed my good arm.

"I have something else planned. Where's your dad?"

"In the barn. Why?"

Jake took the journal and grabbed ahold of my hand, sending a wave of wood-spice my way.

"I don't know, Jake. He's still mad at me."

"He's not mad at me, and I plan to keep it that way." He squeezed my hand.

In the barn, freshly stirred manure overpowered Jake's cologne. Just like I feared Dad's expression might smother my cheerful mood. A shovelful of dung flew out of the goats' pen and landed in the wheelbarrow in the middle of the barn. The goats had been put out in the pasture, so there was none of their noisiness, but the calves stood at the gate. One mooed and the other two followed. Rebecca had said she'd help Dad feed all the animals once I left.

"Hey, Mr. Schmitt."

Dad looked over the gate. Sweat ran down his face. He wiped it off with the sleeve of his work shirt.

"Hi, Jake. Ellie, you look nice. You two taking off?"

"Yeah," Jake said. "We'll get a bite to eat, then run that errand for Pappy, but we'll be close by."

"Do you have..."

"Yeah, I have it." Jake scratched the back of his neck then dropped his arm.

I snapped my head between the two. Jake caught my questioning stare. "What? You don't have to know everything."

"I have my phone if you need me, Dad."

Dad's gaze fell on the journal Jake carried then lifted to my face. For the first time in two days, his eyes softened. "Have a good time."

Back at the truck, Jake opened the passenger door. I gripped the handle above the door with my left hand. "I knew this would be awkward."

"Want some help?"

"No, thanks." It took some effort to get situated. I could make a serious argument for why a skirt was not practical. Jake was back in the truck beside me before I settled.

"You got it?" he asked as I fumbled with the seatbelt.

"Yeah." I laughed, snapping it in place. "I'm no good at being a lefty." I held up my good hand.

"You will be by the time that cast comes off."

"Spoken from experience?"

"Junior high wrestling." He backed up, turned around, and headed down Dillard Hollow toward town. At Subway, I stayed in the truck while Jake went in for sandwiches and drinks.

It wasn't until Jake returned and we started out of the parking lot that I caught sight of Jaxon Reid. Arms folded, he leaned back against his tow truck as he gassed up on the end pump. He made eye contact as we passed by and nodded. I turned away, wondering why he was using the McGraffs and Jeanine to stir up trouble. Seemed fruitless since they were easier to run off than a scared 'possum.

We drove to the southwest corner of town. "Pappy showed me this place we could picnic. It's pretty nice."

We stopped at a private drive with high privacy fences and a locked gate. I watched, intrigued, as Jake jumped out, retrieved a key from his pocket, and unlocked the chains. Then he drove us through and relocked them.

The lane wound down a hill leading to a pond and clearing with acres of tall grass going to seed, their tops like green fuzzy caterpillars.

"This is Hatley's hunting preserve." I gave Jake a sidelong glance, remembering the couple who passed us on the road while I was in a less than dignified position.

"Closed right now, obviously. I called them, and they were okay with us coming here because, and I quote, 'That Ellie Mae is the sweetest thing.'"

"Nice accent."

"Thank you," he said with a cheeky grin.

Jake parked at the end of the stone drive, the back end of the truck facing the clearing with a nice view of the two-acre pond.

"Here, might want to use some of this." He handed me a

can of bug spray. I managed to maneuver my broken wrist and skirt out of the truck without too much of a spectacle and doused myself with the spray and then tossed it back to him. Eyes roving the landscape, I walked toward the pond's edge where bugs danced in sunrays that bounced off the water, veiling the thick forest of surrounding trees. Crickets chirped along with songbirds. Two days of rain and heat left everything lush. The grass grew about waist-high with seeding dandelions and wild violets sharing the space. An old, crumbling dock extended into the pond, between two large weeping willows, and was surrounded by cattails and reeds.

A romantic setting. As had been happening all day, a thrill rushed through me when I thought of spending time with Jake. While I hadn't hung out with a lot of guys, even I knew he was a rare find. How he landed right here in Hush Briar at this particular time in my life seemed as divine as anything I'd known.

"Hey, Lefty, you ready to eat?"

I turned and stretched out my arms, allowing the soft, wispy tops of the seeding grass to tickle my fingers as I sauntered back. I marveled at the joy of feeling pretty and being watched as if it were true.

Leveraging with my good arm, I jumped up on the tailgate and swiveled around to the picnic Jake had laid out on a blanket. Bending my knees, I tucked my feet to the side. "This is impressive."

Jake explained that he and Doc visited the Hatley's this past week. Doc told him when he was a teenager this was a favorite spot for picnics. A place to bring a girl when you wanted to impress her with a nice view.

I unwrapped a half of sub. "Was he talking about my grandma?"

"Yep."

"Did you ask him about Dean Martin?"

"Yes."

"What'd he say?" I placed a chip in my mouth.

"He said, 'Tell Ellie Mae to ask her grandma.'"

I growled playfully. "Why is it such a big secret?"

"I don't know." He took a swig of his Coke. "But I think there's something significant he wants out in the open."

"But he's respecting Grandma's timing?"

"Can you imagine—a secret resurfacing after fifty years? No wonder Pappy's a little scared to talk about it."

"So he wants Grandma to do the talking. That ain't gonna happen."

"Maybe we should help them break the ice."

A grin spread across my face. "What are you thinking?"

"Maybe get them together, set the mood with some Dean Martin classics, and ask them about it. Force them to own up."

I sucked in a deep breath. "Grandma might throw us all out of the house."

"Would she, though? Even I can see the way she dotes on Pappy. She feels something."

"I like your plan. Let's do something next weekend."

Once we finished eating, I brought up Mom's journal. "I found the entry Dad mentioned the other night. Want me to read it to you?"

"Sure. Just a sec." Jake jumped out of the truck, stowed our trash, and returned with the journal.

I opened to the page I had marked earlier.

"Friday, June 24."

"Isn't it weird my accident was on June 29th? Almost the same day."

"Maybe that's why your dad remembers it so vividly."

He pointed to the book I held. "What did your mom have to say?"

Yesterday was the first time Neil saw me a little broken. I had walked several miles southeast of home and stumbled upon some intriguing rock structures I hadn't seen before. Looked like a bit of rock wall fell away and opened up a cavern of sorts. The dirt in the cavern felt like silt, smooth and creamy to touch. I only traveled a few feet when the slippery ground gave way, and I fell several feet, becoming wedged between rocks and earth. I sat there in the semi-darkness, contemplating how to free myself because I had broken my right arm and dislocated my shoulder. Moving dirt and rocks was slow going. Then it started to rain. It didn't take long for water to fill the small space.

I tried to explain the water was actually a blessing. It made moving the earth easier. That was the first time I saw Neil become angry and alarmingly silent. I tried to reassure him this was nothing compared to the rescue team I guided into a coal mine that had partially collapsed on a couple boys. While we were in the mine, more of the structures gave way and buried me under some large rocks. Ended up with three broken ribs, a collapsed lung, and a week in the hospital (S & R *journal, Volume* 2).

Neil wasn't overly impressed.

"A collapsed mine. Your mom was lucky to survive." My heart broke a little for my dad, a victim of loving someone he couldn't protect. "There's more." I picked up where I left off.

> *When we returned home from the hospital, Neil fixed us both a cup of hot chocolate and asked if I planned to make a habit of risking my life. It was the first time I thought about my actions. That my death might have a significant bearing on another human being hadn't crossed my mind.*
>
> *I think it's time to redefine who I want to be. If my death doesn't result in making a difference, then why risk my life? All I've accomplished is hurting the one person in this world who loves me. I promised Neil I would be more careful because I desire to have a family and grow old with him.*

I read this passage countless times, and the last sentence always choked me up. In my mind, Mom in Heaven was happier than she would have been with a family on earth, but my human heart wept for what she lost out on. What Dad and I lost out on.

To give meaning to Mom's death, I desired more than anything to continue what she started, but I had to be safer and smarter so I didn't worry Dad.

I sighed deeply. "No one ever leaves their house thinking today will be their last day. If I had broken my neck, Dad could have lost me, and my death wouldn't have made any difference in the world. It would've only brought more pain into his life."

I closed the journal and held it in my lap, wanting to apologize to Jake for disregarding his advice this past Wednesday. He warned me not to go out, but I didn't listen.

Jake picked up the journal and laid it off to the side. "What do you say we not think about death and dying anymore tonight? Let's have some fun instead." He jumped out of the truck bed.

"I'm no good at having fun." I shimmied to the edge of the tailgate. *How the heck did people move in skirts?*

"Not true, but you're a girl who's had to work hard and grow up fast. I, on the other hand, have been spoiled. I know how to have fun." Jake grabbed my hand. "Come on. We have an errand to run for Pappy."

Chapter Twenty-Two

Grateful for the chance to help Doc, I stowed away all thoughts of the journal and my near disaster. Instead, I embraced Jake's good mood as he entwined my fingers in his. We walked through the woods about a quarter mile, leaving the preserve and crossing over the road to the Hatley's homestead. Goats roamed in a pasture to the right, outside a large red barn. Two alpacas trotted to the fence and looked alert as we walked toward the two-story, gray-sided farmhouse.

The Hatley's raised Nubian goats—the place we got ours—and a hunting line of Irish Setters. They also hosted a slew of seasonal activities, including a pumpkin patch and a petting zoo, which often brought Dad out this way.

We knocked at the front door, and a small dog yipped from inside. A few seconds later, Julie opened the door and scooped up the Yorkie. "Ellie Mae and Jake. How are you? Come on in. Let me get Sam."

She left the living room. We stood looking around at African masks and paintings of the savannah. Jake walked over to a fifty-gallon fish aquarium, and I stepped over to say hello to a gray-and-yellow cockatiel with orange cheeks.

Sam walked into the room. "Ellie Mae. How are ya?"

I held out my left hand. "I'm good. You met Jake, right?"

"Sure did. Good to see you again, Jake. I believe we passed you two on the road the other day." Sam winked at me.

The temperature increased several degrees, and I wanted to crawl under the carpet. I refused to dignify Jake with a glance, because I knew he sported a goofy grin. Julie was kind enough to backhand her husband.

"How's your grandma, Ellie Mae? She ready to breed those goats yet?" Sam swallowed hard, as people do when they're trying not to laugh.

"She's keeping busy. I think she'll have Dad bring 'em over this fall."

"Best dairy goats she'll own. Guaranteed." Sam and Julie motioned for us to follow them through the house to a large, enclosed back porch. Julie retrieved two pair of muck boots out of a wardrobe. "It's a bit muddy. Why don't you two slip these on? If they don't fit, we got others."

"Thank you." Muck boots and a skirt. Now this was more like it.

"I've been after Doc to get himself a dog for years. Glad to hear the two of you are gonna take up bird hunting next year." Sam glanced at Jake. "You came at a good time and have pick of the litter."

"You're picking out a dog?" My excitement bubbled over as we crossed the stone drive to a big red barn, but what stuck in my mind were the words *next year*.

"Actually, you are. Pappy thought you'd be good at it." Then he whispered out of the corner of his mouth. "And I'm not sure I can tell female from male at this age."

Sam slid the large barn door to the side and turned left skirting around an old green tractor attached to a baler. A few chickens roamed loose, and beyond the wooden gates a cow mooed. The pups were under a stairway, cornered off by bales of straw one level high. An orange cat stretched out on a straw bale, staring down at the pups like a centurion prepared to keep order.

The new momma laid in one corner with a dozen pups snuggled up next to her, some climbing over her belly. My heart melted.

"Can we hold 'em, Sam?"

"Surely. Only way to get familiar with 'em. Jump right on in there and give R.G. some loving first. She'll be happy to share with ya."

"What's R.G. stand for?" I stepped over the barrier of straw.

"Red's Girl. Only Red's been gone now for two years. Took R.G. to a breeder up north. Good hunting bloodline."

Jake hunched down, gave R.G. a couple pats, and began playing with the pups.

"Here you go, sweetie." Julie laid a green stadium blanket across a bale of straw and handed me a towel for my lap.

"Thank you." I went over and knelt in front of R.G. "You have some pretty babies." She thumped her tail. "I hope it's okay we look 'em over." I gave her a kiss on the head and returned to the blanket-covered bale. Jake picked up two pups, placed one in my lap, and sat beside me.

"You two go right ahead and take your time. Find one and slip this band around its neck. We'll write your name on it, and I'll take care of business with Doc. Come up to the house when you're finished, and we'll have some coffee."

"Thank you." Jake lifted a pup and inspected it. "How do you pick a puppy when they all look the same?"

"I have no idea. They're all sweet." I lifted a floppy-eared, sad-eyed pup and rubbed the red downy fur next to my cheek. He began to wriggle, so I set him on the straw-covered floor. He waddled back to the litter and his momma. One little pup hopped toward me then yipped and jumped back. I chuckled and scooped her up, but she squirmed, so I set her free.

"She's a little rambunctious, but I think you found a friend." A pup lay sideways, awake and content, across Jake's lap. He stroked it. I reached over and shifted the baby onto its side.

"Girl. That's what you're wanting?"

"That's what Pappy said."

"I think it's great you have him painting, hunting, getting a dog. Jake, you've changed him. Honestly, I think you saved his life, or at least showed him he still has one."

"Hearing that makes all the bad stuff with my mom tolerable."

I looked over the dogs and piled the remaining girls in my lap. They crawled over each other and up my shirt, nuzzling and yipping. I laughed as I cuddled the little potbellies and exchanged nose rubs. "I want them all. Why are you looking at me like that?"

Jake leaned slightly forward, an elbow resting on one knee as he watched me try to corral the puppies on my lap. "It's good to see you relaxed for a change."

"I relax."

"The last week has been pretty intense."

"Puppies." I rubbed noses with one. "Brilliant idea." I handed over a girl fighting to get off my lap.

"Why don't you have a dog?" Jake set the pup on the

floor and weeded out another rambunctious girl. Two remained. I felt the warmth of his arm slip around me as he leaned nearer and inspected the two dogs, both docile.

"We had a lab. She was fifteen. Died last year. With me going off to school, I'm not sure Dad wants another dog. His call."

"Maybe he'll do some hunting with Pappy while we're away."

"You think you'll come home often?"

He shrugged. "Probably. It's only an hour and a half drive. Depends on my schedule, I guess. How about you?"

"I'll be so homesick. I'll definitely come home as much as I can."

"You're anticipating the worst before it's even happened."

"Just being realistic. Thinking ahead."

"Anticipating the worst is not thinking ahead. It's planning for trouble."

"I like this one." I held up the pup. "She has bright eyes and looks directly at us. This one"—I tapped the one nearest him—"isn't making eye contact. She's sort of unaware."

"This one then?" He scratched the alert pup. She jutted out her chin, watching him.

"I like her."

He fastened the pink band around her neck.

Reluctantly, I set her down. She waddled back to R.G. and nuzzled her way in to nurse. We sat and watched until darkness settled outside, and we thought we might've overstayed our welcome. As we exited the barn, I slipped my hand in Jake's. "Thanks for bringing me along."

He squeezed my hand. "You're welcome."

Inside, the Hatley's prepared Ethiopian coffee and homemade cookies. We talked about their mission trips to

Africa before they settled down to raise dogs and goats in what they called the prettiest part of the US of A. When we said goodnight, the sky was black, the animals quiet.

Jake used a miniature flashlight to lead us back through the woods. The usual coyote yips, coon, and 'possum ramblings went on. At the truck, Jake repositioned the blanket and brought out a lantern. We crawled in the back.

"Look at that sky." Cloudless, black, and filled with countless twinkling diamonds. I leaned back against the cab, pulled my knees up, and draped my skirt over them, bare feet flat on the blanket.

"It's a great sky." Jake faced me with his knees pulled up and arms wrapped around them.

"You aren't even looking at it."

He fought a grin. "Same sky I see every night. Do you know that this small scar, right here, reminds me of my tenth birthday?" He touched the left side of my chin and sent chills down my arms and torso.

Not used to such close scrutiny, shyness crept over me, but I liked his touch and wanted more. I held his gaze. "Why?"

"Pappy skyped. You were at his house and passed by the computer screen. He made you say hi."

"I don't remember that."

"Concussion. You fell out of a tree, hit your head, and busted your chin. Your parents were out of town, and your grandma was concerned, so she sent you to spend the night at his place. I remember thinking how much more fun it would have been to climb trees with you than suffer the formal dinner Mom made me sit through."

I had seen Jake as a boy on his tenth birthday. Disappointment washed through me as if I'd been offered a gift and turned it down, only to want it back later. "Did I at least say happy birthday?"

"No, but when I asked about the cut, you described in full detail the maple tree you climbed to return a baby bird to its nest because, contrary to what most people believe, momma birds are not repulsed by the scent of a human hand." He said the last part of the sentence with a superior tone and grinned.

"I said all of that but not happy birthday?"

"You said a lot more, but you were also sort of loopy. Pappy had to shut you down."

I laughed. "You need to show me a scar or give me a story. I'm starting to feel like a one-girl comedy show." He opened his mouth, and I pointed a finger, slightly raising my voice. "You've seen more than one of mine. It's only fair."

He scooted back a little and stretched out his right leg. I sat up and grabbed the lantern, holding it close. He pointed toward his ankle, revealing a nasty three-inch scar.

I traced two fingers over the smooth skin, the hair surrounding it tickling my fingers. "What happened?"

Jake cleared his throat. "Slid into home plate a couple years ago. Caught a sharp corner. That's it. No incredible story to go with it."

"Were you safe?"

"Of course." Somewhere in the surrounding woods a great horned owl called with the typical *who-who-who-whooo*. Crickets filled the silence until a second owl called back.

"Your turn. I didn't get a good look at the talon scar on your belly."

"Why would you want to see that?"

He met my gaze. "Are you kidding? That's probably the coolest scar story I've ever heard."

I rolled my eyes and lifted my blouse a couple inches. Jake held the lantern close and touched the pink raised line. His cool touch, light as a feather, tickled, and I pulled back. His eyes met mine. "You're ticklish."

A tingle of pleasure shot through me. Playfully, I jerked my shirt down and sent a warning gaze.

He held up both hands. "No worries, but it's good to know. So, birds two, Ellie Mae zero."

"No, the birds lived. These scars symbolize success. Your turn."

He set the lantern down and held out his hand. "Give me your hand."

I placed mine in his. He leaned in close as he touched a place behind his right ear. His fingers guided mine until I felt the indentation and remnants of an old scar. Then he let go and allowed his hand to trail down my arm, our faces only inches apart. "Let me guess," I said softly. "You were hit with a baseball?"

He slowly shook his head and swallowed hard. "Bat. I accidently hit a guy with a wild pitch. He hit back."

I gaped and sat up straight, allowing my hand to fall away. "That's terrible. If I'd been there, I would've—"

"Blown out his tires. I know." Jake crossed his arms over his knees and stared at me, grinning.

"Sorry. Just killed the moment, didn't I?" What could I say? When Caleb and I dated, neither of us were romantic. We held hands, kissed, but more times than not, we simply hung out. I'll bet Mary Beth, the southern-belle ex, never showed off her scars or ruined a moment. Stiff, and feeling it, I rolled my shoulders and moved my head side to side, pushing away thoughts of Jake being with someone else.

Jake turned and patted the truck in front of him. "I'm not that easily distracted."

I scooted over and sat facing away from him. He kneaded my shoulders, gentler on my right side. My muscles cried, and I felt my body relax as Jake's breathing grew slow and rhythmic, comforting. I wanted to lean back into his arms, completely block out everything around me, but I also wanted to get rid of the guilt that poked at me.

"Jake, I know it's probably not that big of a deal, but I'm sorry about last Wednesday."

"Sorry for what?"

"Pushing aside your opinion when you said I should stay home. And when I completely ignored any good judgment. That isn't me. Well, it is, but not quite so extreme. I'm ashamed of how I acted."

His hands moved to my biceps and gently squeezed. "I know how important the Bigfoot are to you. I also think you're smart enough to make decisions for yourself." He moved his hands gently down my arms.

"Wait." I shifted to the side so I could see him. "You don't think I was way out of line?"

"No. You got caught off guard. Just like your mom. It could've happened to anyone."

"Dad doesn't think so. He thinks I ignored the danger."

"Even though your dad was scared, he believed in you. He might not admit it, but while we were waiting for you in the barn, he told me this story about a time your family went on a kayaking trip. You apparently tipped your kayak and were swept downstream. He had been afraid he wouldn't catch up to you before you drowned, but you grabbed hold of a rock." He paused, probably because of my dumbfounded look. "You remember this story?"

I nodded. "Go on."

"He said there was no way you should've been able to keep a hold of that boulder barely sticking out of the water, but somehow you managed. That's how he knew you'd make it back."

I remembered how clear Dad's voice sounded in my head, possibly at the same moment he told Jake this story. "Thank you for telling me. It means a lot."

Jake ran a thumb over my bruised eye and down my cheek, the softness of his touch a balm smoothing over Dad's dismissal. I closed my eyes, melting just a little. When his thumb brushed against my lower lip, I stopped breathing, but my pulse jumped to life.

"Just because your dad was scared doesn't mean you should live in a box. You have a right to make your own mistakes. Earn those scars." His thumb touched the nick on my chin.

I searched his eyes and saw only sincerity. He understood me. Believed in me. As warm currents wound their way in and through my heart, I placed my good hand to the side of his face. Jake bent slowly, his gaze fastened to mine. I parted my lips, ready to escape in his touch, to blot out all that was wrong. He touched his lips to mine, soft and slow. The warmth swirled inside me. Nothing else mattered. I pushed closer and felt Jake's hand wrap around my neck. I slipped my hand into his hair. Entwining my casted fingers in his shirt, I pulled him closer.

We kissed over and over. His lips grazed my cheek, my ear, my neck, then found their way back to my mouth. Maybe it was the smile I could feel when he kissed my cheek, or the way his touch completely altered my thinking, that filled me with hope. With Jake, I soared above the chasm of secrets in my family. Being with him felt as right as rain on a hot and humid day.

But when the kiss ended and I laid my head against his shoulder, I wondered for the umpteenth time why a rich boy and hillbilly girl were together and how this relationship would pan out.

We watched the stars and kissed several more times as the moon rose and the temperature dropped. Sometime nearing midnight, Jake whispered, "I think I should probably take you home."

I tipped my chin up and looked at him. "Too much fun for you?"

A slow smile eased into place as his eyes shifted from serious to playful. "You could say that."

"I did have a lot of fun tonight. Thank you."

"Mission accomplished. I had fun, too. Wanna go out again? Same time next week?"

I scooted toward the tailgate. "Yes, but at my place with Doc, Grandma, and Dean Martin."

Chapter Twenty-Three

At the edge of town, we turned onto Main Street and headed north. Jake looked from the road into the rearview mirror. "I think we're being followed. Is that McGraff behind us?"

I glanced in the side view mirror and groaned. "It is."

"Noticed them when we turned into town."

"Must have been waiting near Gunther's Garage. Sits on the corner where we turned. Wonder what they're up to now?"

Jake slowed at a red light and hit the lock button as we stopped.

The two stayed in their truck, but Rodney gunned the engine as if he might rear end us. Both yipped like two hyenas.

"I swear. Two of the stup—"

"How'd they know we'd be passing by there?" Jake looked serious, intent. His eyes moved from the truck to me. "Doesn't it seem too coincidental they picked us up at that intersection?"

"I think it sounds absurd, but these are the games they

play when they have nothing better to do than terrorize people. Could be us. Could be someone else. Let me see your phone. I'll text Dad." I would have used mine except I took Grandma's advice and tucked it away. Retrieving it would require time and a weird explanation.

Within thirty seconds, Jake's phone dinged. "He'll meet us on the porch with the shotgun."

"Nice." Jake sounded more confident than he looked.

"It's an awfully strange way to end our first night out. Sorry you have to deal with this. Rodney's mad at me, and you're caught up in the mix."

He lifted one corner of his mouth, slipped his hand over to mine, which still held his phone, and touched my fingers. "But you and I . . . there's something there, right?"

I hadn't expected those words, but why not? Jake was genuine, and being together was easy and fun. We shared secrets and trusted each other. Not to mention the attraction. Joy filled me, despite the circumstances.

I wound my fingers through his. "Definitely."

That brought a smile to his face and lightened the mood.

We drove through the heart of our dark, quiet town. Rodney followed so close I couldn't see the front end of his red truck.

Jake squeezed my hand. "All the years Pappy sent stories and pictures of you, me leaving home at this time, the Bigfoot returning... The timing just sorta feels like there has to be some reason we met now."

I glanced at him. "I was thinking that at the pond. What do you think is the reason?"

Rodney hit our bumper, pitching Jake and me forward. I turned and scowled at the brothers, which enlivened their stupidity as they bounced around in the front of the truck.

Jake pulled his hand away. Once we hit Dillard Hollow at the edge of town, he drove as fast as the road would allow.

We came upon the Stroh's property, windows dark, the family in bed. Jake tightened his jaw as he gripped the steering wheel, hitting one pothole after another. I winced, feeling each jostle in my sore muscles.

We rounded the bend, going a little faster than the road allowed for. The moment stilled. In the glow of Jake's phone, I saw him clear as day, focused and determined to get us home. Outside, darkness cloaked everything. Only a drop of moonlight silhouetted the trees to our right. The gravel beneath our tires crunched. I noticed everything in the same second a vehicle lurched from the coal mine road. Before I had time to gasp, the vehicle rammed the driver's side. Jake's upper body smashed into the airbag from the impact. I pitched toward him and screamed his name, the sound lost in the crunch of metal and glass.

Jake swore as Doc's truck left the road and careened down the slope. I grabbed the door handle with my loose fingers as Jake clamped a hand around my upper arm. Headlights illuminated the forest and the large oak.

We slammed into the tree. Glass shattered. A ton of bricks slammed into my face and chest. My head snapped back and then nothing.

A fierce pain stabbed my right side and wrapped around my lower back. My eyes hurt even though they were still closed. I tried to breathe through the pain, open my eyes, and make sense of where I was, but my body and mind felt detached.

I heard voices. Too garbled to understand.

Truck accident. Jake. McGraff's following. My mind

flipped through snippets of thought as I tried to recall what happened and how I came to this uncomfortable place.

Something was off. I held my breath.

Don't panic. Don't panic. Think.

These surroundings weren't familiar. I was cold. My fingers brushed nylon, a metal frame. A cot.

Ellie, think first. Don't react. Think. Think. Something's not right.

You were being followed. Jake went off the road.

Jake.

I slowed my respirations to calm myself, but the pain in my shoulders and torso squeezed in on me.

Jake. Where was he? I willed my eyes to open but they felt glued shut.

Don't panic. Think.

I wasn't in a hospital or at home. Voices. Whose voices? Men. Arguing.

I tried opening my eyes again.

Where was Jake?

Panic rose in my chest.

Don't panic. Breathe slow and deep.

It hurt to breathe.

Think.

Wait. Listen.

A door slammed. Footsteps.

"If she don't wake up soon, we're gonna lose our window, and Swanson'll be breathing down my neck."

I knew that voice but couldn't place it. A man's voice.

"Where's Todd with them smelling salts. We need to get a move on. People'll be out looking fer her."

Todd. The voice belonged to his brother. My heart sped up and pulsed in my ears, making my head hurt even more. I whimpered.

"She's waking up." I heard the shuffling of feet and what sounded like a chair scraping across the floor.

"Ellie Mae. You awake?"

That wasn't Rodney's voice. I felt him staring at me. It was hard to think. I didn't want to open my eyes. I didn't want to see this. I felt nauseous.

"Open your eyes, Ellie. I need to talk to you."

"Can't. Hurts too much." Was the croaking sound my voice?

"You haveta. No time for pampering. We're gonna sit you up, and you better rouse yerself, or you're gonna be feeling a lot worse."

I opened my aching eyes, trying to focus. It was dark, but in the light of the battery-powered lantern on a table, I recognized Jaxon Reid's bloody, scowling face and greasy blond hair. The room spun, swirling in a musty stench, assaulting my stomach.

"Sit up. I need to talk to ya."

"What's going on? Why do you have me—"

Jaxon grabbed my upper arm and yanked me into a sitting position. A knife-slicing pain pierced my right side. I hollered and wrapped my good arm around my middle. The moving room picked up speed, and I vomited at his feet.

He shoved me back. "You stupid girl."

I glanced around at what looked like a one-room cabin as I wiped my mouth with my hand. Crumbling stone fireplace, half-boarded windows. One table and a couple chairs. Looked like an oversized sink in the far corner, but shadows draped whatever else they had here.

"Where are we?" I put a hand to my head and winced at the burning pain. Either mud or blood caked my hair on the right side. I looked back at the cot and the dark stain. Hard to tell how much blood saturated it.

Head wounds bleed a lot.

You'll be fine, Ellie. Your thinking is clearing up.

I remembered the airbag. The truck that barreled into us. The impact from slamming into a tree.

Jake?

Jake's side had been hit. How hard? Enough to force us off the road. By the cut on Jaxon's face, I assumed he was the one responsible. But he hadn't been in his tow truck.

"Why are you doing this?" I snapped.

"Hey, someone's coming." Rodney said from the open door. Jaxon popped out of the chair, grabbed his gun, and skirted to the entrance like a fox on the run. The fact he was nervous helped ease my nerves. People were out looking for me.

Rodney and Jaxon stood silent. My head pulsed with each heartbeat, but I was pretty certain even the crickets stopped their trilling. No owls, no frogs, no nighttime rustling. Everything stilled.

Kntock! Who-hoo.

My head snapped to the door, and I focused on the silence. To most the knock-click sound came and went so fast it was forgotten, and the owl cry was mimicry. Meant to sound like an owl so the click would be forgotten. I'd listened to Mom's recordings. She explained the noises, the patterns. On the first night Jake and I went out, we'd heard three slow knocks—a signaling of our unthreatening presence. The following rapid tree strikes answered in acknowledgement.

Only the Nun'Yunu'Wi and those in the know would recognize the click and owl combo was a made-up pattern to signal distress. Trouble in the area. There were no answering tree knocks because whatever made that noise was staying hidden.

The crickets pulsed to life. "There ain't no one coming." Jaxon stormed back to the table. "You're spooked by owls."

"I'm telling you, I heard something." The dim lighting hid Rodney's expression, but Ellie could hear the fear in his tone.

"Let me know when you *see* something." Jaxon pushed aside a chair. "Ellie, git over here. I need you to look at a map and tell me where those Bigfoot are holed up."

Rodney turned from the doorway. "You said once she woke up, I could leave. I'm not gonna be part of no kidnapping."

"You need to shut up. Ellie Mae, you were in an accident, and you wandered off. We're helping you, but I need you to help me first. Now, listen, you mumbled—"

"Why do you have my dad's tranquilizer gun?" My voice came out more controlled than I felt. Probably because I was genuinely curious. There on the corner of the table was the gray case. Beside it, next to a topographic map, was Mom's journal.

"Never mind that. You said something during your sleep about *protecting* Bigfoot. Now, I need you to tell me where they're living."

"What are you talking about?"

He folded his arms and spit off to the side. "Listen, girl, I know'd your momma well. We was neighbors. She kept up with those beasts. Whenever she went hiking for hours at a time, day after day, I knew they was close by. Rodney and Jeanine—they've been watching you, and we know you've been tracking 'em. You need to tell me where to find them."

Mom would never have kept company with Jaxon Reid. "I don't know anything about any Bigfoot. Mom didn't share her secrets with me."

He swore, stood, and picked up his rifle and Mom's

journal from the wobbly Formica table. Far as I knew, Mom's writing in this volume recorded the details of her early traipsing through the mountains but no actual facts on the Nun'Yunu'Wi.

"I don't believe ya. She wrote about them. I seen her journal once, and it had all kinds of stuff about 'em."

I ignored him. "They'll trace the paint scuffs on Doc's truck to the paint on your truck. The glass from your headlights embedded in Doc's side door. The footprints and fingerprints as you carried me from the scene. My dad won't let you get by with this. Your days are numbered because you're too stupid to pull off a kidnapping."

"*If* it was my truck. And, sweetheart, your daddy has a price like anyone else. Wasn't hard to keep him quiet after we sent your momma over that cliff."

I closed my eyes, focusing on his words and their implied meaning. Jaxon killed my mom? Fear faded into anger that was morphing into a slow boiling rage. But I couldn't react or he'd shoot me. I pressed my fingertips to my eyes, pushing at the pain but also disguising the shaking of my one good hand. He might have killed my mom, but he was lying about Dad. Bluffing.

Dad couldn't be bought off.

"Get up. You're gonna show me right now. I need coordinates." He spread a map on the table.

He would kill me anyways. Why give him details? I played dumb on the off chance I hadn't talked in my sleep. In all the weird Bigfoot dreams, I had never protected them.

"What am I supposed to show you? Are you saying my mom tracked a *Bigfoot* monster?" I made it sound like a ridiculous idea.

"I swear, I'll shoot you right here." Jaxon placed the barrel of the gun to my head, and I felt surprisingly calm.

Like his rage nullified mine. Or maybe it was the realization I could die protecting those creatures from *this* monster.

"Hey." Rodney paced from one end of the cabin to the other. "You don't shoot her until I get paid and get outta here."

"You don't get paid until she gives me coordinates."

"I'm not being sent up fer murder. You already killed that boy. I'm not gonna have any part of this."

"Shut your trap, man!"

Killed that boy. What boy? Jake? Tears flooded my eyes. Jake was dead? A roaring sound filled my head. I couldn't breathe.

No. No. No.

"I'm outta here." Rodney walked out of the cabin. Jaxon swore and hurried after him.

Fighting sobs, I stood and tried to balance through the dizziness. Holding my side, I shuffled the table. I flipped open the gray case and picked up the gun and a prefilled dart.

Gasping short bursts of air, I watched the door standing slightly ajar, revealing moonlight and a star-studded sky beyond. The same sky Jake and I watched together, kissed under. He couldn't be gone. I refused to believe it.

A gunshot. I jumped. The dart fell from my fingers. It was hard to manipulate with the cast, but I picked it up.

Oh, God. Oh, God. Please, help. Jaxon walked back through the cabin door. I pushed the dart in the chamber and wasted no time firing the needle at him.

He swore and slapped a hand to his neck. His vision might blur, but he wasn't going down anytime soon. Charging him, I hollered and slammed my casted arm against his head. Pain vibrated through my body. Jaxon crumpled to his knees, dropping the rifle.

Tucking my arm close to my body, I wanted to cry, but there was no time. Blood ran out of my cast, covering my white blouse and dripping to the floor. I bent over, picked up the gun, and shuffled to where Jaxon struggled to get his feet under him. I slammed the butt into the side of his head, but it wasn't hard enough. He grabbed for the gun.

I pulled it out of reach and backed to the door. Sapped of strength, I stumbled into the night as Jaxon pushed to his feet.

Chapter Twenty-Four

The moon illuminated the forest to my left. To my right, a grass clearing opened as far as I could see. I ran through the waist-high brush to the trees, a stinging barbed-wire pressure gripping my left side. I paused at a large tree and listened. Jaxon's footsteps smashed through the brush not too far away. Was that his breathing? So close.

I headed the opposite direction. Ten steps...twenty. "Ellie Mae, stop yer runnin'. There's a drop-off!" Jaxon yelled. The pain ripped through my side, and I fell to my knees, stifling a scream as I hit rocks. The gun clattered and fell away.

Down. Down. Down.

The rifle smashed on the rocks below. I remained still, horrified. That would have been me if I hadn't slipped.

Jaxon didn't want me dead after all. 'Course not. He wanted coordinates that only I could provide. How long could we play cat and mouse before he collapsed? Ten minutes, twenty?

Slowly, I pulled myself up and caught sight of the

lantern thirty feet away. The light blurred and doubled as I ducked back down on my haunches. The smell of a rotting animal churned my stomach. I needed to get away from it.

Jaxon moved slowly. Maybe because of the tranquilizer. More likely he knew the drop-off was nearby. My head pulsed and dark spots blotted my vision. My gut twisted and wrenched, heaving without delay. I shifted to the opposite side of the tree and silently retched, each spasm raking through my ribs and tearing at the inside of my skull. I fell over, trembling.

Nothingness edged in and out as I stared at the canopy of leaves, rattling beneath the moon. A few stars glittered through. An owl hooted. Some believed that to be a premonition of death. But it didn't sound exactly like an owl. Mimicry. No tree knock. That meant—

Jaxon Reid stepped into my line of sight, blotting out the sky. Lantern in hand, his cold eyes scoffed. I attempted to sit up.

"Save your strength." He knelt next to me. Blood dripped from his ear where my cast or the gun had split it. "Your momma would be proud of your stamina even though you failed in your mission. Kinda ironic since the only reason she failed was because of you." He wiped at the blood on his face. "You were her weakness. A distraction." He blinked rapidly and stood, stumbling a bit. I pushed myself to a half-sitting position, my left hand braced on the ground while I held my right arm close to my body.

"She didn't fail, because I'm here, right now. Maybe I failed, but at least you won't win." I ground out the words. "You'll be asleep in minutes."

He laughed and shook his head. "Wrong again. The others will be here soon."

I narrowed my eyes. "Others?" I pushed, slowly rotating

my body, and slid a knee under me to stand up. If others were coming, I needed to get away.

A boot caught me in the gut. My mouth fell open as air whooshed from my lungs. I fell flat, my face to one side, gasping for air through the worst pain my body had known.

"If I can't go, neither can you." Jaxon pulled his booted foot back like he was going to kick again. I squeezed my eyes shut, tucked my knees up to my chin, and covered my face with my forearms.

"Aghrrr..."

Crack! Thud.

The kick never came.

I slowly pulled my forearms down and sucked in as much air as my flaming side would allow. Jaxon's crumpled body laid five feet away, the lantern on its side next to his lifeless face, eyes staring wide into the darkness.

A shadowy figure moved over me, silhouetted against the moonlight. The body was covered in hair with arms that reached to its knees. Standing tall with broad shoulders loomed the monster of my dreams.

My blood chilled. I closed my eyes. This was a dream. I could wake up, but my eyes wouldn't reopen. Nothingness edged in and then retreated. I forced my eyes open. I had to wake up. Had to get out of this nightmare.

The creature bent over me, pushing air in and out of its nostrils as it moved its face from my toes to my head, smelling me. It knelt, no animosity in its stance. With nothing to lose, I opened my fist, palm up, and let my hand fall on the ground in a gesture of submission. "Please help."

With a few grunts and a tap to my palm, long arms slipped beneath my knees and around my back. The stench of rot and mud engulfed me as I was lifted off the ground, but I was too weak to care. My cheek fell next to coarse hair.

Had to be the female. I could feel her breasts, she was shorter than the male appeared, and her touch felt gentle. Where was the male? Where were the young ones? Where was she taking me?

The pulse in my head meshed with the creature's heartbeat, and my body warmed. I missed my momma's touch. Unmoving and secure, I allowed myself to drift off.

I floated on a cloud. No thoughts, no pain, no memories. Darkness surrounded me. A dull ache in my head and torso grew stronger as light pushed at the darkness. I forced my eyes to open and squinted under bright lights.

A hospital room. Dad. Grandma.

Oxygen tubing pulled against my face, confining as if strapping my head down to the bed.

I braced my good forearm on the bed and attempted to lift myself. This wasn't right. It was nighttime. I was outside. I was—

A vice-crushing pain gripped my side. I hollered and fell back. Dad rushed to my side. His face blurred. Was he real?

"Ellie. You're in the ER. Lie still."

Grandma stood behind him. "Thank you, Lord."

"Dad. I . . . Jake?"

"You both were very lucky."

"What? He isn't dead? They said . . ."

Dad's voice echoed around me. "Jake broke a leg and a couple ribs. He sprained his wrist and has a mild concussion, but he's fine."

"He's fine?"

"Yes."

I closed my eyes as memories caved in on me—Jaxon's face, alive then dead, the Nun'Yunu'Wi. "Jaxon wanted coordinates to the Bigfoot cave. He . . . he's dead now. And so is Rodney, I think."

"Dead? How do you know? Where were you?"

"A cabin. Jaxon said he was helping me, but that wasn't true." Memories of that final kick sent a wash of pain through my middle. I grimaced and grabbed Dad's wrist. I attempted to push up, but my head split and swam, bringing a round of nausea. I eased back, wincing, unable to articulate. Dad called for a doctor, and I heard the words blood, tests, and pain medication. Too weak to open my eyes or talk, I drifted back into the dark.

Chapter Twenty-Five

I woke up feeling much less pain and a little dopey. My thoughts were muddled, and my throat parched, but I was alive. The enormity of all that had happened surfaced, and I teared up.

"Dad."

He turned from the window where the morning sun glinted off a corner of the hospital building. I held out my arms. He rushed over and sat on the side of the bed, gently wrapping his arms around me. I cried against his shoulder.

"Hey." He patted my back. "Everything's fine now."

Easing back, I took in several shallow and shuddering breaths. He handed me a tissue then held the water as I drank. I forced a deep breath, one that nearly killed me but felt good in the end. The sterile room came into better focus along with memories of last night.

"Where's Jake?"

"Just down the hall. Been sleeping most of the time. He has a couple cuts and breaks like you, but he'll be okay."

"Where are we?"

"Hazard Regional."

"How did I get here?"

"Simsy called an ambulance."

I squinted and felt the pull above my right eye. "Simsy?"

"She found you outside her door about three o'clock this morning, lying on the porch." His voice cracked on the last couple words. "You woke up once in the ER."

We were alone, so I voiced my speculation. "After the female Nun'Yunu'Wi killed Jaxon, she must have carried me to Simsy." A million questions swarmed my mind.

"Dad, you have to call Kyle and Steve and tell them not to come. I won't be able to tromp though the forest today and probably not tomorrow either." Not to mention I planned to visit the Nun'Yunu'Wi as soon as I could manage it. I couldn't wait to get an up-close look and . . . what? Thank them? They saved my life.

Dad shook his head. "All you need to do is give them the coordinates. They'll take care of the rest." He touched my leg and briefly closed his bloodshot eyes. "But first, we need to decide what to tell the police. Do you feel up to talking about it while no one else is here?"

"Only if you promise to tell Kyle and Steve not to come."

"Ellie, I'm not going to promise anything. You know that."

"Please understand how much this means to me. You should have never called them in the first place. You led me to believe I would have a chance at getting close. But all along you intended for Steve and Kyle to intervene."

"*Please understand* that I'm trying to protect you." He stood and closed the door. "Not just from being injured but from the time and demands the Nun'Yunu'Wi require. They're the reason your mom was gone so much. I don't want to lose you to them, too."

My heart squeezed, and a knot formed in my throat. He was right. Mom left us too much. I remembered watching her pack. I had sat on their bed, asking questions, receiving insufficient answers. Anger usually followed until Dad smoothed it over by allowing me to assist him in the clinic. I couldn't, wouldn't, hurt him by allowing the Nun'Yunu'Wi to consume my time. But I also wouldn't give up on what Mom started. There had to be some middle ground.

I filled Dad in on every detail from the moment I woke up on the cot to Jaxon's death. But I skipped the part of Dad being bought out to keep quiet over Mom's death. Partly because the timing wasn't right and partly because I feared the truth. He might walk out, and I needed him right now more than I needed the truth. Instead, I focused on Dad's major concern. "You don't think they would accuse me of murdering Rodney or Jaxon, do you?"

"Not sure how that might play out. If we tell someone other than JT that the Nun'Yunu'Wi are responsible, they won't believe it. You might be suspected. And once Jaxon's uncle gets wind of this, he might try to pin the murder on you in exchange for the Bigfoot location."

"Yeah, his uncle might be one of the 'others' Jaxon talked about." I lifted my fingers, making air quotes.

"Others?" Dad pulled his eyebrows together. "What others?"

I lifted my left shoulder. "Jaxon said it didn't matter if the tranquilizer put him out because others were coming." Dad ran a hand down his unshaven face. His eyes looked tired. I touched his arm, feeling guilty that I put him through one ordeal after another. "Where's Rebecca?"

"She was here earlier but had some business to take care of. She'll be back. Listen, while you were out, I was thinking over other plausible motives Jaxon could've had for taking you to this cabin, and I came up with one after talking to JT. It involves Caleb."

"Caleb? What would he know about Jaxon's cabin?"

"Enough. If anyone other than JT asks, you need to tell them the McGraff's and Reid had it in for you because of your fight with Rodney and also because Jake is an outsider. But here's the important piece . . ." Dad spoke slowly and distinctly. "You knew something else—Jaxon Reid has been growing and cultivating marijuana at that cabin. You found this out when Caleb was in town. He told you about it. Got it? Jaxon wanted to make sure you didn't squeal to anyone, so he planned to make you disappear. Instead, while chasing you in the dark, he fell and broke his neck."

I shivered, remembering his lifeless face. "He killed someone else, Dad. Rodney mentioned a boy."

"We'll share that, but it's likely no one will ever know who."

"Maybe Todd would know. What do I say about the tranquilizer gun?"

"The truth. I gave it to Jake because he didn't want to carry a rifle or shotgun, and I insisted you have some protection against wild animals while you were out at that preserve."

"I would have carried the gun," I said with force and winced as a wave of pain shot through my head.

He harrumphed, his face softening. "You deserved a fun night out."

"Yeah, well, look how that turned out."

The door cracked, and Doc stuck in his head then barreled through with Grandma right behind him. One rushed to each side of the bed.

"Thank you, Lord." Grandma kissed my forehead. "You sure gave us a scare."

"I'm sorry."

Doc laid a hand on my shoulder. "Glad to see you awake, and your eyes look pretty clear. How ya feeling?"

"Like a rag doll that's been fought over by angry children."

He smiled and looked at Dad. "I'll think she'll be fine. You have a minute to speak to Jake's parents? They have a couple questions."

Dad reached over the end of the bed and laid a hand on my ankle. "I'll be back. We'll work this out, but no talking to anyone about what happened just yet, okay?"

I nodded, hating that I wasn't more sorry about Jaxon's death, but he would've killed me as easily as he pushed Mom over the cliff. After he got what he wanted.

"Hey, Dad," I called to his back. "If you see Jake, tell him I'll come see him soon."

He nodded and walked out with Doc trailing behind.

Grandma sat next to me on the bed, and I hugged her. "Sorry about my blouse and skirt. I think they're ruined."

She rubbed my back. "Don't you worry about that. We'll get you something new. Ellie, it's a miracle you two survived that crash."

"Jake's parents are here?" I changed the subject, hoping to drive the worry from her face.

"They flew in an hour or so ago."

"Have they been hard on Doc?"

Grandma took my hand in hers. "Jake's momma holds nothing but contempt for Ethan, and this only added to her hatred for Hush Briar. It's not fair. This accident could've happened anywhere."

"That's not exactly true, Grandma. Rodney McGraff had it in for me, and Jaxon was plain old mean. But I hear what you're saying. Jake's parents have been unfair to him and Doc."

"It's too bad. She's a woman carrying around a heap of unfounded bitterness." Grandma lowered her voice and glanced at the open doorway. "Best not to talk about it here. We can discuss it more when we get you home."

I fell back asleep and woke to Dad slightly shaking my shoulder. "Ellie."

I blinked several times. Caleb materialized at the foot of my bed.

"Hey, Ellie." He lifted a corner of his mouth.

I attempted a smile. "Hi." My throat was dry and sticky. Dad helped me sit up then held the cup while I sipped the cool water. "Thanks. Where's Grandma and Doc?"

Dad returned the cup to the table and stood. "They left to eat lunch. Caleb needs to talk to you. It's important that you listen and remember what he says."

"What time is it?"

"About one. The nurse left you a tray of food. You hungry?"

"I'll wait." My gaze shifted to Caleb. He held his blue ball cap in one hand, his blond waves hanging over his ears and halfway down his neck. Longer than I remembered.

"You okay?" Caleb's look said he might have asked a stupid question, but he also knew I was somewhat resilient when it came to cuts and bruises.

It pained me to think he might be inadvertently involved with Jaxon. "Did you know what they were up to?" If he lied, I'd be able to tell. During our last year as a couple, I'd caught him in so many lies. He'd make light of the situation, downplay the significance of whatever happened, and avoid eye contact.

He shook his head and held my gaze. "No. Your dad just filled me in."

I snapped a questioning look toward dad.

"He knows everything."

"Everything?"

Dad nodded and put a hand on Caleb's shoulder. "We spent the last hour talking. Caleb has some important details to go over with you. I have a meeting with an old friend of your mom's, name's Harvey Swanson. He's out of Frankfurt and heads up the rangers across the state. He got word from dispatch of a girl injured in the forest, and he's following up on it this morning. He wanted to know if he could stop by and ask you a few questions. Does his name sound familiar?"

I nodded. "Mom mentioned him a few times. He gave her clearance to hunt out of season." To shoot wild game for the Nun'Yunu'Wi. "I thought he was too old to still be working."

Dad half-chuckled. "He's not that old. I'll return his call, see what he wants, but I'm sticking to our story. I'll be back this evening." He looked from me to Caleb. "You have about a half hour or so before Doc and Grandma return. Use the time wisely. And by the way"—Dad looked at me—"Caleb's your brother if the nurse asks."

He slapped Caleb on the back and left. Caleb moved around to my right side and sat on a straight-back chair. He leaned forward, elbows on his knees, twirling the ball cap between his hands.

I played with a couple loose strings on my cast. The fact Caleb came running when Dad called showed he cared. His face was serious, mouth a straight line, pinched at one corner, the way it did when he was angry or mad at himself.

He half stood and scraped the chair across the floor

until he sat as close to the bed as he could get. "Your dad wants me to tell you that I knew about the cabin and the weed growing there. Which I did, and which I avoided talking about for a lot of reasons. He said it's important the police think I told you about it."

"You won't get in trouble, will you?"

"Maybe. We'll see how it all pans out, but I'd rather suffer the consequences than see you get blamed for something you didn't do. Jaxon's uncle will be looking to lay blame unless he has something to hide."

"And you think he'll want to hide the marijuana?"

"Oh, yeah. They're growing way more than is allowed. He won't want the feds out there snooping around."

"What's going on with Jeanine?" A rush of regret and confusion accompanied those words.

"She's in Knoxville. Dad brought her down midweek. I guess something happened at church last week and he decided it was time to get her away from McGraffs. To my knowledge she doesn't know about anything that's happened to Rodney and Jaxon. I'll tell her when I go back."

Relief washed through me. "I'm so glad she's not involved anymore. Caleb, Jaxon was going to kill me." A chill slithered down my spine, and I'm guessing it happened to Caleb, too, because he visibly trembled.

"Jeanine had no clue they planned to kidnap you. I could almost swear it. When I took her home from Willie's that night they threw bottles at you, I made her tell me why she and Rodney were hanging around Jaxon. She said he promised to pay them if they followed you."

Which explained why they showed up at church. "But your dad . . ."

"He also made a deal with Jaxon, roped off the tracks so

hunters could find them, and pointed him in the right direction, but he wouldn't take part in anything like this. He didn't know Jaxon was going to involve you." Caleb looked sick. "At least I hope not."

I stretched my good hand over my belly. The taped IV tubing pinched slightly. Caleb slipped both of his hands around mine as if I were a delicate flower.

I gave him a reassuring squeeze. "I believe that, too. I'm sorry you're knee-deep in this."

He shrugged. "Feels good to do something right for a change. Ellie, if you'd been killed, I would've—"

"Don't. No sense going there. It's over." I pulled my hand back.

Caleb motioned to my body like a mechanic trying to pinpoint the source of trouble in a car engine. "So what all's happening here?"

"I have a bruised rib, a concussion, and a nice gash right up here." I lifted my hair on the right side. "That earned me four more stitches beyond the beer-bottle incident." I lifted my broken arm to show him the cut that began where the cast ended. "Six stitches. Three different times now. Between the airbag and falling on my face, I look like something out of *The Walking Dead*."

"Most badass zombie these hills have ever seen. How'd you break your wrist?" He offered an affectionate smile that stirred an unexpected shyness inside me.

"Fell down a hill. My wrist stopped moving when it wedged between a couple rocks, but my body kept going. I'm scheduled to have it x-rayed again. Pretty sure I re-broke it on Jaxon's head." I pulled back the blue cover and showed him the crack.

He made a face. "Does it hurt?"

"It's tolerable."

"You always were tougher than me." We laughed and reminisced about our many adventures jumping out of hay mows and trees, the times we should have been killed doing reckless stuff like propelling down cliffs using kudzu vines, and playing on their pond when the ice was only an inch thick.

"We've both had our hind ends warmed more times than I can remember. I blame you."

I chuckled. "I'll give you that, but only because you're helping me out."

Caleb glanced at his ball cap then made eye contact. "So, can I ask about Jake? He's not been here long, but you two seem close."

His neutral expression meant he didn't want me to know what he was thinking. I pulled the sheet taut, folded it down on my lap, and smoothed it out. "He's a great guy. We have a lot in common, and I trust him. He doesn't put up with my temper or allow me to best him at everything."

"Like me."

"Yeah. You're a pushover. You let me get into all kinds of trouble."

And I could have said when I kiss Jake, there's a euphoria that takes me to another place, but I didn't want to be rude.

"I talked to him last Saturday morning. Day before I left. Guess he was picking up your four-wheeler at the police station. Anyway, I was on my way to see JT and there Jake was. We talked a little bit. He seems down to earth, smart, and he likes you an awful lot. I made sure he understood that if he hurt you in any way, I'd come calling."

I rolled my eyes. "Pretty sure I can handle myself, but thank you."

Doc and Grandma returned. Caleb stood. "Remember,

you know where I'm at if you need anything. I mean it. I want us to remain friends."

I smiled. "You watch your back."

"See ya later." He nodded to Grandma and Doc as he left the room.

Police and friends visited throughout the day. The same was true for Jake because every time I asked about going to his room, someone else was in there. At eight thirty, when visiting hours were over, the nurse strictly enforced the rule for everyone, including both our families, to leave. I waited until nine to call the nurse in and explain I wouldn't be able to sleep unless I got to see Jake.

"He's in and out, but I'll give you fifteen minutes, and then I want you back in bed."

Chapter Twenty-Six

Wrapped in my purple-and-gray flannel robe, I pushed my squeaky-wheeled IV pole three doors down and entered Jake's room. The head of his bed was slightly inclined. He lay motionless, eyes closed. His left leg was elevated in a system of ropes and pulleys, his left upper lip cut and swollen, three stitches holding it together. Another gash ran along his left hairline from forehead to ear where a portion of his hair had been shaved off, and his left arm lay across his abdomen in a sling.

Even bruised, cut, and lying helplessly in a hospital bed, the sight of him stole a little of my breath. It took an enormous amount of effort to keep my tears in check. I walked around to his right side so I could touch his free hand and get closer. His eyes drifted open, and he attempted to lift a corner of his mouth.

"I came to show you how to text one-handed." I slid my hand in his, careful not to disturb either of our IVs. "It's not as hard as you might think."

He stared at my face long enough I began to feel self-conscious. His eyes fell to my re-casted arm, sporting a red cover, then back to my face.

"I'm sorry, Ellie. I promised to keep you safe."

"What are you talking about?"

"Hatley's—a date behind locked gates. Your dad insisted we take the tranquilizer gun. Otherwise, he wouldn't let me take you anywhere. But I didn't see the truck until it was too late. How banged up are you?" His speech was a little muffled, possibly the cut or pain medication. Either way, at the moment, I felt little regret over Jaxon's demise.

"How could you have seen it?" Foregoing the metal folding chair, I slipped onto the bed, holding my breath as I shifted through the pain in my side, careful not to put too much weight on my casted arm. When I settled, I held his hand in my lap and partially faced him. "Jaxon had his headlights off. Do you remember any of the crash? He and the McGraffs had been communicating all along. They wanted me to show them where the Bigfoot were staying."

"I don't remember anything. No one's told me much except it was an accident."

"No accident. Those lowlifes left you for dead and kidnapped me. Todd and Rodney had been watching us, using Jeanine, too. They reported back to Jaxon. Jaxon's also responsible for my mom's death. At least, he hinted that he was. He killed Rodney. And . . . and . . ." Should I tell him the truth surrounding Jaxon's death or wait until he was better? What if the pain meds caused him to slip up and say too much? But I hated holding out on him. "Jaxon's dead, too."

Jake looked pained. "I didn't know what happened to you. I woke up here. No one would tell me anything."

I gently squeezed his hand. "I'm here. I'm fine. They say I'll go home in a day or two. You, on the other hand, were out cold, and you didn't need my account to be the first words you heard when you woke up."

He let go of my hand and touched my face. "You were my first thought."

Such sweet words. I swallowed my tears. "You were mine, too. Think you'll still be able to play baseball?"

"Doctor said it was a clean fracture. Dad seemed optimistic."

"That's good."

"You were unconscious?" He placed his hand back in mine.

"A couple different times. But believe me when I say I did more damage to myself last Wednesday than what happened in the truck last night. I have a bruised rib and a couple more stitches. You, on the other hand, have some major recovery ahead of you." I nodded at his leg.

His eyes closed briefly then opened a sliver. "Surgery tomorrow morning, physical therapy after. Not exactly how I wanted to spend my summer."

"Don't worry. I have hundreds of stories to entertain you with."

"Mom wants me to come home."

"To New Orleans?" My heart tightened in a panicked vice . "But you don't need to go. You can stay here until the cast comes off. Six to eight weeks, right? You can even do your physical therapy here, be with Doc." *Be happy.*

"All of my family came up here to be with me. It's important to them. It makes sense right now. But I'll be back."

People never came back to Hush Briar. The chasm separating me from the people I cared about opened and threatened to suck me in. Like when Mom died and when Caleb left. I didn't want to go there again and feel that suffocating pain. I tightened my jaw, afraid to voice the words and expose myself. Be seen as weak and unreasonable. Selfish.

"None of this should have happened to you. I'm sorry you got caught up in it. I understand why you would want to go home." I stopped a tear with the fingers sticking out of my cast and sucked in a ragged breath. Jake tightened his grip on my hand, and I caught a tear from my other eye before it dripped down my cheek.

"Hey, I am coming back. You promised me a camping trip, remember? And there's college."

I nodded, but it didn't ease my fear of being the girl he went out with once then soon forgot. Nothing to get broken up over. I tried to smile. "I remember."

Heavy-lidded, his eyes opened slowly, and I saw the longing and sorrow in them as he tried to hold my gaze. It gave me hope.

Blinking back the tears, I rubbed my thumb over Jake's palm, memorizing how good it felt to be near him. I stayed put, listening to the muffled sounds of the hospital, until he fell asleep.

The next morning, as light began to peak through the blinds, my door opened and Doc sauntered in. I'd been awake since an earlier blood draw, contemplating how to best shower before any more visitors arrived. It wouldn't be easy since every muscle in my body screamed for me not to move. As I struggled to sit up, I caught sight of Doc's droopy face.

"You okay?"

"Shh, just lie still. It's early." Doc leaned over and kissed my head. "Jake's in surgery, and I needed a place to escape the wrath of my daughter."

Ah. That explained the frown. Did he know Jake was returning to Louisiana? If so, he had to be feeling the sting, too. Made me want to tear into Jake's mom and ask if she ever thought of anyone but herself, but Jake wouldn't want that. Still, I was one hundred percent on Doc's side. As long as I was breathing, I wouldn't stand by passively while others hurt him.

I shifted and raised the head of my bed a little more. "Glad to help. Any word on Jake?"

"He just went in. Pretty straightforward surgery. Should only take a couple hours."

I pushed my call button. After the nurse helped me to the bathroom and back, I sat up in my robe.

Doc moved my bedside table over my lap. "I brought you this." He slid a disposable cup of McDonald's coffee nearer to me. "And your grandma sent these." He pulled a baggie of small apple turnovers out of his jacket pocket and set them on the table.

"Thank you. I'm sorry about your truck," I said as Doc sat down next to the bed, facing me. "It's not likely Jaxon had insurance."

"No, but I do, and I'm glad you were in the truck versus the car. Not sure the two of you would have made it out alive otherwise."

I shuddered and moved away from such gruesome thoughts to the one weighing heaviest on my mind. "Jake said he's going home for the rest of the summer. How do you feel about that?"

Doc scrunched up his forehead. "I'll miss him, but he'll be back in the fall, and we'll be in touch. How about you?" His eyes weren't smiling, and I heard the sadness in his tone. I handed him a turnover then retrieved one for myself.

"I don't want him to go, but I guess I understand. Doc, why did you write to Jake about me? Why did you tell him all of those stories over the years?"

He stared at the IV monitor, a contemplative pose, then patted my leg. "I didn't realize I talked so much about you. You've been a constant in my life—the granddaughter I wasn't allowed to have."

"What do you mean?"

He took a bite of the pastry and studied my face as he chewed. "My granddaughters barely acknowledge me. Kim's convinced them I never loved her or their grandma." He shrugged. "I've grown accustomed to it and accept it for what it is."

"That's not fair. Why didn't you talk to me about them this past year? Why don't you have any pictures in your house?"

"It's complicated, and when I say complicated, I mean layer upon layer of unfortunate circumstances mixed with poor choices and years of disappointment."

I rolled my eyes and wanted to growl in frustration. "The truth isn't complicated, but dancing around it gets tricky. Why are you doing it?" I couldn't help my prodding.

He shook his head and looked at me as if he expected nothing less than the most difficult conversation. "It seems one reason falls into another until it becomes the norm, and anything different would upset the balance. But I tell ya"—he shook a finger at me and eased back in his chair—"Jake brought a little victory into my life."

Because he brought the truth with him! I wanted to shout it. Wasn't it obvious there was no longer a need to keep secrets? Jake's mom might have poisoned everyone's mind to think Doc was evil, but all Doc needed to do was speak up. These lies and secrets didn't make any sense.

"It feels good to have someone on your side, doesn't it?" I lifted the coffee.

"It feels good to have my grandson. And now that you mention it"—he winked—"maybe fate was at work. I think there might've been a reason why I sent those stories to Jake. Since he's met you face-to-face, I'm confident he'll return and maybe even call this place home."

I should've felt embarrassed that he implied fate at work —that Jake and I were meant to be together—but I think I believed it, too. Not to mention Doc always offered unconditional support. I had no reason to be embarrassed with him. "You think he'll want to come back?"

"I'm sure of it."

After Jake's surgery, Doc said he was going to charm his way into recovery for a brief visit and then leave while the rest of the Harris's were still hanging out in the chapel. That was the last place he saw them.

After about ten minutes, curiosity won out. I called my nurse, told her where I was headed, then rattled my way down the hall, pushing the IV pole.

Chapter Twenty-Seven

Outside the chapel door, I peeked through a long, narrow window. Five people sat in chairs, one beside the other, facing an altar and crucifix like disciplined soldiers.

The somber tone and dim lighting gave me the creeps. Jake had been in surgery, not on death row. Had to be Jake's dad on the end. They shared the same profile. He only had one brother, so the guy planted between the two girls had to be Ty, seven years older than Jake. He looked like Jake but thinner with blond hair. Both hands were interlocked behind his head the way I'd seen Jake do. The youngest girl sat on Ty's left, and the woman next to her had to be Jake's mom. That left Andrea, the older sister, on the end, nearest me. I could only make out long brown hair about the shade of Jake's.

Temptation won out over common sense. I entered the small room and sat down in the chair closest to the door, saying a prayer for Jake's recovery and a *thank you, Lord* for non-permanent injuries. Then I prayed for Jake's family and the healing that needed to take place. I prayed for my dad, Doc, and Grandma—the family that needed to be, but instead held onto a nonsensical secret so the woman in front of me wouldn't have to admit to the scandal in her life.

Would it matter if the truth came out? If Jake was right, and his mom believed a lie, she deserved to know the truth. They all did. Wish Grandma had talked to me. Then there'd be no doubt about what happened in the past. At least in my mind. I'm sure this family accepted Gertie's story without question. Without all the facts, they had no other option.

Jake's mom turned and caught sight of me.

My mouth moved way faster than my brain. "Doc said Jake came out of surgery and is doing fine."

The woman nodded. "Yes. *Thank God.*"

"Kim, it was a leg, not a vital organ," Mr. Harris's gaze flipped between me and his wife.

Ty chuckled. He dropped his hands and, with the two girls, turned to look at me.

"Are you Ellie Mae?" Ty asked.

I swallowed hard. "I am."

He and Andrea smiled. The younger girl, fourteen maybe, with bangs nearly covering her eyes, showed no expression. Dad looked friendly, but Kim looked as if she wanted to pop the top off a dandelion stem with my head as the flower. Was she being a lawyer or a mom looking to lay blame?

"Just so you're aware," Kim said, "the officers said the accident was the fault of that Reid fellow. He's responsible for all of the damages. So, if you're thinking about a lawsuit, you won't have a leg to stand on."

The comment was a dig at hill people. A stereotype

meant to imply we were nothing but lowlife money grubbers. Heat rose from my toes and burned inside my skull as I met Mrs. Harris's gaze square on.

Be the bigger person, Ellie. Don't do it.

But those accusatory brown eyes drilled me with contempt, and I felt the words leave my mouth before I checked them.

"Why would I sue Jake? He didn't do anything wrong. And Jaxon Reid has already paid. After I shot him, he fell and broke his neck. I hardly expect any of us to get a single penny from whatever assets he had, but where he's at, he'll definitely be held accountable. In the meantime, it'll be Doc's insurance and my dad covering the cost of things. That is how these things are handled, correct?"

My shock factor worked on four of them who reacted with wide eyes and slack jaws. Kim bristled.

"Kim, don't." Her husband laid a hand on her shoulder. "The girl's been through a lot."

She shrugged it off. "I've already spoken to your father. I believe he understands."

At least I stopped myself from smirking at her lame comeback. I looked down the line of Harris's. Ty hid his eyes with a hand, shaking his head. Andrea looked mortified.

"What she means"—Andrea stood up and came to sit beside me—"is that she's happy you weren't severely injured. I'm Andrea, by the way."

"I'm Ty." He extended his hand across the two rows of chairs separating us. I stretched and shook it with my left hand. Ty's smile matched Jake's, but none of their eyes matched his kindness. "This is Janey, the youngest. She's thirteen. Our Mom, Kim, and Dad, Felix."

Felix nodded. "We *are* glad you're okay."

I wanted to say it was nice to meet them but thought I might come off sounding hypocritical.

An awkward silence ensued. Thankfully, a nurse cracked the door. "Ellie Mae, can you come back to your room, please? You have someone here to see you, and the doctor will be in soon. I think he's looking to write discharge orders."

Standing slowly, I adjusted my robe then wrapped an arm around my ribs. I wanted to tell his mom so many things, but she would reject me and probably resent the fact I knew anything about her life. Still, this might be my only chance.

One hand on the IV pole, I looked her in the eye and prayed my feelings wouldn't overshadow my words. "You should know Doc nearly died grieving for Gertie. Jake saved his life by coming up here to be with him."

Mrs. Harris's taut face, and her rigid, unfriendly stature as she looked down her nose at me, dredged up unfiltered and envious feelings. I lost my battle with self-control. "I know you think Doc is my Grandpa, but I hadn't heard a word about it until Jake told me. If it's true, then Doc chose you instead of my dad."

I should have stopped, but there was no one to scowl at me or clamp a hand over my mouth. "It's how he showed his love for you because he already gave you a home, a life, his devotion. And because of his love for you, I didn't get to have a grandpa . . ." Only I did. Doc had always been there for me. I just didn't know why. Until now. Doc had willingly inserted himself in our lives the only way he knew how.

Steam rolled out of me like a balloon letting out air. I wanted to wilt to the floor.

I turned to leave but paused at the door. I remembered

how Jake wished his mom could wipe out her bitterness. He wanted to help her find peace.

For Jake, I said, "Doc's a forgiving man. He's the most honest and fair person I know. Y'all should talk to him. I think he would like that."

"He had an affair with your grandmother." Her voice, slick with confidence, meant to intimidate. But it's hard to be intimidated when the truth's on your side.

"Kim, not here! Not now." Felix nearly jumped out of his seat.

I held my ground, one hand on my IV pole, the other on the door. "My dad was born before Doc even married Gertie, and while he might have loved my grandma, he never acted on it. And he did love Gertie. I saw it growing up. I watched them interact every day."

I made eye contact with each of the family, sorry they missed out on a relationship with a good man. Then I slipped out the door and shuffled down the hall, my muscles screaming at me to lie down.

"Ellie Mae."

I turned. Andrea jogged after me. "That was awesome. All of us have tried to tell Mom to let the past be the past. Move forward and be happy with the family she has, but she's bent on finding fault. Which is why she mentioned that bit about the lawsuit. It's how she thinks."

"I understand. It's okay." I still disliked her.

As I shuffled down the hall, Andrea slipped an arm over my shoulders. A couple inches taller, she looked down as a sly grin crossed her face. "You should also know Jake's really into you."

A little heat crept up my neck. "Not after he hears about this. Has he told you how blunt I can be? Comes from being raised by a single dad who spends all day with animals."

And the frustration of being on the tail end of family secrets.

Andrea lightly squeezed my shoulder. "He said you tell it like it is. I think we'll get along well."

Doubtful. Ten minutes in my company and Andrea would wish she'd kept her distance. For Jake, I swallowed my opinion and gave her a tight, agreeable smile.

As I passed through my hospital room doorway, Simsy stood from where'd she been sitting next to the window. I closed the door.

Her large, dark brown eyes roamed over my face and body. Gray hairs straggled along the sides of her face. "Lord of Heaven and Earth. I wasn't sure what kind of shape you'd be in. Your daddy filled me in on everything except how you ended up on my doorstep."

"The one answer I can't give you." I shuffled past her with my IV pole and scooted onto the bed, thankful for a friendly face after being cold-shouldered by Mrs. Harris. But seriously, what had I expected from Jake's mom?

"Judging by the way you smelled, either the garbage collectors dropped you off or . . . maybe the Nun'Yunu'Wi?" She lifted a brow, tipping her head to one side as she placed the folding chair next to the bed.

"The female. She . . . she found me, saved me from Jaxon. I lost consciousness once she picked me up. That's all I remember." I scrunched my brow. "That smell . . . I forgot about it. Disgusting. What did the EMT's say?"

"By the time they arrived I had rubbed you down with rosemary. That and the night air took away a good bit of the stink."

I laughed and winced, wrapping an arm around my middle. Never had I ever been rubbed down with rosemary.

"I was afraid they might ask too many questions. I'm sorry for what you went through, but, Ellie Mae, this proves you did something right. The Nun'Yunu'Wi wouldn't have helped you unless they felt a connection."

Excitement bubbled inside me. "I'd been circling their cave like Mom used to do, hanging out in an area where they could see me. You think they recognized me as Mom?"

She shook her head. "I doubt it, but they might've been curious, wondering what you were up to. They probably sensed the familiarity and that you weren't a threat."

"The blood." I sat up taller, eyes widening.

Simsy tipped her head in question.

"My blood. I left a long trail of it when I fell last week. Then again last night."

"Ahh, so they did recognize you."

"As what?"

"Just what you are. A friend who wants to interact. But they know you aren't your momma. In fact, your daddy asked if I'd come talk to you about her upbringing. He thinks understanding her motivation to work with the Nun'Yunu'Wi might release you from any obligation to follow in her footsteps."

I narrowed my eyes, almost certain his motivation for staying silent was a bigger secret than Mom's motivation for working with the Bigfoot. "Why isn't he talking to me about it instead?"

"*Hmpf!* There's a good question that's gotten me into trouble more than once. I won't go guessing at his reasoning.

Neil doesn't understand you're called to this life. It's in your blood. Or maybe he does, and that's why he made me promise not to say anything to you before."

"What's the big secret?" I pushed a piece of wayward hair out of my eyes and settled into my pillow.

"Davis was my family's name. My momma was half Cherokee. Carl's parents were both part Cherokee. They moved up this way from Virginia and settled in southern Clay County. For generations the Simms' and Davis' worked to protect the Nun'Yunu'Wi, so when your momma came into our care, she was introduced to them. And there was no keeping her away. She took to those critters like coons to a corncrib. Wasn't a summer day she didn't spend camping out, learning everything possible about the way they lived. Sometimes she even traveled with them. It was her way. I think what your daddy wanted you to know, what he couldn't admit out loud, was that the Nun'Yunu'Wi was also her family. This gave her an advantage when it came to working with them."

"An advantage I don't have." I processed her words, visualizing my mom at a young age interacting with the Bigfoot. I knew the Simms's found Mom in the barn when she was about five years old. She had been huddled under an empty feed sack with a broken leg, feverish, and near starved to death. No one knew how she got there. Simsy and Carl called a doctor-friend who came out and set her leg.

Authorities speculated Mom's parents had died because she was never reported missing. Jodi Simms wasn't even her real name. The doctor agreed hill people took care of their own, so he helped the Simms's work with children's services to provide foster care.

"I just couldn't see putting that baby in a place where

she couldn't be out in the hills and forests. Best decision Carl and I ever made, but your daddy doesn't agree. He feels like your momma missed out on all sorts of opportunities. And he might be right. But she wouldn't have been any good locked up in a foster home with a bunch of other kids. She was too independent, too wild for society."

I wasn't sure I agreed being isolated from society was a good thing. Maybe if some of Mom's wildness had been tamed, she wouldn't have ventured off alone so much.

Both of Simsy's sons warned me that becoming involved with the Nun'Yunu'Wi would be all-consuming and steal my life. They agreed with Dad, but they also respected Mom's wishes. And she had wanted me to follow in her footsteps. There was no way I'd get sucked in to doing something I didn't want to do, but the idea of getting close and interacting with the Nun'Yunu'Wi gave me a thrill greater than I could imagine.

Simsy looked like she expected me break out of the hospital and run into the hills. "What do you plan to do next?"

I glanced at the door. All was quiet so I grinned. "I want to go see them. Get close. See if I can talk with them." Chills ran up and down my arms. "Until the female picked me up and carried me to safety, I didn't think I stood a chance of interacting with them. I was so scared at first." I recounted the experience Jake and I had our first time out and how I expected to see the monster from my dreams. "But now I'm intrigued."

Simsy clapped her hands together and touched them to her lips. "Your momma hoped you'd carry on her legacy. Everything she did was to protect the Nun'Yunu'Wi. They were her life."

The words pricked at my heart, and my excitement took

a nosedive into a knotted mess of emotions. This was exactly the kind of stuff I wanted Dad to share with me, but I never expected to feel second to the Nun'Yunu'Wi. Simsy's words hurt in the same way I hurt every time Mom walked out the door and wouldn't tell me where she was going. Was this life of protecting the Nun'Yunu'Wi really all or nothing?

I bit the inside of my cheek. Dad wanted me to have a different life. Or at least a shot at a different life. But maybe this was my life, my destiny. How would I know unless I tried? Still, I wasn't sure I liked the way Simsy presented it. I was my own person, making my own choices.

"Dad's calling Steve and Kyle. He wants me to tell them where the Nun'Yunu'Wi are at."

"You let me take care of the boys. They won't show up 'til you're ready for 'em."

That sounded fair. Visit once or twice before school started. Make up my own mind on what to do next.

"Thank you." Knowing the doctor would come anytime, I asked a question that Mom hadn't answered in any of her research. "So where did the Nun'Yunu'Wi come from? Were they just always here?'"

Simsy smiled, wistful-like. "I can only tell you what my daddy told me.

"Long, long ago the Nun'Yunu'Wi shared hunting grounds with the Native Americans. They lived together in this land long before the white man came. It's in our Cherokee blood to protect them. You mustn't forget that. You have Cherokee blood running through your veins. Same as your momma. Same as me."

I was just about to ask how she knew for certain mom had Cherokee blood in her when a knock came from the open door. A middle-aged woman in a white lab coat walked in with my nurse trailing behind.

Simsy stood and kissed me on the cheek. "My dearest. Do not give up. They're counting on you now."

With that, she walked out.

Chapter Twenty-Eight

Once home, I went straight to bed and didn't wake until noon the next day, which happened to be the Fourth of July. Dressed in blue shorts and a white tank top, I stepped down the stairs, coming to a complete stop between each one. Every muscle in my body rebelled with the movement. Grandma stood in the kitchen, busy as usual.

"Morning." I shuffled to the fridge for my antibiotic, pushing my hair back out of my eyes as I opened the door.

"Morning, sweetheart. How are ya?" She pressed ground beef into patties between her hands.

I held up two bottles of medicine. "Ready for breakfast."

"There's some juice in the fridge, and eat a banana, but don't eat too much. Your daddy fired up the grill. Ethan's coming over for a hamburger."

"Rebecca coming, too?"

"Maybe this evening. I believe she and your dad might be headed over to Rick Matthews's ranch for a party."

I rubbed one gritty eye after the other, sensing a need to share the conversation I had with Jake's family before someone else beat me to it. Doc and Grandma deserved to know what presumptions I made public. I also wanted to end this stupid charade. Surely, there was no longer a need to keep Grandma and Doc's past relationship a secret, but I needed to wait on Doc.

I slipped on a pair of flip-flops and carried my juice outside. Dad had pulled the grill onto the cement pad in front of the pole barn along with a couple lawn chairs and cleaned the grate with a long-handled brush.

"Need a hand?"

"You have one to spare?" He lifted his gaze.

I looked down and wiggled the fingers of my casted hand. "Nope."

"Then I guess not. How are you feeling?"

Like a load of crap. "A little sore and tired, but otherwise okay. Heard you're going to a party tonight."

"Maybe. Unless you want us to stay home."

"No way. You deserve a break."

He tossed a sympathetic look my way. "Ready to slow things down a bit?"

"Yes! Good day for a nap in the sun." I tipped my head back, eyes closed, and absorbed the warmth on my face.

"Sleep would do you good."

I relaxed, contemplating which of the million questions in my mind I wanted to ask Dad first. Or whether I should leave it alone for now. A shadow glided across my eyelids. I cracked my eyelids and watched the red-shouldered hawk skim beneath the blue sky, circle, and land on top of the light down at the barn housing the animals.

"It's like he knows I took his mate. I've seen him three times now."

Dad looked from the bird to me. "He's probably confused. His job is to feed their little ones, but the nest is empty. Too early to migrate. He's not sure what to do with himself."

"Sad."

We both watched the bird, then I cleared my throat. "Throwing focus on the drugs to avoid talk about the Bigfoot was brilliant. How did you know Jaxon was growing marijuana?" I lifted my glass of juice and swallowed a couple gulps.

"JT. When we talked about how Jaxon died, he told me about the drugs. Apparently, last time Caleb was in town, he told JT that Jaxon was growing the stuff at his cabin."

"So you and JT came up with the story that Jaxon wanted to shut me up."

"That's right."

Even though I was touched by everyone's concern, my insides churned with regret. "Dad, Caleb isn't safe. Whoever Jaxon's working with will figure out he squealed."

Dad closed the grill and hung up the brush. "Maybe, but that's a risk he's willing to take."

I swallowed hard, not sure I could accept other people sticking their neck out for me. "How'd JT figure out it was Jaxon who hit us?"

"The abandoned truck was registered to someone he recently towed. Truck never made it to the intended garage."

"I knew they weren't smart enough to cover their trail."

"I'm sure Jaxon figured his uncle would cover for him. Especially if there was some profit to be made." He spat out the words.

I set my glass on the grill stand next to dad's iced tea and slowly pulled a leg up so my bare foot rested on the fabric of the chair. When pain from the movement subsided, I spoke slowly, praying with each word that Dad wouldn't get mad.

"Dad, when Jaxon had me out there, he implied that he killed mom and you were paid to keep quiet about how she died. Is that true?"

The pinched expression returned as he looked toward the hawk posted on the light pole then turned his sad green eyes back on me. There was a lot of emotion and maybe some extra moisture in them. I almost relented and apologized for bringing it up, but he owed me an explanation.

"I wasn't bought off to keep quiet about your mom's cause of death. I was blackmailed. If I had told anyone the truth, Reid would've hurt you."

I went cold. "So Mom was murdered?"

Dad nodded.

Jaxon more or less admitted to it, but hearing Dad confirm the truth ripped my heart wide open.

"Your mom had been leading him and some others away from the Nun'Yunu'Wi. She had texted me her location along with pictures of the people following her and details about Reid. I should have forwarded it to the police right then. Instead, I put together some men and we went after her to help, but we arrived too late. Reid threatened your life if I disclosed any information to the police. I had to give him the evidence."

"You lied to the police?"

"I couldn't protect you any other way. You would have come up missing, and no one would have been the wiser. And that almost happened."

I watched him, tired eyes, cheeks weatherworn from keeping up with the outdoors. "You feel responsible for her death. That's why you never talk about her, isn't it?" His avoidance made sense.

"That's where I go every year. You wanted to know. I visit the cliff, trying to somehow reconcile what happened." His eyes took on a sheen, and it caused an ache in my throat. I swallowed the knot. "Dad, you didn't do anything wrong. You tried to save her."

"I should have insisted she stay home or at least gone with her."

I stood and wrapped my arms around his middle. "It's not your fault. You couldn't have stopped her. And if you'd died, too, where would I be?"

He gently squeezed my shoulder with one arm. "Ellie, if I'd known Jaxon had any part in this, I would've never let you look at those footprints."

My mouth fell open as I recalled Jaxon's arrogant grin the day he gave me the lock. I snapped it shut. No way would I say anything and place more burden on Dad. But Jake was in the hospital with a broken leg, his scholarship on the line, because I didn't say anything. Because I didn't want anyone to stop me from doing what I wanted.

I gnawed at the inside of my lower lip. Is this what I wanted? For everyone else to pay for my poor decisions?

"Dad"—I swallowed hard, dreading his disappointment—"the lock came from Jaxon. I took him the vet bill the day the footprints appeared, and he gave me the lock. He wanted me to tell you to call him. I told him I would, but then I didn't want to because I was mad. And I didn't want you to stop me from investigating."

Dad's mouth fell open. He tipped his head back and covered his eyes with the heels of his hands. I watched, scared I'd really messed up.

"I'm sorry! I didn't think it was important at the time. Are you mad?"

He dropped his hands and glanced at me. "I'm not mad,

but I could've maybe prevented this." He pointed an open hand at me, raising and lowering it to take in my injuries.

"Telling you where the lock came from wouldn't have changed anything. I would've asked more questions about Jaxon, and he would've blackmailed you in some other way."

Dad's face softened as he gazed back at the hawk. "You're right. When those footprints were found over at Hansen's, a part of me shut down. That evening, I started reliving a nightmare. I should've been the one out there looking at those prints with you, not Jake."

I shook my head. "You weren't ready. But it's not too late. You can go out with me now."

Dad returned his gaze to mine and shook his head. "I hear what you're saying, but I can't put us in any more danger."

I wrapped my casted arm around my middle. "Did you already call Steve and Kyle?"

"They'll be here tomorrow."

"Tomorrow! I thought I'd have a week." I couldn't believe he wasn't even giving me a shot at this.

"Once you're healed you can visit. Go out with them. But take it easy for now so you don't do some real damage to yourself. I'm going for the burgers. Can we just avoid this topic for the rest of today?"

I nodded silently and watched as the hawk shifted on the pole and jumped into the sky. Shading my eyes against the sun, I looked on as he circled and disappeared over the hills.

Grandma had spread out lunch on the dining room table. After I washed, I slipped onto my chair and measured my words carefully, waiting until everyone filled their plates with burger, potato salad, and baked beans. Then I started.

"I have a question. Something I cannot live another minute without knowing."

Dad shot me a side glance. I placed a hand on his arm. "It's not that dramatic, but it's important to me."

"What's on your mind, Ellie Mae?" Grandma smiled sweetly. I silently prayed this would go well.

"Should I step out?" Doc asked, humor visible in his face.

I shook my head. "No, because it involves you. I'm gonna get straight to the point because, well..." I shrugged. "It's easier. I hope you'll answer me right out, too."

I took a deep breath and focused on Grandma. "Is Doc my grandpa?"

Dad choked on his iced tea, and Grandma became serious as she carefully set her fork beside her plate.

Doc chuckled. "Ellie Mae, you never disappoint."

Twisting my fingers together in my lap, I waited. The three looked at each other as if they weren't sure who should be the bearer of such news.

"Okay. Let me make this easier. Grandma, is Dad Doc's son?" She sat stoic while Dad glared at me. Doc looked down at the floor, fighting a grin. Their hesitation spoke volumes, and I felt a measure of satisfaction at Dad and Grandma's discomfort. Served them right for not telling me the truth after Gertie died. Still, their hem-hawing seemed ridiculous.

"Grandma, I don't mean to disrespect you, but please tell me the truth. I don't want to keep speculating over the gossip I've heard, and if I have a grandpa, I want to celebrate."

She gave me a cross look of affection, telling me she loved me even when I caused trouble.

"Truth is, I had a run-in with Jake's mom yesterday. Well, the whole family, and the subject came up." I put a hand to my chest and looked at Doc. "I may have misspoken when I accused you of choosing Kim over my dad."

I glanced at Dad who drilled me with a hard look. I think I saw smoke rolling out his ears, but I pressed the issue because if they didn't start treating me like I mattered, I would tear my hair out.

"And I'm sorry, but Kim insulted all of us. I had to speak up. I hurt most for you." I looked at Doc. "You don't deserve to be treated the way she's treated you. We're a better family to you than she is."

Doc started to speak, but Grandma cut him off. "Ellie Mae, Doc is your grandpa and your dad's father." Her gaze fell to her lap. Doc reached over and squeezed her hand, a smile spreading across his face.

I got up and went around the table and hugged her. "Thank you for telling me." Finally! I wanted to throw my hands in the air, but I felt Dad's disapproving glare. Not to mention the pain from such movement would send me to my knees.

I moved to stand before Doc and placed a hand on his shoulder. "How many times in my life did you almost spill the beans?"

"Every day, Ellie Mae."

I gave him as hard a hug as my body would allow. "Thank you for being in my life. You have always been the grandpa I was never allowed to have." I repeated the words he used yesterday. I pulled back but kept my hands on his shoulders. "I love you. I hope you aren't disappointed in me."

I sat down and frowned at Dad. "How long have you known?"

He frowned back, likely frustrated because I pressured my elders into telling the truth.

Grandma sniffed. I looked over in time to see her dab at her eyes with her napkin.

"Grandma, what's wrong?" Her sadness broke my heart. I didn't intend to hurt her.

"I've caused a lot of unhappiness. Because of me, you've all had to sacrifice and suffer at one time or another. I'm so sorry." She scooted away from the table and went upstairs.

I followed, partly to escape Dad's scathing glare, but mostly because I couldn't stand to see grandma hurting.

"Grandma?" I gently pushed open her bedroom door. She sat on the edge of her perfectly made bed, wiping her face with a tissue. A knot formed in my throat. I went over and sat beside her on the multicolored quilt. When I was younger and had a bad dream or missed my mom, Grandma let me climb in bed with her. She would offer me tidbits of wisdom and make me believe life would turn out "pretty as a posey."

I placed my arms around her. "I love you, Grandma. I'm sorry I hurt you."

"It's not you who did the hurting. I was selfish by keeping facts from you, just so I wouldn't have to dredge up the memories."

"But I forced it on ya."

"You were right to do it, Ellie. You came to me a while back asking questions, and I wouldn't give you answers."

"It's okay. You've been my rock through the worst times in my life. You could never do anything that would make me feel ashamed or think less of you." I rubbed her back.

She dabbed at her eyes with her hanky. "There're so many things I would have done differently had I known a single one of my family would be hurt. Things a young girl doesn't realize will impact life later on. I tell ya, our defining moments are found in the darkest corners of our lives. I thought finding out I was pregnant at sixteen and marrying a man I didn't love had been my darkest place. Now, I'm convinced it was keeping the truth from you."

I didn't see how one compared with the other. Her father sacrificed her life to a man she didn't love. Interesting how the consequences of keeping the truth a secret hurt more than the abuse she endured.

"If you need me to say it, *I forgive you.* But I have wonderful people in my life because of you. Come back downstairs and tell me how you and Doc met and fell in love, about the dances at city hall."

"I'll do no such thing." She looked horrified, like I wanted to place her centerstage in the spotlight.

"All right," I relented. "Then just come and eat with us, but no more secrets. You and Doc don't have to hide your feelings anymore."

Chapter Twenty-Nine

After lunch, I slipped out to Mom's office and packed my backpack. I stowed it in the four-wheeler then waited until Rebecca and Dad left for the Matthews's party. The sun was touching the tree-tops in the west when Doc left to visit Jake at the hospital and Grandma went out back to work in the garden.

Knowing the time was now or never, I changed into my hiking clothes, bandaged my cuts to keep out sweat and grime, and downed a couple painkillers. I descended the stairs and left a note on Dad's chair before grabbing my gun and slipping out the front door. Grandma would hear the four-wheeler, but she wouldn't be able to stop me.

I hated to disappoint Dad and cause more worry for everyone, but Simsy's boys were coming tomorrow. I didn't have a lot of faith Simsy would be able to change their minds. Right or wrong, I needed to go out, or I'd regret it. Studying Mom's journals, walking in her shoes—literally—helped me understand her thought process. Simsy helped me understand Mom's motivation. Now, I just needed to experience what Mom wanted to share with me—a meaningful face-to-face encounter.

Around dinner time, I sat down near the cliff's edge at Lucas Gorge and placed the gun at my side.

Sweat broke out on my brow and back even though I was only wearing a lightweight flannel over a T-shirt. I pulled the outer shirt off and took my phone out of my back jeans pocket. One bar. I sent off a message to Jake.

Me: How's your leg?

I regretted my tears and the pity party I forced on him last night. He had been right. Even if I didn't see him the rest of the summer, it wouldn't be the end of the world. The thought hurt, but I'd survive.

I pulled Mom's Bigfoot language book out of my backpack and studied the knocks, grunts, and hand motions. An hour later, I exchanged the book for my sketchpad as the sun touched the ridge off in the distance. Another hour passed. My stomach rumbled, and I guessed it at about seven o'clock. Finishing the details of the mom and child picture, I considered it quality first-grader work, but that didn't matter.

Still no text from Jake. Probably busy with his family. My back grew stiff, and my rib ached. I put down the drawing pad, bent side to side, rolled my shoulders, and leaned back on my good hand. Lifting my face to the breeze, I closed my eyes. The drone of cicadas rose and fell. I joined their chorus and sang what I knew of a Carrie Underwood song, picturing my mom as she sang while relaxing in the porch swing or driving in the car. I heard her voice in mine as I sang "Mama's Song," one I'd memorized after she died.

Memories of Mom and her sweet voice left me refreshed and happy. Despite my ups and downs, I decided no better place existed than right here, right now. Mom felt so close. And when I opened my eyes, I wondered if her spirit wasn't nearby because one of the Nun'Yunu'Wi had left the cave and stared right at me.

My mouth went slack. I stared back in shock at the larger male and moved slowly until I sat upright. He waited. Three, four, five seconds. We watched one another until I remembered he expected me to acknowledge him.

Was I doing this? Taking the risk? All the studying, the trekking, the hunting. The questioning, the arguing. It culminated to this moment, and I wanted to shout and scream and throw up.

Pushing to my knees, I shoved my phone in my back pocket then tied my shirt around my waist. Everything else I stored in my backpack except for the picture of the momma and child.

Down in the gorge, the Nun'Yunu'Wi stood tall, waiting for my response to his obvious recognition of me. I lifted my casted right hand as if to wave, then turned my hand and placed my palm over my heart.

He watched, stiffened, and stretched to his full height as a man preparing to square off in a fight. Only this wasn't a man, and his reason for exerting himself was dominance. At my elevated position, he possibly felt threatened. I turned to the side so as not to look at him straight on and sank to my haunches. Then I stood halfway, partially facing him, made the gesture, and sank to the side once again.

I heard him repetitively and loudly snort from the distance. The action wasn't hostile. Mom speculated at uncertainty, curiosity. She believed they would have interacted this way around their own kind. And in a world where they might be the only living beasts of their kind, it made sense they would accept Mom, others, and possibly me as their own.

I made the gesture again and waited.

The snorting continued, and then in one fluid motion, he lifted his arm and crossed it over his chest.

My breath caught. The movement wasn't distinct and orderly as my movements had been, but more as an ape might do—sloppy movements made in haste.

But I saw it.

A confirmation.

Deep breaths. You can do this. I slipped on my backpack.

What was he thinking? That I was Mom? He invited me to come share their space, but why? Shivering anxiously from head to toe, I picked up my rifle and walked. I lost sight of the cave for a while and paused as I took a few deep breaths, coaxing my heart to calm down.

I retrieved my phone and texted Jake with, "We did it." I added in a separate message, "I'll be as careful as I can. Pain in my side isn't too bad."

I climbed to the bottom of the gorge. The large patch of Kudzu descending from the northern slope ended at the base of the cliff. I side-stepped to stay out of the roping plant and stifled a gag over the rotting flesh of the cows as I hid my rifle in a bush not yet covered by the vine. Giving a wide berth, I all but tiptoed as I rounded to the front of the cave and stopped next to the creek that gathered in a pool of water just beneath the shelf outside the cave entrance. I pushed away the images from my dreams, reminding myself those figments of imagination held no ground in reality.

The cave opened ten maybe twelve feet above the canyon floor, pitch black. The size of a single-car garage door, the space looked deep enough to offer absolute cover.

About twenty yards from the larger-than-life male—what was he, nine, ten-feet tall!—I placed the picture on a boulder. I backed away, forcing myself to breathe evenly and keep my eyes on his enormous feet.

He grunted a call to his mate. I knew this because Jake and I had listened to one of Mom's CD's and laughed hysterically as we tried to mimic the different clicks, knocks, and grunts.

I stood still and observed, lifting only my eyes as the female and her young emerged from the cave. She knelt down on her haunches and scrutinized me. The teenager did the same but stayed behind his momma's back. Entranced, I studied her feminine features—softer, less protrusive brow, pretty eyes, and long dark lashes. I lifted my right, red-casted hand and crossed it over my chest. She looked at the big male, grunted and motioned to the picture.

He kept his eyes on me as he jumped down into the pool of water then advanced, slightly hunched, swinging his arms for balance, but not as drastic as an ape. He picked up the paper, smelled it, and carried it to the female. Instead of handing it to her, he reached up and helped her and the baby in her arms down. Then he helped the older child as naturally as any father would help a child.

Amazing. Like he was introducing me to his family.

The female snatched the picture away from him, also smelled it, and cocked her head as she looked from the paper to me. She squinted, either confused or in recognition—the way a squirrel looks when trying to cross the road in front of a car. To this female, I looked and smelled familiar—I drew pictures, sang, and called them using familiar methods, but I wasn't Jodi. I was the bloodied girl who circled the camp and whom this momma saved from a bad man.

I offered a series of grunts and clicks hopefully translating: "Jodi—my mother. Jodi dead."

They looked at me, and the male's eyes dilated, a sign of anxiety. He snorted loud and quickly. I gave them a second message, hoping they wouldn't mistake my intentions and squash me like an intrusive bug.

"I live here. I—protect you."

The mother walked toward me, but the male let out a low guttural sound and put his arm out. She pushed it away and stood before me, a foot-and-a-half taller than me. She smelled foul, like the rot they'd been eating, but I didn't move. I took in every inch of her coarse reddish-brown fur hanging straight and neat, well groomed. Her face and hands were dark brownish gray, leathery. Long fingers and toes. She lifted a hand and placed a hot, rough-as-sandpaper palm against my cheek. My heart pulsated, vibrating through me as her fingers wrapped around the back of my head. She could easily break my neck like she had Jaxon's, but the look in her eyes, the tilt of her head, showed nothing but curiosity.

She touched me with a gentleness that felt caring and nostalgic. Motherly. Tears pooled in my eyes. I cautiously reached out and touched her face.

The male grunted sharply. She dropped her hand and returned the grunt. Turning, she handed the baby to the older child, who watched with fully dilated pupils as he wrapped long arms around the infant. The female scaled the rock wall to the ledge outside the cave and disappeared, returning as quickly. She jumped down and walked back to where I stood rooted in place and handed me a child-sized, beaded comb, no bigger than a matchbook, with half the beads missing. She uttered the sound for mother.

I gasped and flipped over the comb in my hand. Was she saying this comb belonged to my mother? Obviously from a time when the Simms's first introduced her. Why did they still have it? Overwhelmed, more tears slid down my cheeks at the unbelievable realization. We were communicating . . . about my mom.

I held the comb in a fist next to my chest and stretched out my casted hand, palm up, as a sign of appreciation. She softly tapped my fingers with hers.

The male lifted his eyes to the ridge, grunted with urgency, and pulled his family into the cave.

I shifted my gaze upward and felt my blood run cold. Two men stood motionless on the cliff where I had been sitting. One a stranger, but next to him stood Todd McGraff, a rifle propped against his shoulder.

Chapter Thirty

As darkness edged in, my heart pounded fast and hard. The men watched, still as ducks on a morning pond. No way they followed. Unless they came in from another direction. From the north maybe? But not without exact coordinates.

"Well, Jaxon Reid, even from the grave you did it."

The men pointed in various directions as they talked to one another. I glanced inside the cave and saw nothing but black. The family of four made absolutely no sound. My eyes went back to Todd, holding up the binoculars. He scanned the landscape, while the other guy talked on his cell phone.

I texted Dad.

> Me: Need help. Coordinates are on your recliner. Men on the cliff. They have BF and me trapped. Thirty minutes until they reach us.

I slipped the phone in my back pocket. He'd freak, but I didn't have a choice.

Thirty minutes. Maybe longer. The first time Jake and I found our way down into the gorge it took about forty-five minutes. Today, I had made it in twenty.

So, what were my options? Run and take myself to safety? That's what Dad would want me to do. I'd covered this area enough to know my way around. I could easily hide. But if I didn't stay and intervene, these creatures would be killed. That was no more an option than hiding. So that meant I needed to stay.

Glancing around at my surroundings, I strategized. Sweat ran down my forehead, into my eyes, and stung. I wiped it away with the tail of my flannel. Somehow, I needed to communicate to the Bigfoot my plan so they would stay inside.

Mom hunted with them, she warned them, but to my knowledge, she'd never fought people alongside them. Would they stay hidden? Would they trust me? I faced the black mouth of the cave and offered a series of grunts, hopefully warning them to hide and that I would protect them. Was that enough?

I ran to the bushes and retrieved my gun, praying help would arrive soon. With the creek flowing off to my left, I waded across the waist-high pool of water and climbed up the rocky ledge to the mouth of the cave. Laying my gun near the opening, I slowly crept into the cave, half-hunched. Facing the dark shapes huddled along the back wall, I prayed my discreet approach came off as unthreatening. I couldn't see a thing, so I used the flashlight on my phone and dimmed it as much as possible.

Moving slowly, I placed the light on the cave floor and signed the gesture for family and went to the mother. Light from the entrance reflected off her dark eyes. I stared at that reflection. Slowly, I stretched out my arm and placed a hand to her cheek. She returned the motion. I placed a hand to the cheek of the baby. The momma picked up the baby's hand and placed it on my cheek.

Swallowing hard, I approached the male. I tipped my head forward and stretched out my hand, palm up, avoiding eye contact. Standing before him, vulnerable, caused my knees to weaken. The female snorted and whined. The male touched my hand, ever so softly. Acceptance. I moved to the young male. Mom had no notes about how to approach young Nun'Yunu'Wi. Neither the mother nor father made a sound or gesture. Not sure what to do, I decided to err on the side of caution so I didn't spook him. I tipped my head forward and held out my hand. The mother made the same sounds, and he lightly touched my hand. Acceptance.

I sidestepped over to the cave wall. My eyes had adjusted to the dark enough I could make out the pile of bones, sticks, and rocks. As Mom's drawings indicated, I picked up three sticks and laid them in a triangle design, stacking four rocks in the center. The symbol for family. I added another rock and touched my chest. Then I took two matching pieces of wood, resembling a pair of canes and banged them in a series of Morse code-type taps, hoping to communicate my promise to protect them.

Family. Protect.

I turned and exited the cave, opened my backpack, and stored the child's comb. I retrieved four shotgun shells and put two in each of my jeans pockets. I had four in my gun and four in the sidesaddle. My phone buzzed.

> Dad: On our way. Keep yourself hidden.

No way would Dad get here in time. We had maybe ten minutes.

Sorry, Dad. I have to do this. They're family.

I put the binoculars around my neck, grabbed my gun, and climbed to the top of the cave where larger rocks and trees allowed me to hide. Up here, I had the advantage.

Todd and his sidekick crossed the canyon. One pointed at the cow carcasses. When they stood within earshot, I yelled. "I suggest you stop right there." Both carried high-powered rifles. Thank God, they couldn't see me.

They stopped and looked around. Todd spoke up. "We don't mean no trouble, Ellie. We come to have a look. That's all. Don't want anyone to get hurt."

"Turn around and go back, and no one *will* get hurt, Todd."

Cell phone man made another call.

Todd hollered, "Why don't you come out here and talk with us a bit?"

I rolled my eyes. *So you can shoot me and get on with your hunt.* I aimed at the ground between their feet and fired, gritting my teeth as the butt of the gun kicked back into my shoulder. Buckshot hit the ground, sending up particles of leaves and dirt. Both men sashayed back two steps.

"Ain't necessary to shoot at us!" Todd scowled in my direction.

Their eyes roved the area, searching. I wasn't about to speak, but I pumped the shotgun and released a shell ready to fire again if they moved any closer. They stepped toward the canyon wall in an effort to hide but couldn't get close enough to be out of sight. The kudzu stretched out too far and too high. It'd take them an hour to get through it, and then I'd shoot them right off the side of the ledge as they tried to ascend.

I heard them talking about what they should do.

"Wait her out . . . others . . . hour."

I texted Dad.

> Me: There are others out here somewhere.

I put my phone in my back pocket and lifted my gun. The men stood in the open contemplating their next move.

"Unless you both want to lose your lives right here, my best advice is to turn around and live to hunt another day. I have no problem defending myself against two grown men threatening my life."

"We aren't threatening your life. Calm down. Come on out here and talk civilly."

"I know what you're after, Todd, and it's not happening today. Leave or you'll force me to shoot ya."

Swear words flew between them as they turned around and headed back toward the ridge. Cell phone man walked with the phone to his ear. I lost sight of them for a short while, but they came back into view as both stopped halfway up the climb to the ridge. The man on the phone shook his head vigorously. He pointed to a spot behind me.

I turned, and on the opposite ridge, near the place I had trekked, fell, and broke my wrist, a party of four men hiked our way. I closed my eyes and tried to slow my breathing. I wiped sweat from my forehead. These men were at a higher elevation and would be able to see me. I scuttled down the rocks and hid inside the mouth of the cave. Now I couldn't see the other two.

Please, Dad, hurry. I looked back at the Nun'Yunu'Wi, the only sound the low rumble of the male. I hummed softly, intending to soothe the tension and ease the pain burning through my right side. Just muscles stretching beyond their comfort. Nothing major.

It'd take about thirty minutes for the four men to reach the cave. They'd have to cross the creek at its deepest point unless they traveled to the north or south. Dad would arrive sooner. Maybe the men to the west could see me, but they wouldn't have time to reach me.

In a few minutes, they'd be out of sight, forced down into a ravine before they headed upward again. I climbed back on top of the cave and located Todd and the other guy back on the ridge. Others stood with them. I took out my binoculars. Dad, Rebecca, JT, and Travis. Dad looked my way, Rebecca at his side. I pulled out my phone.

> Me: I'm on top of the cave. 4 hunters to the west. They haven't crossed the river yet. They've lost sight of the canyon. When u get the guys out of here, I'll take the BF South.

> Dad: No, Ellie. They might think you want to leave with them. Come up here. We'll take care of the others.

> Me: I have to. U can't stop the others without more help. Go home. Wait for my call. I love u. See u soon.

I waited until JT and Travis left the area. The men to the west wouldn't be visible again for quite a while. We had plenty of time to move south if the Nun'Yunu'Wi would follow me.

I reentered the cave and carefully moved my hands, motioning for them to come out.

"Follow." I clicked and tapped a stick simultaneously

then hooted in the same way the female did at Jaxon's cabin when she indicated there was danger nearby. Then I grunted in an almost hostile manner. "Go, now! Follow!"

The three of them stood. The mother placed the small child on her back. I walked out and made the sound again. I slipped my backpack over my shoulders, ignoring the pull. I left the bulky shotgun.

The family emerged from the cave. I climbed down and dropped into the cool, waist-high water, trudged through, then took off running on dry ground, calling for them to follow. Over and over, I screamed the sound, moving as fast as my feet would carry me over the uneven terrain.

I heard the splash of water then felt the ground vibrate as large pounding feet picked up speed behind me. I turned my head as the male Nun'Yunu'Wi grabbed the older child and threw him on his back. The younger child held tightly to the mother. My backpack pulled against my shoulders as the Nun'Yunu'Wi wrapped his entire hand around it. I gripped the straps to keep it from being ripped off and realized my mistake. A few more strides and my feet left the ground.

I turned and caught sight of my dad standing on the cliff. Rebecca held her hands over her mouth. Then I landed with a thud on the hairy back, clinging for my life with one hand and a few fingers.

Chapter Thirty-One

I flopped like a ragdoll in the wind, wincing with each step the big male took. When a branch nearly took off my head, I buried my face into the giant's wiry and smelly hair and wrapped my left leg around his middle. Water splashed up when he crossed the creek and entered the thicket, heading southwest. Plastered against his back, I avoided the gauntlet of thrashing brush but lost my sense of direction.

The forest passed around me at frightening speed. My heart kept pace with the pounding of the Nun'Yunu'Wi's feet as they hit the earth. The male's arms swung as he batted aside saplings and ran through brambles without a flinch. Amazed and frightened, I clung to his fur, certain my fistful of hair pulled and hurt his skin, but he didn't appear to feel it. My grasp weakened. If only I could reach up and wrap an arm around his neck, but there wasn't opportunity to reposition. I'd fall for sure.

He kept running and running, crossing water twice more. No way were men following. The Nun'Yunu'Wi leaped over rocks and climbed steep cliffs. Those powerful arms hauling us up, up, and over a rocky ledge. Long legs catapulting down. If the male noticed our weight, it didn't slow him.

My arms and fingers burned as I tried to hang on. I glanced beside me, gritting my teeth under the strain. The young male seemed to have no problem since his long toes curled around the hair as well as his hands. And he was about ten times stronger than me.

I slipped as my hand cramped. They ran uphill, deep in brush thick with wild roses and tall thin trees. I tightened my leg around his waist, but it did nothing to ease the pain in my hand. This was going to hurt.

I fell, opened my mouth to holler, but the air left from my lungs when I smacked the ground. Thorns scratched my hands and arms as I rolled a short distance. At least I had the wherewithal to cover my face with my arms. The dense brush stopped me. I didn't roll far, and there was no vibrating pain of broken bones. Good sign.

The couple stopped, and the male started toward me. I promptly stood and swayed as all the blood rushed to my toes. I fell back to my knees, spots dancing before my eyes. With my head down, I blinked rapidly and waited for air to come. Once it did, I hollered a sound I hoped communicated, "No! Leave me alone."

Their next documented stop was about fifty miles south near the Virginia-Tennessee border. Near Steve's home—if they chose to stop there. Occasionally, they skipped a documented area and kept going to the next. If they passed up Steve's territory, I could end up in the middle of a huge forest oblivious to which state I'd landed.

I bent my head and held out my hand. He touched it quickly and sharply, not tenderly as he had earlier in the cave. Acceptance. It meant I could speak.

I motioned with my hands. Simple words. "You go. I stay. My father alive. You go. I stay. My father alive."

The adults looked at me. The older child kept out of sight on his father's back. The female whined and shuffled to where I stood. She grunted at me.

"No." I repeated the soft grunts. "My father alive. I stay." She put a hand to my face. This time I backed up a step. I lowered my head in the less intimate form of respect. "You go. Hurry. Danger. I stay."

They looked confused, so I turned and began to carefully climb my way out of the sweet-smelling sticker bushes. I didn't look back until I stood at the bottom of the hill. When I turned around, they were gone.

I sat down and took off my backpack. My entire body shook, first a tiny tremble, then an uncontrollable quake. I rubbed my arm with my left hand.

Calm down. I sucked in deep, relaxing breaths.

Then I laughed.

And laughed.

Oh. My. Sweet. Lord.

I fell backward and faced the bluish-black sky. A few stars had made an appearance. Riding on the Nun'Yunu'Wi's back had been the scariest roller coaster and kidnapping rolled into one.

"Thank you, God. Today could have ended badly, and it didn't."

I sat up. Darkness surrounded me. Where in the Appalachians was I?

I pulled my phone out of my pocket.

No service. No wonder. I sat nestled between two hills. I needed to find a high point. I plugged my phone into the portable charger, stowed it, and retrieved my flashlight. Heaving a sigh, I stood and started back up the thorny hill.

Three hours later, I called Dad.

"Ellie, where are you!? You okay?"

"I'm fine. You are *not* going to believe this."

"Try me please."

"I'm in a town called Greensburg. I'm standing across the street from a place called the Lucky Duck. I smell too rotten to go inside."

There was a thud and muffled noise.

"Dad, you there?" Hopefully he fell into a chair and not on the floor.

"Sorry. Dropped the phone. Greensburg is about ten miles as the crow flies. Are you okay?"

"Only ten miles? Felt like fifty. Yes. Physically, I'm fine. Might need a shrink, though."

"I'll be there in about thirty minutes. Sit tight."

I hung up and plopped on the window ledge of a closed attorney's office, my backpack between my feet. I'd already put on the flannel to cover my scratched arms. Sipping on a bottle of water, I watched people come and go from the bar, the smell of onion rings taunting me every time the door opened.

Thankfully, I'd only wandered about an hour before I happened upon a road. One wrong turn and I could have wandered through dark trees all night long. An hour after hitting the road, I entered Greensburg, population about a hundred. A few people cast me curious looks, so I pretended to study my phone, not really able to concentrate on anything as the evening kept replaying in my mind.

Twenty minutes later, Dad stopped along the curb. He'd broken some laws to maneuver through the mountains that quickly. I loved him for it. All bravado left me as I pushed away from the building. Hot tears threatened to burst free. I didn't care what others thought. I stood and tucked myself in Dad's arms.

"I don't think I can do that again."

He pulled back, scanned the stitches above my right brow, then opened the passenger door. "I sure don't want to see it again."

On the way home, I recounted every last detail. Dad listened and paled a little with each piece of the story.

Chapter Thirty-Two

Dad hadn't even pulled to a complete stop in front of the garage when Rebecca rushed out of the house. I climbed out of the truck, and she placed a hand on either side of my face. "You are the most courageous woman I know, but don't ever scare me like that again." She pulled me into a hug.

I hugged her back. "Don't plan on it."

I blew out a breath as I stepped through the front door. Grandma immediately smashed me in her arms. "We are gonna have a talk about this." Then she wrinkled her nose. "After you take a shower. You smell like you've been wrestling a billy goat."

Doc lifted himself off the sofa and folded me into a hug. "You all right? How'd you get all scratched up?" He touched my cheek where a thorn had found a way through my arms and nodded at the back of my good hand.

Leave it to him to notice something so trivial. "Long story, but I basically fell in a patch of wild roses. How's Jake doing?"

Doc shrugged. "His mom wouldn't let me in. She's not

allowing visitors or phone calls. Says it's too much for him right now."

"It's my fault. I shouldn't have talked to her like I did."

"No, it's not your fault. Kim's not happy unless she's in control. But don't you worry none. Jake still has a mind of his own."

"Provided she doesn't cart him off to New Orleans while he's sedated." I grimaced at my rude tone. Being patient was hard, so I changed the subject as I dug through my backpack. "Dad, look at this." My excitement built as I pulled out the comb, placing it in his hand. Resting in the center of his palm, it looked even tinier. He turned it over and studied it.

"I think I've seen this before. You go clean up. I want to check out something."

"If you're going out to the office, would you mind getting my journal off Mom's desk? I have so much I need to write down before I forget."

After my shower, I returned to the dining room and found everyone leafing through scrapbooks. The sweet apple-cinnamon smell of turnovers hung in the air, mixed with the aroma of fresh coffee. No instant decaf tonight. The maker gurgled and popped, spitting out the last bits of what my body craved.

I headed for the kitchen, but Doc was there and shooed me out. "I'll get your coffee. You go sit."

I gladly obeyed, loving my family.

"Feeling nostalgic?" I sat across from Dad.

"Look at this." He turned the album, positioned it in front of me, and tapped a picture. "I saw it over Jake's shoulder the night you two were poking around in the office."

The picture accompanied a newspaper article about the

missing girl. I hadn't honed in on the headline before. *Two-Year-Old Goes Missing After Parents Burn In House Fire.*

Two-year-old? Dad placed the comb next to the album. "It's speculated the girl died in the fire as well, but no remains were found."

The picture showed the lopsided smile of a toddler wearing a beaded comb in her thick dark hair. "Jennifer Evers." I held the hair trinket in my hand, comparing it to the one in the picture.

"Unbelievable. You think Mom was this missing girl?"

"I remember this story." Doc placed a cup of coffee next to me and spoke over my shoulder. "People scoured Clay County for weeks but never found a trace of her. Most assumed she died in the fire even though there wasn't a body. I didn't know Jodi had this article."

I lifted my eyebrows, stunned. "I'm calling Simsy. Either she found mom sooner than she's telling us or the Bigfoot did." The others sat quietly as I punched in her number.

"Hello?"

"Simsy?"

"Who's this?"

"Ellie Mae. Question for you, but first I need to tell you something." While I told her what happened to me, Doc filled cups and started a second pot of coffee while Grandma plated the apple turnovers and set them in the middle of the table. Dad and Rebecca stayed put, hanging on every word I shared.

I finished by describing the child's hair comb and how it matched the newspaper clipping. Simsy laughed, and it sounded like she clapped her hands. "You did it. I knew you could. Your momma would be so proud."

"Simsy . . ." My somber voice cut off her celebration.

"Did you really find my mom in your barn when she was five?"

The connection fell silent, all laughter gone. Cool air from the air conditioner pushed through vents in the floor buffering ticks from the mantel clock, but I still counted eight until Simsy spoke.

"Since you called and let me know about your adventure, I feel it's only fair to tell you the whole truth."

"Hold on. I'm putting you on speakerphone so Dad can hear you, too." I pointed at Doc, Grandma, and Rebecca and put a finger to my mouth. "Okay, what *really* happened with Mom?"

"Truth is, we found your momma with the Nun'Yunu'Wi when she was about five. She had a broken leg and had a terrible high fever. That's how we got her away from 'em. They knew she was near death. We carried Jodi back to the house and called ole Doc Randolph to come help us out.

"He suggested we keep her. Let Jodi ease out of running wild. But we couldn't tell anyone where we found her, so we invented a story."

With his elbow on the table, Dad's hand covered his mouth. Rebecca laid a hand on his other arm. Grandma sat quietly at the other end of the table, her eyes welling with tears. Doc stood behind her with his hands on her shoulders.

My brain tried to wrap around the slippery details. "How long was she with the Nun'Yunu'Wi, do you know? Was she the Evers girl that supposedly died or wandered off from that house fire at age two?"

"Jodi dug up that article when she was a teenager, hoping to find out where she came from. Seemed the only likely event that fit her circumstances. She tried to connect with the rest of the Evers family, but none of them cared whether she came around or not."

Dad dropped his hand onto Rebecca's. "How were you able to keep her? Didn't people wonder where she came from?"

"Back then, we lived out on Clayton's Hollow. Not many folks out that way. We didn't even let on Jodi lived with us for several more years. Got in a little hot water with the county, but Doc Randolph and his attorney helped us out."

I leaned forward on my elbows. "What was she like when you found her? I mean after the fever wore off. Was she scared? Did she accept you?"

"She was scared, and no, she didn't accept us. The only thing that kept her from running off was that leg and everyone keeping a close eye on her. After a couple days and a dozen chocolate bars, she finally understood we wasn't gonna hurt her. How could we expect anything less? The Nun'Yunu'Wi were the only family Jodi could remember. Took years for the wild tendencies to wear off enough we could take her out in public. You can't take the wild out of a child until they're ready to let go of it. Society would have destroyed her. Now can you understand why I didn't throw her into a public school?"

Dad and I exchanged a look, understanding Mom so much better now. Dad sucked in a deep breath. "Dorothy, I owe you an apology. I came between you and Jodi, but I thought—"

"No one kept Jodi from being right where she wanted."

"But I could have been more tolerant if I'd only known. Why didn't she tell me the truth?"

"She feared it would change your relationship. Jodi

didn't want you to know because she was afraid you'd reject her."

"I'm sorry I haven't treated you more like family," he said. Rebecca slipped an arm over Dad's back and rested her chin on his shoulder. It felt good to watch her care for him. He deserved the comfort.

Simsy snickered. "Here I thought your rudeness was because you considered me family."

He let out a strained chuckle. "No, that's not how I like to treat my family." His brow pinched as he glanced at me. "Not anymore, at least."

"Well, I look forward to starting over."

The doorbell rang. Grandma left the dining room as we said our goodbyes. After hanging up, I circled the table and hugged Dad from behind. "Thank you for being here for me. You inherited a lot of trouble between Mom and me."

"No." He shook his head. "But I did receive a blessing in a daughter who is a good person capable of accomplishing great things."

"He's right about that." Rebecca rubbed my shoulder.

Grandma returned with JT Long. Dad reached over and pulled out the chair at the end of the table. "Hey, JT, have a seat."

JT nodded to each one of us. "Sorry to interrupt at such an awkward time, but I have some questions for Ellie Mae."

I shook my head. "I'm not answering a single one unless you sit down and eat one of my grandma's apple turnovers with a cup of coffee." I pushed the partially eaten plate of turnovers toward the open chair.

He smiled and took the seat. "I reckon I can do that."

Doc handed him a cup of coffee and refilled everyone else's.

I told him everything that happened from the time he

left the gorge with Todd and the other hunter minus our conversation with Simsy. JT shook his head as he swallowed half a turnover.

"There's just no predicting you, is there? You find more trouble than the rest of this town put together. Maybe the county. You okay?"

"I'm fine. Thanks to you. You saved my life."

He blushed a little. "Just doing my job, but it'd be a shame if something bad happened to ya. Listen, I'm sorry to burden you anymore tonight, but Todd offered up some information. I need to see your phone, please." He nodded to where it sat on the table. I handed it over.

"Seems someone paid off Rodney and Todd to bug you." He worked until the phone case popped off then pulled a small tool out of his shirt pocket. "We don't have the name of who, but this is how they found you in the gorge." He slipped the back cover off and showed us the underside of the lid where a small black dot had been placed. "GPS tracker. We maybe can find the source behind this, but once we go pressing charges, the *full* truth needs to come out. It might not be just about the drugs anymore. That what you want to do?"

I looked at dad, and he lifted a shoulder. "It's your call. I'll support you either way."

My gaze went back to JT. "No." I took the GPS tracker out of my phone and dropped it in my coffee.

He snorted a laugh. "You obviously don't know they're waterproof."

"Oh." I looked in my cup. "Then I guess I'll smash it with a hammer."

JT stood. "Fine by me. Wasn't looking forward to explaining this one to a judge."

I walked with him to the front door and gave him a tight

hug. "You've been a good friend, JT. The best. I won't forget it."

"Good. Enjoy your family. It's good to see everyone together finally."

Most everyone.

Chapter Thirty-Three

Two days later, I sat in the barn on the top board of a gate and spoke to Daisy and Lulu about whether I should go out and move the pile of cow bones.

"It's going to be such a foul job. The kudzu's about to cover them anyway."

Daisy bleated, seemingly indifferent to my plight, so I handed her another piece of apple. I also gave one to the more docile Lulu. I had already gone to the cave yesterday, retrieved my shotgun, and erased evidence of the Nun'Yunu'Wi. The trip was bittersweet since the gorge had become a big part of my summer and was linked to so many new memories of my mom. But those memories would carry me forward as I carved my own path.

Harvey Swanson had called Dad yesterday for an update on my condition. Dad and I both felt weird about the timing, especially since we didn't know who was behind the GPS tracker. And I couldn't say why exactly, but the Swanson name stirred a strange feeling inside me. We told Harvey the Bigfoot moved on, and I wouldn't have time to keep up with them because of my schooling. Besides, we didn't need his help.

Daisy turned in a circle and came back to me, lifting herself up on a board between my knees so that we were nose to nose. I kissed her. At the same time, my phone buzzed. I gave the remaining two apple slices to each goat and glanced at my phone.

"Dad needs me." I tucked the phone back in my pocket and patted Daisy's nose. I held my breath through the pull in my side as I eased my legs over the gate.

Sarah had left early to take her son to the doctor, so Dad asked me to be on call for the afternoon. I jogged out, noting Simsy's Buick, and grinned. What sort of critter had she found this time? I pushed open the clinic door. Simsy sat on a chair holding a bird cage.

"Hey there, Simsy, whatcha got?" I knelt down beside the half chipmunk, half squirrel. He was sort of red and gray and looked a lot like a rat with a bushy tail. Folks around here called 'em boomers. They were deceptively cute but could be real pests.

"This little guy's been following me around for days. I give him crackers, and he sits in my windowsill chattering up a storm. I've fallen in love with him. This morning out in the barn, he got underfoot of the cows. Not sure how bad he's hurt, but he's limping awful."

I took the boomer from her, cage and all, and walked into the exam room. Dad looked at me and rolled his eyes.

"You're giving her happiness, Dad."

"Yes, well, slip on those gloves, and we'll see how happy this little guy is. People and wild animals—"

"Are Simsy's life. And she's family."

The corners of his mouth quirked up as we held eye contact.

"Hey, Dorothy?" Dad motioned for her to come into the room. "Ellie and I wondered if you might stay for supper."

A smile spread across her face. "I would love to. I brought peach pie, but you're sure I won't be intruding?"

"Not at all." Since our call, I couldn't wait to hear more about Mom and even Simsy's life with the Nun'Yunu'Wi.

Dad jerked his head in the direction of the house. "Mom's inside. If you want to go on in, Ellie and I will take care of your boomer."

Simsy walked out with a big smile on her face.

"Nice move. I'm proud of you."

Dad rolled his eyes and opened the boomer's cage door.

Mom's organizational skills had been as primitive as her outdoor adventures. But sorting through her stuff was proving therapeutic, opening a channel of conversation about Mom and the Nun'Yunu'Wi that Dad and I wouldn't have otherwise had.

I sat at her desk—my desk—and inserted an SD card into the computer, uploading photos. While waiting, I opened a Word document, thinking on a project I wanted to start. It had only been three days since my encounter with the Nun'Yunu'Wi, but so much had happened. I wanted to record all of it. What I learned about my family, my mom, and myself.

While the tiny life lessons seemed mundane, I saw them as jewels I wanted to preserve. Overcoming my fear of failing Mom, staying true to what I deemed my calling, taking necessary risks, but only with the right amount of planning. Even though Dad didn't agree, I found peace obeying my convictions to make contact with the Bigfoot.

How else could I explain why I'd had no dreams the last couple nights?

Fighting for my best relationship with Dad, Grandma, and Doc almost ripped us apart, but we became closer. I wanted to remember those conversations when Grandma spoke through her tears, sharing how she endured hard times. And how, once she and Dad let go of their fear of the truth, healing spread over our family like the spring rains watering the earth. If I didn't write it all down, I feared these precious memories would get shrouded by the major events of being kidnapped, acquiring broken bones, and falling in love.

But one gem eluded me. I desperately wanted to learn patience so I could think about a future without speculation. Grandma told me not to speculate. Let the facts speak for themselves. Okay. Fact one, I was no closer to being patient than the day those footprints appeared on Hansen's land. Fact two, my impatience could simmer and erupt into fits of anger only settled by beating a stick against a tree. Fact three, these fits usually revolved around a certain New Orleans boy who was being discharged today. Only I didn't know if home was Hush Briar or New Orleans because his mom had continued to keep a tight rein on visitors.

I created a folder called Ellie's Journal and saved the document. I stared at the white page thinking how to start. Finally, I shrugged and began:

Grandma said a person's defining moment could be found in life's darkest corner. In my case, I found it at the bottom of a river gorge. It was when I'd come face to face with my greatest fear and decided risking my life was better than not finishing what my mom had started...

A tap sounded at the door.

"Come in," I said as I finished my thought, knowing Dad would slip in anyways as he did on occasion. He and Rebecca were about to head out to dinner, and I told them to let me know before they went.

I had moved the desk so it faced the door and glanced up, doing a double take. Jake stood in front of me, walking cast up to his thigh, crutches underneath both arms. His hair was cut uneven, shorter on one side where it'd been shaved at the hospital. His upper lip still held a couple stitches as did the cut from his temple to ear. Dark circles rested under his eyes, blending with a couple other fading bruises, but he was up on both feet . . . here . . . in front of me.

My pulse picked up speed. The desire to hug him rushed through me, but doubt tampered it due to the uncertainty of how this meeting might end. Had he come to say goodbye? We stared at one another. Jake lifted a corner of his mouth.

I forced myself to hold eye contact and speak in an even, controlled voice. "Are you just stopping by before you leave? Come to say goodbye?"

"No, I didn't come to say goodbye."

My face broke in a grin, but his short-lived smile didn't touch his eyes. Something was wrong. I studied his face, remembering just five days ago in the hospital when he told me he planned to return to New Orleans. The sad eyes. They looked the same now.

"Let me get you a chair." I retrieved one from the waiting room and placed it opposite my side of the desk. Jake pulled it back to give himself enough room to sit down and stretch out his leg. He placed the crutches on the floor and looked around the room.

"You cleaned this place up."

"Dad helped."

"Pappy said you and Neil were on better terms?"

I nodded, entranced in his presence, waiting for him to continue.

"I'm glad. You both deserve a good relationship."

The way he sat stiff and rubbed his palms on his shorts told me the unspoken words—the real reason he stopped by—caused him discomfort. I prepared for the worst as he drew in a deep breath.

"I just spent a horrible few days with my mom and dad. As it stands, they're talking divorce." He grimaced and looked down at the floor.

"I'm sorry," I said, drawing his eyes back to me.

He shrugged. "They've been tolerating one another for a long time. We all knew it. But it's been hard to watch my family crumble. Everything I thought was real dissolved into this unknown reality. Not to mention there's this tendency to blame myself, because it all broke loose when I moved up here."

"You came for Doc."

"But I opened a can of worms." Jake snatched the framed four-by-six selfie he'd taken of the two of us off my desk and looked at it. He met my gaze, aware I'd stolen it from his belongings.

"Your mom asked Doc to pack up your things. I was at his place this morning and found that in one of the boxes."

"When Dad found out she did that, he lost it. She was already driving everyone crazy by hovering every second. Yesterday, when Pappy came up to visit, she wouldn't let him in, so he and Dad went off and talked. I think my dad apologized for everything that happened over the years." He returned the picture to the desk. "If you hadn't spoken up, no one would have known the truth." His eyes lit up a tiny degree.

"I'm sure what I said in the hospital was offensive."

"Dad wants you to know that standing up for Pappy was one of the bravest things he's ever witnessed. It gave him the courage to finally dig for answers instead of accepting her accusations. Mom's bitterness has poisoned our family.

"Anyway, Ellie, even though life sort of spiraled out of control the last couple days, I couldn't get you out my mind. Not you, or Pappy, or Hush Briar. I'm not leaving because this is where life makes sense, where I feel at home. And Dad's going to stick around and help me get settled. Mom and the others went home today."

No longer able to stop the surge of emotion rising in my gut, I walked around the desk and leaned against the edge in front of him. "I'm so glad. Losing people is hard. I was afraid I might not see you again."

"I'm sorry I didn't text more."

I bent down and picked up his crutches. Why be sad over a lost couple of days when Jake was sitting right in front of me? I wanted to help him cope with the pain in his family and share the peculiar details of mine.

"How about we get out of here and go up to the house? I'll make you some decent coffee to go with Grandma's turnovers."

He took the crutches and hoisted himself up, his eyes never leaving mine. I placed my hands on the desk behind me as the crutches caused him to lean forward a bit. The chicks typically running wild in my belly danced to a melody. Something happy like Frank Sinatra's "Fly Me to the Moon."

I swallowed, feeling a little off-center at his nearness. "I also have a boatload of stuff to catch you up on. First being this . . ." I reached across the desk and opened the top drawer, pulling out the small, beaded comb. "Guess where I got this?"

He took the comb from my hand and examined it. "Looks familiar, but I'm not sure where I've seen it."

I stood straight. "I'll tell you. But first . . ." I gently slipped my arms around his middle and leaned in, careful not to set him off balance. I needed to be close, feel the beat of his heart and his comforting touch. He set the comb down and propped the crutches against the desk on either side of me. He pulled me close, tightly wrapping his arms around me and pressing his face to the top of my head. I buried my face in his chest and breathed in the scent of cotton and wood spice.

"I'm so glad you're not leaving." An understatement since not a single second went by when I didn't feel the hole in my heart or think about how perfectly Jake fit into my strange world.

He pushed back and held me by the shoulders.

"How could I? I was a gonner the first time you dumped me off the four-wheeler."

"Which explains why you didn't run when I mentioned the Bigfoot."

"I was fascinated by your desire to trust me. No one has ever trusted me like you. I want to help you with the Nun'Yunu'Wi in whatever way I can."

"Thank you."

"So, where do we start?"

I picked the comb up off the desk. "Let me tell you a story, and then we can decide."

Epilogue

Propped up on one elbow, Jake tossed a rubber chicken ten feet across the lawn. Florida Georgia Line played in the background from the wireless speaker on a corner of the blanket. We laughed as Fiona and Belle, the two nine-week-old Irish setter pups, tripped over their feet chasing the toy. Dad and Doc each bought one, intending to train and hunt. Jake would join in whenever he had time.

Seeing Dad and Doc bond openly warmed my heart. I asked Dad when he learned Doc was his real father. He said after his stepdad died, Doc came to him in private and told him how he and Grandma tried to run away when she was sixteen. They got as far north as Detroit before her dad found them and brought her back. Soon after, Doc was drafted into Vietnam. When he returned, Dad was two-and-a-half years old. Doc went off to the University where he met Gertie. She was already pregnant. Grandma and Doc tried to move on by ignoring the fact they still loved each other, but Gertie was the jealous type and wouldn't let it go. When Kim moved away, Doc offered Gertie a divorce.

She chose to stay, but he put a condition on it. He wanted Dad and I in his life.

It hurt my heart to think that for so many years, Grandma had to watch Doc and Gertie together. But those times were in the past, and Doc was trying to make up for it. Just the other day, after Grandma pitched a fit about two hunting dogs in the house, Doc invited her to come live with him. She clammed right up and turned beet red. But I didn't think it'd be long before a wedding happened, and Doc would join his pup at our place.

Fiona made it back first, her wavy reddish blonde ears bouncing. She was a mite bigger than Belle and more rambunctious. Belle plopped on the blanket, stretched out against Jake's belly, and yawned.

"Are you still sleepy?" I scratched her head then pulled Fiona in my lap so she'd leave Belle alone. I tossed the chicken, and the pup took off.

"Hey, you two..." Dad and Felix rounded the corner of the house, "Rebecca's on her way over with the hawk. Might want to take the pups inside."

"Sure." I bounced up, the pain in my side completely gone. And I was pretty sure my wrist had finally healed. The cast would come off next week—right before school started. Jake had two more weeks in his cast. His dad had stayed with him and Doc in Hush Briar to help him set up treatment with doctors in Lexington and make arrangements for physical therapy on UK's campus.

Working remotely, Felix touched base daily with Ty, allowing their parents a much-needed break. A good thing, since Jake said they stopped talking divorce and decided on counseling. Felix was headed back tomorrow for their first session, but he promised to return and help Jake move into his dorm on campus. Today's get together was sort of an informal send off. Plus, no one really got to celebrate the Fourth of July. We weren't setting off fireworks but returning a rehabbed bird to her home in the wild. I couldn't think of a better way to celebrate freedom.

Jake sat up and bent his good knee, the other stretched out in front of him. We'd perfected this technique over the past month, taking naps in the sun whenever possible.

"Ready?" I held onto both of Jake's hands.

"Yep. Be gentle." He winced as I pulled him into a standing position. I moved my hands to his waist for stability, and his hands went to my shoulders. Actions not really necessary anymore, but it'd become a routine. Normally, we'd kiss or playfully dance, but our dads stood on the back deck talking. I pulled away and picked up his crutches.

"Chicken."

I whipped around. "What?"

"I said, 'you forgot the chicken.'" He bent and picked up the plastic toy Fiona retrieved, giving it a squeeze.

I rolled my eyes and picked up Belle. "Come on, Fiona. Time for an indoor nap."

Once the pups were settled in the living room pen, I followed everyone out the front door. Doc and Grandma sat on the porch swing. Dad, Felix, and Jake stood on the cement pad in front of the garage. I stood at the front steps, waiting.

Simsy slipped an arm around my waist and squeezed. "Excited?"

I squeezed back. "I've been waiting all summer for this."

"The light in your eyes shows."

"How's Steve doing?" I glanced over to the garage to make sure Felix was still engrossed in conversation. He was the only one who didn't know about the Nun'Yunu'Wi.

"Steve's doing great. He knew they arrived when a

neighbor's calf went missing. He's been out every day a hunting. You still planning a visit?"

I could hear the hope in her voice. I wanted to help, but I also wanted to get ready for school, spend time with my family before I left, and help Dad in the clinic and Rebecca at the Rescue. Since the Nun'Yunu'Wi moved on, Dad and I had grown closer. I wasn't sure I wanted to compromise that.

Regardless of what Simsy thought, I didn't believe my obligation to help the Nun'Yunu'Wi stemmed from my Native American blood. Both my parents raised me to care about all vulnerable animals. Besides, if patterns held true, the Nun'Yunu'Wi weren't likely to come back to Hush Briar for another five years, so I didn't feel bad taking a step back, at least for the time being.

"If it works out, I might visit him over fall break." But I also had plans to go camping.

Simsy stared at me for several seconds. "You have many talents. Your momma would be proud no matter what you decide to do with your future."

"I appreciate hearing that."

Rebecca pulled into the drive in her white dually. Raptor Rescue was written in red on the side with a pair of talons appearing as quotations. Dad and I walked out to meet her while the others watched from the house.

She stepped out of the truck. "Hey, there. How are y'all? Having a good time?" She showed off a pretty smile that found me but settled on Dad. Instead of the typical green-and-khaki uniform, she wore white capris and a sleeveless teal blouse. Her blonde hair hung long and straight.

"An even better time now that you're here." I said it so

Dad didn't have to. I loved seeing them together, such a perfect fit.

"Great." Rebecca lowered the tailgate, revealing a steel cage with a green tarp over the top. She climbed in and removed the covering. The hawk skittered from one side to the other, uncertain of her surroundings. "Can't say she's been the best patient. I would've had her out here two weeks ago, but I think I mentioned she reinjured herself early on. She's more than ready to go home." Rebecca jumped down and retrieved gloves from the cab.

"Being patient is hard." I sat on the tailgate, spun, and stood beside the hawk.

Rebecca reappeared. "I'm not sure who's more excited, Ellie Mae or the bird."

"Well, I know who's more impatient."

"Hey." I scowled. He threw up his hands. "I didn't say it was you, but . . ."

"I'll unlock the cage." Rebecca offered the elbow-length gloves. "We'll disappear around the front. Once we're out of sight, pull the door up and back. Let her take as long as she needs. Ready?"

I nodded, and Rebecca pulled the locking pin. As she and Dad moved out of sight, I eased the door up and laid it back over the top.

"Slowly walk to the back of the cage," Rebecca said.

The brown-speckled hawk had been rambunctious and scared the day I found her. Today, she didn't even startle as I slipped behind her. She watched with big brown eyes. I lifted my hands on either side of the cage. When I touched the wire, she hobbled forward on thick yellow feet and inch-long black talons.

"There you go," I whispered. "That's it. Time to go home." I stayed on my haunches as she stuck her head and broad rounded shoulders out of the opening. In one quick motion, she jumped to the ground. Immediately, she leapt into the air. I jumped off the tailgate and watched as she climbed, her three-foot wingspan impressive up close. Reddish-peach tones washed her underside, deeper in color across her shoulders. Black bands across her tail and wing tips were distinct and stunning against the blue sky.

"Spectacular, isn't it?" Dad slipped an arm around my shoulders as the others stepped away from the house to watch.

I nodded as she circled higher and higher until she flew over the trees then off to find her mate.

I looked up at Dad. He gently squeezed my shoulder and kissed the top of my head before he let go and turned to Rebecca.

"Nice work, boss."

"My pleasure, but Ellie's the hero. The hawk would have starved to death if she hadn't brought her in. It also didn't hurt to have an excellent surgeon." She smiled at Dad.

"Guess we make a great team."

I took off the gloves and laid them on the truck bed. "Thank you for letting me help."

Jake hobbled over to me on his crutches. "How does it feel?"

"Like all the scars are worth it." I glanced over the trees bordering the barnyard. "A couple together at last."

"Seems to be the theme around here," Jake said. Dad and Rebecca and Doc and Grandma walked indoors, followed by Simsy and Felix. "But there's one more bit of unfinished business." Jake grinned, mischief in his eyes.

"What are you talking about?"

"Dean Martin." He said it with a hushed tone. "I have an idea. Get the wireless speaker and meet me on the deck."

With everything else going on I kept forgetting about that long-ago summer. I walked around back and picked the speaker up off the blanket. Grandma, Doc, and Simsy carried food out the door to the octagon picnic table on the deck. When Jake came through the patio doors, fiddling with his phone, I climbed the steps and placed the speaker on the far railing.

As the eight of us gathered around the table, Jake straddled the bench seat, facing me. He texted.

> Jake: Doc told me about this song.
> Watch your grandma's face. Then ask
> her about Dean Martin.

Dad prayed, food started making the rounds, and the wireless speaker fired to life playing "I'm the One Who Loves You," an old tune I'd heard Grandma play numerous times. Doc let out a quiet chuckle, but Grandma remained as indifferent as a turtle atop a log on a sunny day. I grinned at Jake. He smiled back, motioning his head her way. Then he plopped a large mound of mashed potatoes on his plate.

I cleared my throat. "Grandma, I keep forgetting, but Doc said I should ask you about the summer of '63 or '64 when Dean Martin was in Hush Briar. And this is the best pot roast I've ever had."

Jake bumped my knee, a good-job gesture. Grandma's face jerked to Doc's, and I feared she might lay into him, but his grin and unapologetic shrug silenced her.

She took a drink, flushed. "Is it hot out here?" She picked up her napkin and fanned her face.

Dad glanced my way and tipped his head, silently asking what was going on.

Simsy spoke up. "I remember hearing about that. Never saw him, but lots of folks talked about that night he sang at City Hall."

"Dean Martin came to Hush Briar?" Rebecca placed a roasting ear on her plate.

"More like he passed through." Grandma eyes met Doc's. "It was the summer of '64. I'm guessing about the end of August. Hot enough tar boiled on the roads."

"How old were you?" I dished gravy onto my potatoes and scooted the bowl to Jake.

"Young enough to be a bit too rebellious for my own good."

"I don't know about that." Doc's admiring gaze warmed my heart. "We were as deeply in love as two teenagers could be."

"We spent a lot of time down at the creek—that summer in particular."

"I'm surprised you were allowed to go," I said.

"If my papa would've found out, I'd have likely been skinned alive and locked in the cellar, but I got to be pretty good at sneaking around. Before I returned home, I would go to Ethan's house and change my clothes. His family always kept apples, mushrooms, and berries in the cellar. I often carried half a bucket home to prove I'd been out 'working.'" She lifted her hands, making air quotes. "Anyway, on this particular day, Ethan and I were on our way back to his house when we saw my folks coming down the hollow toward town."

Doc's face lit up and he joined in the telling. "We were about to where Stroh's live, near the ol' coal mine road. No houses there at that time."

"No, but there was a big old barn. We ran behind it to hide, and you stole a kiss." She faced Doc.

He shrugged. "I was an opportunist in those days. What can I say?"

"That's what Dean Martin said, too."

"What?" Dad looked at Grandma, perplexed and enthralled.

Felix paused, an ear of corn halfway to his mouth. "You two spoke with Dean Martin behind a barn?"

"He was out for a walk." Grandma buttered a piece of bread. "Correct me if I'm wrong, but I believe he stopped in Hush Briar to visit a friend. Somehow or other, he cut his hand deep enough it needed stitches. Rather than go to the hospital and create a fuss, they brought him to your daddy, who was Doc at the time."

Doc nodded. "Hand was wrapped and he was smoking a cigarette when he happened upon us sitting behind the barn. Scared the living daylights out of me."

"I thought I'd fallen asleep and was dreaming." Grandma's eyes sparkled. "Once the initial shock wore off, we thought it was no big deal he caught us kissing, because we'd never see him again. So we thought. But as we walked along, he followed us. All the way back to the house. We didn't know what to think until he explained about cutting his hand."

"We thought we'd be in a heap of trouble, but he never did say a word." Doc forked a piece of meat into his mouth.

Grandma nodded. "Later in the evening, he performed at City Hall. I made arrangements to spend the night with a friend. Ethan and I were able to dance the entire evening."

"You remember he dedicated a song to us . . ." Doc smiled at her, and it warmed my heart.

I touched Jake's leg with the fingers sticking out of my casted hand. So kind. He'd brought their memory to life as the song looped and kept playing.

"Yes. He said, 'To my young opportunistic friends.'"

Jake switched to a swing band mix that played while we ate. Not long after dinner, Jake's dad went back to Doc's to pack. Simsy went home, and the two remaining couples cleaned up the dishes and stayed in the house while Jake and I sat on the back deck steps watching the puppies chase grasshoppers and then fireflies.

Jake slipped a hand in mine. "So, can I start calling you my girlfriend now?"

"Sure you want to commit to a backwoods girl? What happens if I embarrass you with my hillbilly accent?"

He lifted his brows. "Then I'll embarrass you right back." He turned the music up using his phone, stuffed it in his back pocket, and stood.

"What are you doing?"

He pushed himself up and pulled on my hand. "Creating a moment. C'mon."

With no crutches, he hopped a few feet into the yard, carful of the pups, and wrapped his arms around my waist. "Ever danced under the moonlight?"

"No, but how are you going to move?"

"Just watch." He hop-shuffled, hop-shuffled, hop-shuffled, until one of the pups ran behind him. "Oh, shoot!"

He lost his balance. I reached out to grab his torso, but the momentum pulled me forward. As he hit the ground, I landed on top of him. He groaned. I quickly moved off his sore ribs, instantly attacked by puppies. Fiona crawled on my head and licked at my face with her soft tongue, squirming every which way to get to my mouth. Jake sat up and added Belle to the mix.

I laughed, covering my face as I shifted side to side. "Make them stop." I tried to sit up, but Fiona barked and playfully attacked, encouraging Belle.

"You haven't answered me. Are you my girlfriend?" Jake tickled my good ribs. I dropped my hands to stop him, offering access to the pups. One caught me in the mouth.

"I am so"—I laughed—"paying you back." I rolled out of his reach and sat up, pushing my hair out of my face and wiping puppy slobber off my cheek. A lightning bug between us caught Fiona's attention, and she jumped at it, following it toward the garden. Belle chased after her.

I grinned at Jake. "Quite the moonlit moment."

He pulled himself toward me, dragging his casted leg. "I cannot wait until this comes off." He turned, facing me like he'd done on our first date in the truck when we compared scars. We'd both added a couple new ones since then. I ran a finger down the one next to his ear, my thumb grazing the pink line above his upper lip. How could scars make a person even more attractive? His face became serious, but his eyes danced.

"So?"

"Yes. I'll be your girlfriend. Even when you embarrass me."

"Promise?"

I nodded once affirmatively.

"Then I'll kiss you, even when you smell like puppy breath."

And he did.

Author's Note

I first wrote *Hidden Truths* as a short story for my daughter. She was living in China over her nineteenth birthday. Knowing the boxed gift I sent might never reach her, I also wrote a short story featuring her favorite cryptid.

The story was about a girl who tracked Bigfoot to redeem her mom's character. I modeled Ellie Mae slightly after my daughter and Jake after her boyfriend. I created Ellie Mae with an intense need to protect her mom's integrity—to stand up for her while her dad turned a blind eye. But I also created Ellie with bitterness and vulnerability because this story is really about Ellie's relationship with her dad and her desperate need for him to tell the truth.

A year prior to writing this story for my daughter, I went through a divorce. People suddenly regarded me with a "there's-two-sides-to-every-story" expression. My reply was, and still is: "Yes, there are two sides but only one truth." My daughter became my strongest support. She wasn't the only one to stand by my side. Other family and friends—you know who you are—reminded me that, because of my faith and resolve to thrive, I was strong enough to walk through a crumbling world.

Thank you, friends and family!

I also wrote this story because I understand how much the truth hurts. Burying it can feel safe and like the right thing to do, but it often complicates matters or prolongs inevitable pain. At the very least, lying forces us to carry a more heavily weighted burden. The only proper way to lighten the load or extinguish the pain associated with any kind of loss or change is to walk through the pain and deal with the consequences. The key is to not give up on others when they tell the truth. This is what Ellie and Jake's story teaches their families.

I hope you enjoyed reading *Hidden Truths* as much as I enjoyed writing it.

—*Tammera*

Acknowledgments

This book was over five years in the making with several stops and starts as life interfered. Thank you to my family and friends for putting up with me and my ideas all these years. You let me share when I probably should've kept my mouth shut. I had a couple early readers whose names I wrote down but have misplaced. I remember you though, because you gave me hope this story could one day be something special.

Thank you to my daughter, Mel—lameness detector and travel partner. You were so gracious to listen as I read chapters over and over. Thank you to my son-in-law, Antoine. You read this book when it was a short story (when you were still only Mel's boyfriend) and didn't run away embarrassed. Thank you, both, for laying a final pair of eyes on my back cover copy. Thank you to my sister-in-law, Denise, for proofreading. We did our best to find those pesky typos!

Kathy McKinsey, you so graciously read the story and offered encouragement with each installment of chapters. A huge thank you to the Armorers at the Forge—Kat Vinson, Conrad Stilling, Wendy Heuvel, Kandi Wyatt, Cadi Murphy, Stacey Womack, and Laura Zimmerman. This book would not be what it is without your expert help. And Kat—you read it more than once and offered so many great suggestions. I am humbled by your willingness to help others. There are two more professionals that have gone unnamed for privacy. I hope you know who you are. Your insights were invaluable.

Thank you to my editors, Leslie L. McKee and Laura G. Johnson. You are remarkable. Any typos or errors in this text are my fault alone. Lastly, because a picture speaks louder than words, I want to thank my cover designer, Lynn Andreozzi. You asked all the right questions and patiently helped me navigate foreign territory to realize my dream. You are a special individual.

About the Author

Tammera Mart grew up a street rat in the small state-divided town of Union City, Ohio. By seven, she and her brother had memorized back alleys and the best places to find glass pop bottles. They spent summer days exploring on their bicycles, swimming at the pool (or corner puddles after a heavy rain), and hiding out in their fort next to the railroad tracks. As with most kids in the 80s, they narrowly survived childhood <wink>.

At age ten, their mom remarried and moved their small family onto a farm, where life took a dark turn into a world of mental abuse and hard work. Enter writing and escaping into worlds where hurting teens overcame obstacles using faith, grit, and resilience.

Today, working as a licensed social worker, Mart writes for joy instead of escape. Daily encounters with incredible people help shape her stories and characters. Her first writing award and publication came in a local county magazine at age sixteen. Since then, she's won several writing awards and published many true-to-life stories in various venues. At present, Tammera Mart writes from her small Midwestern home not far from where she ran barefoot in the streets as a child. You can connect with her at https://tammeramart.com or on one of the following platforms.

Abandoned Legacy

Coming Soon

Curse or Fate. Both require sacrifice.

What do you do when the man who gave you away pulls you into a world of mysterious legends and curses to clean up the mess he left behind?

Eighteen-year-old and Berkeley-bound Andrew Pearson wishes he could run. But with parents bent on using real experiences to teach life lessons, he finds himself on a plane to the New Jersey Pine Barrens with one goal in mind: sell the creepy, three-hundred-year-old manor and return to civilization as soon as possible.

But Legacy Manor is different than Andrew expects. So are the people who manage its B&B, including Haley, their free-spirited daughter who is determined to save her home and help Andrew understand his unique family history. When a grandpa he never knew reveals a curse that will use Haley as a pawn, Andrew is forced to choose between his future and hers.

As a plot to destroy a creature who calls Legacy Manor home unravels, Andrew makes a life altering decision—one that will not only challenge his views on life and love, but will explain a centuries-old connection between his family and the local legend of the Jersey Devil.

Other Works

Prequel to Hidden Truths:

The Art of Peacekeeping: Jake's story

(free when you join my email list. Sign up at https://tammeramart.com)

Published Short Stories

(free on Website)

Into the Light

Delivering Hope

Miracle at Sea

Surrounded By the Enemy

Quick On His Feet

Coming soon in the Living Lore Series:

Abandoned Legacy

Never Alone

Broken Pieces

Read excerpts at https://tammeramart.com

Non-Fiction by T. S. Mart and Mel Cabre

The Legend of Bigfoot: Leaving His Mark on The World (Red Lightning Books, 2020)

A Guide to Sky Monsters: Thunderbirds, the Jersey Devil,

Mothman, and Other Flying Cryptids (Red Lightning Books, 2021)